W9-DFZ-788

"I'M NOT GOING HOME."

The flame that always burned deep in his eyes seemed to leap to angry life and his brows drew down, as his face darkened.

"You can't stay here," he said harshly. "You're tampering with things you can't possibly understand. Go back to the States where you belong. Japan is not for you."

She slid out of the chair and went close to him. "Last night you wanted me. Why is it different now?"

The anger in his eyes frightened her and for just an instant she feared he might strike her. Then he pushed roughly, furiously past her and went out of the room. A few moments later he had left the house and the shadowy room seemed to crowd in upon her, thrusting at her with hateful, alien hands. It was as if it were repeating Jerome's words, "Get out! Go home!"

ALSO BY PHYLLIS WHITNEY

The Quicksilver Pool
The Trembling Hills
Skye Cameron
Thunder Heights
Blue Fire
Black Amber
Window on the Square
Seven Tears For Apollo
Sea Jade

*Coming Soon from HarperPaperbacks

PHYLLIS A. WHITNEY

The Moonflower

A NOVEL

HarperPaperbacks
A Division of HarperCollinsPublishers

If you purchased this book without a cover, you should be aware
that this book is stolen property. It was reported as "unsold and
destroyed" to the publisher and neither the author nor the
publisher has received any payment for this "stripped book."

This is a work of fiction. The characters, incidents, and
dialogues are products of the author's imagination and are not
to be construed as real. Any resemblance to actual events or
persons, living or dead, is entirely coincidental.

HarperPaperbacks *A Division of* HarperCollins*Publishers*
10 East 53rd Street, New York, N.Y. 10022

Copyright © 1958 by Phyllis A. Whitney
All rights reserved. No part of this book may be used or
reproduced in any manner whatsoever without written
permission of the publisher, except in the case of brief
quotations embodied in critical articles and reviews.
For information address Dutton, a division of Penguin
Books USA, Inc., 375 Hudson Street, New York, N.Y.
10014.

This book is published by arrangement with E.P. Dutton,
a division of Penguin Books USA, Inc.

Cover illustration by R.A. MaGuire

First HarperPaperbacks printing: June 1991

Printed in the United States of America

HarperPaperbacks and colophon are trademarks of
HarperCollins*Publishers*

10 9 8 7 6 5 4 3 2 1

For Patricia Schartle
Gratefully, affectionately

ONE

OUTSIDE THE AIRPORT TERMINAL BUILDING PALM TREES rustled shaggy leaves in the breeze and brilliant February sunshine flooded Hawaii. To Marcia Talbot, standing in the wide, open end of the waiting room, the mountains looked unbelievably green against the sky. Delicate tracings of cloud brushed the high ridges toward which she faced, while behind her lay the blank reality of the sea.

It was hard to stand there quietly, watching the beguiling panorama, when with all the urgency in her she longed to hurry time toward the moment of take-off when she would be aloft again, flying over the Pacific toward Japan. A day and a night in Honolulu had broken the long flight from San Francisco, and it had given her young daughter Laurie pleasure. But Marcia had not been fully prepared for the impact Hawaii would have upon her this time.

Eight years ago she had honeymooned here with Jerome. There were reminders on every hand to stab sharply, to increase her awareness of the uncertain future. Last night on the ocean terrace of their Waikiki hotel, when Kanaka boys had lighted the tall Hawaiian torches against a darkening sky, memory and pain and yearning had swept over her frighteningly. She and Jerome had been so marvelously happy during those weeks in Hawaii. He who was such a stranger to laughter, had been able to laugh with her, to share in her young excitement over all that was new and lovely and amusing. Even later when they'd gone home to Berkeley, the spell had held them for a while, and the strangeness that had ridden Jerome since the end of the war had faded in the early delight of their marriage. He had surely been a different person then. For a time he had been a different person.

It could not be over now, she thought—not in eight brief years. She would not believe it had come to an end. Once she saw Jerome she would know what to do, she would be able to take some action.

For a little while she stood looking off toward the mountains, a slim, rather tall young woman in navy blue, with a feathered blue hat hugging brown hair that lay in a soft natural coil on the nape of her neck. At twenty-six Marcia Talbot still wore the candid, eager look of youth and as a rule a smile came easily to her lips.

Disquiet drove her and she turned to look through the big waiting room for her daughter. Laurie lingered eagerly near a group which had come to bid one of its number good-by. If given time, she would manage to become part of the group, her mother was sure.

She was a tall child for seven, and her legs stretched long and bare beneath a red plaid suspender skirt. Above the round collar of her blouse her brown head with its two long braids was tilted back, and her brown eyes watched entranced as the departing visitor bent to receive a weight of leis about his neck.

His friends were apparently not waiting for take-off time. They exchanged handshakes, waved a final "aloha" and went out to their waiting cars. He watched them go, then turned to find Laurie regarding him with that enchanted look no one could ever resist. He responded with a ready smile.

"Hello, there," he said. "An Hawaiian pixie, I do believe."

"You look beautiful," Laurie said raptly.

He was a tall, broadly built man, perhaps in his mid-thirties, with sandy hair and gray eyes that crinkled at the corners as he laughed out loud at Laurie. His laughter had the exuberant ring of good health and good spirits, and Laurie laughed with him. She never minded whether she laughed at herself or someone else.

"Madam, you are indeed kind," he said with mock formality. "So kind, in fact, that I wonder if you would do me a favor?"

"Sure," Laurie said, always ready to do anyone a favor any time.

The man removed three of the four leis from about his neck and lowered them gently over Laurie's head— a scarlet chain, a white one, and one of ginger-colored blossoms. He stood back judiciously to study the full effect. The garlands hung to her knees in front, and looped down her back behind, bedecking her as if for a parade. He did not laugh now, but adopted an expression of stunned admiration.

"Now you are beautiful too," he said. "Will you do me the honor to wear them?"

Laurie's gasp was one of pure ecstasy. Then some do-not-accept-presents-from-strangers warning must have flashed through her mind and she looked quickly about for her mother.

Smiling in amusement, Marcia moved toward the two. "You look like a fiesta float," she told her daughter.

"Can I keep them?" Laurie demanded. "Is it all right if I wear them?"

The lei-bestower looked at Laurie's mother cheerfully. "You don't mind, do you? My name's Alan Cobb, bound for Kyoto, Japan. And I can't see myself boarding a plane looking like a winner of the fifth at Pimlico. It takes an islander to wear a lei with aplomb. No one from the mainland can manage it at first try without looking foolish."

He had an engaging lack of pretension about him and Marcia found herself meeting his smile with her own. But Kyoto . . . she was thinking. Did he live there? Did he know Jerome?

"You've made my daughter happy," she told him. "I'm Marcia Talbot from Berkeley, and this is Laurie. Of course she may wear your leis if you really don't want to yourself."

She said nothing about Kyoto. There was no point in mentioning that their destination was the same. Kyoto was a city. It was probable that their paths would not cross again once they were there.

Under the circumstances it seemed natural to

wander through the building with Alan Cobb and stand looking out over the flat, reclaimed land of the flying field, waiting for their plane to be announced.

Laurie said, "I went swimming at Waikiki yesterday." And Alan Cobb said, "So did I. Went out on a surfboard too, and fell off three times. Head first."

The two were good friends by the time the loudspeaker proclaimed the flight to Japan, Hong Kong and Singapore. With other passengers they hurried out into the whipping wind. A stewardess met them at the plane door to welcome them aboard and gestured Marcia and Laurie up front in the tourist section. Laurie waved to her new friend, two seats back across the aisle, and bounced into the window seat while her mother settled more quietly beside her.

This was the last lap, Marcia told herself in relief. Tomorrow—Tokyo. And surely Jerome would be at the airport to meet them. At the very thought her breathing quickened and her natural optimism and confidence surged back full force. Of course he would meet them, and the disturbing things he had written in his letter would be nullified. After all, she had been through just such a crisis once before. She had solved the problem then and she could solve it now. *Oh, hurry, hurry, hurry!* she told the plane.

Now that she was back in the air she felt hopeful again and ready to enjoy the adventure of this flight across the Pacific.

"Look, there's our hotel!" Laurie cried, looking down and squirming against the pull of her seat belt.

The long curve of Waikiki beach with its creaming surf lay below, and the familiar jagged point of Diamond Head. Then the plane banked away from Honolulu and the view vanished beneath a tilted wing as they turned out over the ocean. They were really on the way now, toward the islands of Japan. One stop for refueling at Wake, then Haneda Airport.

"Will Daddy be there to meet us?" Laurie asked.

Lest Laurie be disappointed when the time came, it was better not to speak too hopefully. After all, Marcia had not dared to give Jerome advance warning of her plans for fear he might cable her not to come. She had simply cabled him at the last minute that she and Laurie would arrive in Tokyo on such and such a plane and date. By the time he received the message, he would have no choice but whether or not to meet them.

"We have to remember that it's an all-day trip from Kyoto to Tokyo, and he may be too busy to come," she told Laurie. "We mustn't count on it. He'll come if he can."

"Oh, I know he will," Laurie said, and her eyes glowed in anticipation.

Jerome had never fallen naturally into the role of father. Perhaps that made him seem all the more fascinating to a father-hungry little girl. It had been hard for Laurie to contain her eagerness to be with him, once she knew they were to make this trip.

Marcia leaned her head against a pillow and closed her eyes, listening to the steady roar of the motors as the plane ate away the miles. Behind closed lids she could see Jerome's face with disturbing clarity. The intense dark blue of his eyes with winged black brows above them, the mouth that could tighten so grimly in anger, yet which she had always been able to coax into a smile. Would he be angry with her now?

She had seen him angry at others only once or twice

and had been frightened by his cold fury. But he had never turned that fury upon her, no matter what the provocation. And sometimes she must surely have provoked him. What a child she had been when she'd married him at eighteen—seventeen years younger than he.

When Jerome Talbot had first appeared in her father's house she had been little more than Laurie's age. That was at the start of the war with Japan, when Jerome was the most gifted of her father's "bright young men" of science. Her father, Merrill Vance, had been unknown in those days, except in certain circles, just as the words "atom" and "radiation" had no significance for the general public. But Jerome had studied under Dr. Vance, worked with him in the university laboratory, and been a welcome guest in the Vance home. And he had seemed a hero out of a story book to an impressionable little girl.

What an exciting young man he had been in those days, with all that nervous drive and energy, all the brilliance and promise her father had seen in him. Dark and lean and slender—too lean for his height—he was like a thin steel blade that rang with vibrancy.

By the time of Hiroshima, Marcia had been thirteen and romantically, secretly, "in love" with Jerome. Where other girls her age had worshiped movie actors from afar, she had focused on someone who came in and out of her own house.

Since Jerome Talbot was too valuable a man to be permitted out of the laboratory during the war and since he was working on some project of hush-hush importance, he did not get into uniform. Often he went on long trips across the country, meeting with other men of science, going to Washington on secret missions.

Dr. Vance was one of the few who had worked knowingly on those secret plans. Yet when the bombs were dropped on Hiroshima and Nagasaki, he had not been able to face the consequences. Illness had betrayed him in the last year of his work and with his lowered vitality he could no longer achieve the objective, long-range view that was, under the circumstances, necessary. He had withdrawn from his work to the unhappy life of an invalid and Marcia remembered her father in those years with sadness.

Jerome went out to Japan with the Occupation forces and made straight for Hiroshima. Radiation was his business and he wanted to know more about it firsthand. He had stayed in Japan. Stayed until Merrill Vance's death, some four years later. That had brought him home to find Marcia grown up in his absence.

The roar of plane engines recalled her to the present and in the seat beside her Laurie stirred and prodded her mother.

"Look at the clouds—they're like a king's court, aren't they?"

Marcia played the cloud game for a while, counting queens and ladies in waiting in the vast cloud world massed on the horizon and beneath the belly of their plane.

At least once every half hour Laurie would climb over her mother's feet and get a drink at the water cooler just ahead of their front seat. And sometimes she stretched her legs with a walk up and down the aisle. The stewardess had furnished a plastic bag for the leis and they were still the basis for friendship. Several times Laurie stopped to speak to Mr. Cobb, with whom she was now on heart-to-heart terms.

"He's been in Japan before," she reported. "He's a writer or something and he's going to work on a book out there. He's going to teach too, in a college in Kyoto for a year."

Marcia fixed her daughter with a sympathetic but knowing eye. "He volunteered all this information, did he?" Laurie grinned, unabashed.

The meal made a welcome interlude, and afterwards, when the stewardess began bedding everyone down for the long night flight, handing out pillows and blankets, turning off the overhead lights, Alan Cobb came across the aisle to Marcia's seat.

"It occurs to me," he said, "that this young lady might sleep more soundly if she could stretch out on two seats. There's a vacant one next to mine and if she'd like to take over I'll be happy to change places with her."

For just an instant Marcia hesitated. Alan Cobb seemed pleasant enough, but he might like to talk and she wasn't sure she could face conversation with a stranger just now. She looked up at him uncertainly and found that he was watching her with a quizzical air, his eyes amused.

"I promise you I don't snore," he said. "And if you chatter in my ear I'll squelch you. I mean to get some sleep."

He had easily read her mind and she thanked him a little sheepishly. When Laurie had been made comfortable, Marcia slipped into the window seat and curled up with her pillow resting against the wall of the plane.

Alan Cobb, in the seat next to her, wrapped himself in his blanket and appeared to fall asleep at once.

Marcia could not resist parting the curtains and peering out at the vast starry sky, with edges of daylight still to be seen on the horizon, and all that roiling black ocean beneath. She felt a sense of wonder and excitement and she could not sleep. What fun it would have been to make this trip for the first time with Jerome. She had done so little traveling with him.

How clearly and achingly she could remember him as he had been after her father's death, when he had first been aware of her as a grown young woman plainly in love with him. She had realized at once the change in him when he returned from Japan. He had never been a gay, or lighthearted person, but now he seemed more somber and serious than ever. At times she had thought him oddly haunted. Perhaps by the shadow of Hiroshima? She did not know. She knew only that she had been able to tease him into laughter and that he had responded as if, through her, he could forget whatever it was that lay behind him in Japan.

Her mother had seen well enough what was happening and she had thrown her weight against it. "He reminds me of Lucifer, Marcia," she had said one time. "It gives me an uncomfortable feeling to have a dark angel flitting in and out of my house."

Marcia had seized upon the poetry of that image and it had added to Jerome's fascination for her. It was true that he burned bright as Lucifer and that there was a darkness in him as well.

Her mother said, "For heaven's sake forget him, darling. He's too old for you. Besides, no woman in her right mind should marry a scientist. Science is much worse than the medical profession, or even golf."

"You married a scientist," said Marcia.

Mrs. Vance nodded sadly. "Yes, and eight nights out of every seven I couldn't tell whether or not he would be home for dinner."

But Marcia knew her words were loving and that she would never have traded places with any other wife. Adoring her father as she had, Marcia felt she could hardly have asked for a husband who would better suit her than Jerome.

At first their marriage had seemed a wonderfully satisfying thing. If he turned to her for youth and laughter and life, she turned to him for wisdom and adult counsel. During the first year or so she had had the feeling that he clung to her as if she held something of salvation for him, as if there were some safety in her arms that he could find nowhere else. She had not understood, but she had held him close and had built her life wholly around him and for him.

There had been one especially strange thing—his reluctance to talk of Japan. Or at least he would talk of it only superficially. Once she had asked him if he would ever go back and he had looked at her with a sudden anger that had frightened her. But then he caught her in his arms and she knew that whatever had angered him, his displeasure had not been with her.

And yet, soon after Laurie's birth, he had returned to Kyoto. At first Marcia had not been concerned. He had talked little to her about his work—as her father had talked little to his wife and daughter—but she knew he was interested in the experiments of one Kyoto scientist in particular. It did not seem strange that he felt he must return to Japan and continue the work he had dropped after her father's death. He would send for her eventually and she would go eagerly to join him.

But he did not send for her and he was home in a few months, restless and unable to settle down to life in America. After that he had commuted in a sense between Kyoto and Berkeley, with the stays in Japan growing longer as time went by. Whenever she had broached going with him, he had turned from her coldly and she had learned not to make the suggestion. If she were to hold him at all, she knew it would have to be on his own terms. When he had come home a year ago he really frightened her with his mood of despondency. It was no use, he had told her—he loved her, but to continue this way was only to injure her. He must work in Japan. It was no place for her and she must release him from their marriage and allow him to return to Japan for good.

How hard she had worked that time to bring him back to sanity and the enfolding warmth of her love. She had laughed at his "solution," refused to be lugubrious and despairing. She loved him too. Whatever the price, it was marriage with Jerome Talbot that she wanted. Not for a moment would she consider that marriage at an end. As long as he loved her, that was all she needed to know. Gently, coaxingly, she had brought him out of the morass of gloom. And she had not let him see her worry when once more he returned to Kyoto. Now nearly a year had passed and his letters had grown few and noncommittal. Until this one. She carried it with her in her purse, but she knew the words only too well without looking at them:

"Thank you for being the very dear and courageous person you are. Now I am asking of you something more. My freedom. It is impossible to continue like this, torn between two worlds. I find I must give my allegiance to one or the other. But I am thinking of you, as well as of myself. You are caught in a marriage that is not a marriage . . ."

There had been more, a lot more. He had tried to use the knife gently, to tear the flesh as little as possible on the way to her heart. But all her being had cried out in pain and disbelief. Where had she failed him? To what in Japan did he owe more allegiance than to his wife and daughter? What held him there? Or who?

She had never been one to weep silently in a dim room. "My little actionist," he had called her once, teasing because she was so ready to go after what she wanted without troubling to do much thinking first. And once she was on her way, she could hold on blindly and never give an inch.

Upon reading his letter, she had acted quickly, telling herself that she had brought him out of such delusions before, and he had thanked her for it. She could do it again. Only the coward gave up his life without a struggle, and she was never that. So she had taken Laurie out of school and made swift preparations for this trip. Her mother had been against it, but Marcia would not listen. She could hear her mother's words now: "Darling, we all have to learn when to let go. It isn't always possible to make things come right by hanging on blindly." But her mother had never truly liked Jerome, and Marcia could not let go. She had never learned how, nor wanted to learn.

Action had brought confidence and hope sweeping

back. Nothing could stop her in her flight across the ocean to Jerome. And once she was in his arms, all would be well again. Comforted by this ability to take some action, she had even been able to enjoy the new experiences of the trip, and to look forward to seeing the country Jerome's letters had told her so little about, but which she had read of voraciously, so that she might share his background through the printed word.

Here in the plane she felt increasingly keyed up. Yet she must have dozed fitfully through the hours, for she was suddenly startled awake when the lights came on and there was a stirring throughout the cabin. The loudspeaker announced that they were about to land on Wake and would be on the ground for an hour. The seat belt sign, with Oriental characters beneath the Occidental words, clicked on, and Alan Cobb rose quickly, picking up his blanket and pillow.

"You haven't done much sleeping, have you?" he asked frankly, and went to change places with Laurie.

When they had landed on Wake, Alan did not urge his company upon them, but Laurie had adopted him as their friend and benefactor. For a little while they stood together in the strong Pacific wind and looked up at the close, bright stars.

"Laurie tells me you've been in Japan before," Marcia said idly.

"My father was Army," Alan Cobb said, "and I was born in the Orient. We went to Japan now and then on vacations, but I don't know it well. I understand you're going to Kyoto too?"

"To be with my father," Laurie put in before her

mother could answer, and added proudly, "My father is a very famous person."

Alan Cobb cocked an eyebrow at her. "Is that right? Talbot—Kyoto?" He glanced quickly at Marcia. "Is your husband Jerome Talbot, the physicist?"

"Yes, he is," Marcia said, and let it go at that.

But Alan Cobb's interest had come keenly to life. "I know about your husband's work in nuclear science. We have some mutual friends in Washington. Perhaps you know the Brewsters?"

"I've heard him speak of them," she said guardedly. She had a feeling that Jerome had cut his ties with most of his friends at home.

"In fact," Alan Cobb went on, "Mark Brewster asked me to look him up if I went to Kyoto. Though of course I'd have wanted to do so anyway."

"In that case you must certainly come to see us," Marcia said, but she could not put much heart into her words. She did not know whether Jerome would want to see anyone from home. Perhaps not even his wife.

Alan made no response to her invitation. "I've read a lot of your husband's things in scientific journals. I've always had a good-sized admiration for his work. Though I haven't heard much about him lately." He looked as if he wanted to say more, then decided against it.

Laurie glanced up at him with interest. "Why do you want to teach in Japan?" she asked. "Why don't you just teach Americans at home?"

He seemed to weigh the question carefully in his mind before he answered. Then he said, "I suppose because it will give me a chance to find out something about myself."

"About yourself?" Laurie echoed, puzzled.

"Why not? Are you so sure you know everything there is to know about you?"

"Of course," said Laurie, and Marcia smiled at her youthful confidence.

Nevertheless, Alan Cobb's words had an enigmatic ring and Marcia found herself growing curious about him.

"What subjects are you going to teach?" she asked.

He chuckled ruefully. "Just modern American literature. And it's going to be a tough course. For me. Of course I'm only teaching part time, so I hope we'll all survive."

The loudspeaker summoned them back to the plane and Laurie was tucked into the double seat again, sleepy now from the wind and air. Marcia too found herself drowsy and she curled up against her pillow and closed her eyes. For a moment or two she found herself wondering idly about the man next to her. But sleep came quickly and she forgot him.

It was Alan Cobb who lay awake and quietly thoughtful.

TWO

CLOUDS BLANKETED THE ISLANDS OF JAPAN AS THE plane came down in a flurry of snow at Haneda Airport outside Tokyo. Laurie peered eagerly through the window at the observation deck, where a little crowd of people stood in the open, with snow falling about them as they waved and smiled at the plane.

A bit breathlessly Marcia leaned over her toward the window while they waited to disembark, but she could not see Jerome among those on the deck. Not that his absence meant anything. If he had come to meet them he might well wait inside on such a day. Her heart was thumping now in anticipation. She had a feeling that she would know the fundamental answers the moment she saw his face.

When the quarantine officer had finished his sketchy inspection, Alan Cobb was beside them again. He helped casually with their hand luggage and went with

17

them into customs. She was grateful for his presence, for here, suddenly, was a strange land, strange faces, a language she did not understand.

"I suppose your husband is meeting you?" Alan Cobb said, when they were ready to leave the restricted part of the airport.

"I don't really know," Marcia faltered. "He may not have been able to get away. If he's not here, we'll go right to the Imperial Hotel, where I have a reservation."

"That's where I'm heading," he said. "If you're not met, I can see you that far."

When Marcia and Laurie entered the waiting room there was still no sign of Jerome, but a Japanese stepped up to ask if their companion was Alan Cobb. Plainly surprised, he admitted his identity, and at once several reporters and a photographer surrounded him.

He gave Marcia a look of mock despair and rolled his eyes heavenward. "I hardly expected this!"

"Don't worry," she told him. "We'll get to the hotel all right."

"He must be awfully famous," Laurie murmured as they left him to his admirers and boarded the limousine.

The Imperial Hotel was an indestructible landmark in Tokyo. No earthquake had ever managed to shake it down, and bombs and fire had also spared the low, sturdy stone structure.

There was no message from Jerome waiting for Marcia at the desk. It appeared that once more the moment of reckoning had been pushed ahead and Marcia hardly knew whether to feel relieved or more anxious than ever. When the phone rang in midafternoon Alan Cobb's voice answered hers.

"Hi!" he said, cheerfully informal. "Did that husband of yours show up?"

"Not yet," Marcia said. "I—I'm afraid there's been some sort of mix-up."

"Japan's the place for that," he said lightly. "Can I help by getting your tickets to Kyoto when I get my own?"

He could indeed, and by the time he hung up, it had been arranged that they would take the train to Kyoto together in the morning. Marcia was happy enough to have the details taken out of her hands.

When she hung up the phone she thought of trying to call Jerome in Kyoto, then rejected the notion. He knew the time of their arrival. If he had wanted to meet them, if he had wanted to get in touch with her, he would have done so. And if she spoke with him and he told her flatly not to make the trip to Kyoto, what would she do then?

She and Laurie might at least begin to enjoy Japan and the evening in Tokyo. They got into coats and galoshes and went out into the cold and muddy snow of the streets, equally fascinated by the shops and the Japanese crowds, though it was disappointing to find nearly everyone in westernized dress. Laurie even loved the excitement of noisy traffic that tore up and down the Ginza with a steady beeping of strident horns. From the doorway of a shop a radio blared one of the latest hit tunes from the States. Movie facades displayed the familiar face of Cary Grant and Gary Cooper, and neon lights shone brightly everywhere.

At times it was hard to believe that they had really left the States.

In fact, Marcia had no sense of being truly in Japan until the next morning, when she and Laurie were seated in the last car of the train to Kyoto, with Alan Cobb on the seat facing them.

As the train left the dingy city environs behind and the snowy Japanese countryside began to slip past the train windows, a sense of delight filled her. Bare branches of cherry trees made a delicate black tracery against the snow-blanketed landscape, and green pine forests climbed the mountainsides. A sudden flash of vermilion from some shrine or torii gate, the tall clustered stalks of a bamboo grove—all these began at last to give her a feeling of having arrived in Japan. The train ran between sea and mountains and the views of each were like the scenes of all the Japanese prints she remembered.

Once she spoke idly of the delegation that had met Alan at the airport the day before.

"I didn't expect a reception," he said. "I'm afraid I wasn't able to play up to the role they handed me. But how could I know someone in Japan would remember a book that was published years ago?"

"What was the name of your book?" Marcia asked.

Alan stared out the window at frozen paddy fields. He had a habit of lapsing oddly into silence at times and she felt that he did not want to answer her question. After an interval he skirted the subject somewhat carelessly.

"It wasn't a good book, really. It was written too soon. And it's long out of print in the American edition. I don't recommend it to anyone. I'm much more interested in the one I'm working on now. Maybe your husband can help me with that."

She glanced at him in surprise. "In what way?"

"He may know something about my subject matter. I suppose my theme is recovery from disaster. Any sort of disaster dealt with in human terms. It's not difficult to find material these days. Your husband was here after Hiroshima, as I recall. He may know stories, or even some of the people—" He broke off and smiled at her frankly. "The book's an excuse to meet Jerome Talbot. Not just because the Brewsters asked me to look him up, either. I suppose I'm curious about him."

"Curious?" Marcia asked uneasily.

He looked at her for a moment and then seemed to turn his back upon the subject. "Actually it's none of my business," he said. "What about lunch? Are you hungry, Laurie?"

A little later they went into the dining car and had the company of a young Japanese businessman at their table. Alan struggled with the problem of giving their orders to a pretty waitress who spoke no English, and they laughed together over finding a cheese sandwich listed among the desserts.

During the afternoon Alan amused Laurie with riddles and puzzles that led to frequent bursts of laughter. No, he had no children of his own, he told her at one point. He was not married, but he liked to borrow his friends' children now and then just to keep his hand in with the young. Perhaps her mother would lend Laurie to him sometime in Kyoto, so they could go sightseeing together.

Marcia let all this flow past her and over her, lost in her own thoughts as she tried once more to plan the details of her first meeting with Jerome and exactly what she would say to him when they were alone. The trip seemed endless.

Once she came out of her reverie to find Alan's eyes resting upon her thoughtfully and knew that he had sensed her preoccupation and that he had deliberately taken Laurie off her hands so that she could be free to think about whatever was worrying her.

In the late afternoon the train turned away from the sea toward a valley that lay between mist-shrouded mountains, and the journey was at an end. The loud-speaker announced Kyoto.

"The university wrote that someone would meet my train," Alan told Marcia. "If no one comes for you, you can get to your house all right, can't you?"

She felt suddenly unsure. "I—I don't know. I mean if the cab driver doesn't understand English—"

"You'll be all right," he said almost curtly. "Just show him the written address. You're not really scared, are you?"

His tone pulled her up abruptly. He seemed to be pushing her away, as if he felt that it was time for her to stand on her own feet.

"I'm sorry," she said quickly. "We've been an awful nuisance to you. And of course we'll manage on our own."

"I'm sure you will," he said. "There's no reason to expect anything but the greatest friendliness in Japan. Queer, isn't it, when only a handful of years ago—"

He left the sentence unfinished and she wondered if he had been in the war—perhaps in the Pacific, fighting against the Japanese. He turned away from her to put on his coat, and once more she had the feeling that this seemingly open-mannered man could suddenly close a door and leave her outside, smiling at nothing.

The train rolled to a stop beside a long, sheltered platform. Tickets had to be shown at the exit gates, then at last the trip was over. This was Kyoto. Alan Cobb held out a casual hand to Marcia, accepted her thanks as though his mind were on other matters, and said, "I'll be seeing you, Laurie."

Marcia stood in the station with the crowd thinning about her, feeling strangely abandoned. Alan Cobb's presence had gone further to make things comfortable than she had fully realized. He had begun to seem like a friend and his sudden dismissal of them had come as a surprise.

"I don't see Daddy anywhere, do you?" Laurie asked, standing very close to her mother.

"We really couldn't expect to," Marcia said. "He won't know what train we're arriving on."

Taxis, she found, came in assorted sizes and assorted prices. She picked a middle-sized one and discovered that the driver spoke not a word of English. He was cheerful and enormously eager to be helpful, but she felt uneasy as they got under way. She had read that Japanese addresses were apt to be vague, with neighborhoods rather than streets designated. But their driver sped his car along with the horn blaring and pedestrians fleeing their path in the gray, slippery snow of churned streets. The cold was raw and damp and the heater in the taxi seemed not to be working.

In the murk of late afternoon Marcia could see little of Kyoto as they followed winding streets between Japanese houses, over bridges, along car tracks, beeping and blaring. She gripped Laurie by the arm and held her breath. Somehow the pedestrians always leaped in time, the other cars missed them by a hair's breadth and they slowed at last to follow a narrow residential street with high bamboo fences on either side.

The taxi stopped at a wooden gate that had come straight out of a Japanese print. It had a sloping tiled roof, so that one might stand under shelter, and its unpainted wood was weathered to a dark, grayish brown. In the background, beyond a space of garden, rose the eaves of a great spreading house. There were no lights in the upstairs windows and the first floor was hidden by the fence.

A small bell hung inward from the gate, suspended by a strip of flexible metal. When the driver pounded on the wooden gate, the bell jangled urgently. At the sound Marcia could feel the quick, suffocating beat of her heart. Her hands were damp and she could not trust her voice. This was the moment—nearly.

The gate opened and a Japanese man peered out at them. There was an exchange of bows and a lengthy discussion. He was a short, stocky individual with a vaguely unfriendly air about him. An ugly scar puckered the skin of his forehead from one black eyebrow to the hairline. He was not discourteous, but his manner showed little interest in the cab driver's problem.

The driver returned to the cab shaking his head. Beyond him the gate was about to close. Marcia opened the cab door and stepped hastily out into the snow of the narrow lane.

"Wait!" she cried. "Please wait a moment!"

The man paused with the gate half shut and stared at her blankly. In the dim light of a street lamp he looked stolid and far from encouraging. But this had to be the place. She knew nowhere else to go.

"I'm looking for Mr. Talbot." Her tone was almost beseeching now. "Mr. Jerome Talbot."

Still he looked at her blankly, without comprehension.

"Talbot-san," she repeated. "This house is home of Talbot-san?"

A glimmer of recognition crossed his face. "Ah, *so desu ka?*" he said. "Tarbot-san. Not here." And he gestured indifferently into the gloom.

"Can you tell my driver?" she asked. "Where is house of Talbot-san?"

"He's my father!" Laurie called helpfully from the cab.

The Japanese man looked from Marcia to Laurie and back again, as if what he saw disturbed him in some way. He bowed and spoke again to the driver, pointing. Then he firmly closed the gate in their faces. The driver held the cab door for Marcia. There was nothing to do but get in.

The cab followed the long bamboo fence to a corner, then turned up a still narrower lane until it came to a halt before another gate. This entrance was somewhat wider and more elaborate than the one at the other house. Again there was the business of bell ringing, and after an interminable wait a Japanese girl came to the gate, bundled into a quilted, padded coat, her cheeks bright with the cold, her breath steaming.

This time Marcia got out of the cab quickly. "Talbot-san?" she said, making it as simple as possible.

The girl smiled and nodded readily. "*Hai*, Tarbot-san."

Marcia motioned to the driver to take out their bags. But when she started through the gate with Laurie, the little maid barred their way, shaking her head and chattering to the driver.

"Never mind," Marcia said firmly, "this is the right place and we're going in." She pushed gently past the girl, pulling Laurie with her.

Neat stepping stones curved through the snow toward an entryway where a lamp burned overhead. A large, oblong stone from which all snow had been brushed offered a step up toward the level of an entry hall with a narrow veranda ledge. The driver piled their bags on the ledge, accepted the yen bills Marcia handed him and escaped before anyone could have a change of mind. The maid was still protesting in Japanese.

"It's our shoes now," Laurie said. "She wants us to take off our shoes."

So they sat down on the step and pulled off galoshes and shoes, while the maid brought them house slippers. The girl was still concerned about letting them come in, and she backed away uncertainly as they entered the wide, uncarpeted hall. A polished floor gleamed darkly beneath a shaded electric globe hanging far above from the high ceiling. It was almost as cold inside as it was in the garden and their breath misted the air.

The girl made gestures which indicated they must wait there while she went for help. Plainly Jerome was not in the house, or he would have heard the commotion by now. In a moment the little maid returned, bringing an older woman with her. The second woman wore a brown kimono and a dull obi around her waist. Only her eyes, which looked curiously at Marcia and Laurie, were bright and lively.

"I'm Mrs. Talbot," Marcia explained, and found that she spoke a little too loudly, enunciating as if they were deaf. "I am the wife of Talbot-san. This is Laurie Talbot. We are here from America. Where is Mr. Talbot?"

The older woman exchanged looks with the younger. "Tarbot-san not here," she said. "You no stay."

"But we're going to stay," Marcia said firmly. "We'll wait for Mr. Talbot to come home."

Again there were quick exchanged looks. The older woman spoke to the younger in the manner of one giving an order. "Horner *Okusama,*" she said. The girl smiled and nodded with an air of relief. Then she hurried out the front entryway.

"It's awfully cold in here, isn't it?" Laurie said.

Marcia nodded. "I know, darling. We'll just keep our coats on till we find out what we're going to do."

She looked about the bare wide hall. At the rear a flight of stairs went upward into darkness and near the bottom step was a small table of carved teakwood, with knobby claws for feet. The table held a brass card tray on which lay several envelopes.

Marcia walked quickly to the table and picked up the handful of mail with a sense of foreboding. It was all addressed to Jerome Talbot and none of it had been opened. Halfway through the stack she found her cablegram from the States.

Jerome Talbot could have had not the faintest notion that his wife had left home and was on her way to Japan.

Marcia set the envelopes down with hands that trembled and turned toward the front door. She could hear voices as the maid came back through the garden, followed by a tall, rather angularly handsome American woman with a blue scarf tied over her head. She paused at the entry stone to kick off her shoes and then came into the hall. She was a thin woman, perhaps in her late thirties. Her face was broad at the high cheekbones and she had beautiful large dark eyes. Her expression was no more welcoming than had been that of the Japanese man at the other house.

"Hello," she said. "I'm Nan Horner—a neighbor up the hill. Sumie-san says you're having a bit of language trouble. Can I help you find the place you're looking for?"

"We've found it," Marcia said. "I'm Marcia Talbot. It seems the cable I sent my husband didn't reach him in time, so he had no warning of our coming."

The woman pulled the scarf from her head and ruffled her short, gray-sprinkled hair. "That's who Sumie-san said you were, but I'll confess I didn't believe her. Well, you'd better come in here, while I see if we can get some fires going in this icebox. The servants have their own quarters and they prefer a native *hibachi* to keep them warm." She turned her attention on Laurie and this time flashed a quick smile that made her face seem suddenly alive and warm. "You're Laurie, I suppose? I've heard about you."

She flung open a door into a great gloomy room and went briskly about switching on lamps. Over her shoulder she spoke in Japanese to the maid, who ran to light the fire ready laid in a grate.

Marcia followed her uneasily into the room. Who

was this Nan Horner that she came so readily into Jerome's house to take charge and give orders to the servants? Somehow all her own confidence and courage was fading in the face of this woman's assurance and air of being completely at home in Jerome Talbot's house.

Was this the one? Marcia asked herself bleakly. Was this woman the answer to the question she had always thrust away to the back of her mind?

Nan Horner turned from the fire and looked at her appraisingly. "So you've finally come," she said.

THREE

NAN HORNER'S WORDS WERE A STATEMENT, NOT A question. What lay behind them Marcia could not tell and she resented their being spoken. She looked about the big room without answering.

It had apparently been intended as a drawing room and was of drawing room proportions. In spite of its size, it was overcrowded with Victorian furniture that might have come out of a period play. In the middle of an ancient Oriental carpet stood a round table covered with a red plush cloth, an overflowing potted fern set upon it. There were two plush-covered sofas and one small one of black horsehair. Burdened whatnots cluttered every corner, and various stiff chairs and bits of bric-a-brac were strewn without taste around the room. From the ceiling an old-fashioned chandelier, now electrified, shed a dingy light from two or three bulbs. It seemed an improbable room to come upon in Japan.

Nan Horner stood near the marble mantel, from which a gilded clock watched the room in silence. Her hands were thrust deep in the pockets of a loose coat and she wrinkled her nose as she looked about her.

"What a dustbin! I don't know how Jerry stands it. He has gone down to Hiroshima for a couple of weeks. Something to do with his work, I suppose. The ABCC's down there, you know. Atomic Bomb Casualty Commission."

Jerry? Marcia thought. Jerome had never been a "Jerry" sort of person for as long as she could remember. Her sense of resentment toward this woman was increasing.

"Do you know when my husband will be home?" she asked, a little stiffly.

"He didn't say. He never does. But before too long, I should imagine." Nan Horner walked to a tall, narrow window and looked out at the snow-hidden sky. "Can't tell tonight, but the moon's due to be full in another week. And he's always home by full moon."

That seemed a curious remark. "Why should he come home for the full moon?" Marcia asked.

Nan Horner shrugged thin square shoulders. "Oh— we're a moon-ridden people in Japan. We pay more attention to such things out here. In the meantime, let's see what can be arranged for you." Once more she spoke in Japanese to the two waiting women and then nodded at Marcia. "Tomorrow Sumie-san will clean the guest room and get it in order for you. Nobody's used it for years. But for tonight they'll make up Jerry's bed and set a fire in his room. You'll find it more comfortable than this mausoleum. Lord, what a place!"

Marcia nodded in agreement. How strange that Jerome should occupy this big house, when his needs were so simple.

"It's like Jerome not to worry about his own comfort," she said.

There was wry amusement in Nan Horner's eyes. "Yes, I know. I met Jerome Talbot when he first came to Japan. Before he married you, in fact. This house dates back to the '80's. It has quite a story. The man who built it belonged to one of the great ruling families of Japan, but he was educated abroad in Europe. By the time he returned to Kyoto he had developed an admiration for the Victorian styles of his day and he insisted upon building a big, foreign-type house."

Nan gestured, taking in the huge place.

"But he had to satisfy the rest of his family," she went on, "so he attached a Japanese wing to the villa. After he died in the early 1900's the house was turned into a hotel for a while. So it's had a history as mongrel as the architecture. Some of the furnishings in this room must be almost the original vintage. Lord knows what they did with it when the Occupation moved in. Anyway it suited Jerry's purpose. Most Japanese houses are tiny, you know."

"Why should he want anything big?" Marcia asked.

Nan was watching Laurie absently as the child explored the room, and seemed not to hear.

"How did you find the place anyway?" she asked Marcia.

Marcia held her hands to the blaze, letting the warmth seep into her, ready to be scorched a little after being cold and discouraged.

"I showed the written address to a cab driver," she explained. "But he took us to the wrong house first—

around the corner on another street. A Japanese man came to the gate, but he wasn't very friendly."

"That would be Ichiro Minato," Nan said. "It's all the same house, though Jerry has partitioned it off. The Minatos are . . . well, I suppose you'd call them tenants. They live in the Japanese half, and Minato-san has his own troubles, I imagine. He's not a very sociable sort. What about food, Mrs. Talbot? You can come up to my place for dinner, if they can't fix you up here."

It was not the warmest of invitations and Marcia shook her head quickly. "I'm sure they can find something for us. We had a big meal at noon on the train. Soup—anything at all will do."

Nan Horner spoke to Yasuko-san, the cook. The woman bowed and shot a quick bright look of curiosity at Marcia.

"She'll fix you up," Nan said. "There's fish and rice and vegetables, and you'll find her a good cook. She's been with Jerry for years. Anything else you need?"

"No, thank you very much," Marcia said. "I don't know what we'd have done without you." The words sounded stilted in her own ears, but she had lost the power to be natural.

Nan Horner gave her a long straight look. "That's all right. Jerry's an old friend. You can reach me by phone if you need me. But you'd better get Sumie-san to call the number, or you'll never make it past the Japanese operator."

While the two women talked, Laurie had been circling the great museum of a room with curiosity and interest. Nan looked after her soberly.

"Doesn't resemble her father much, does she? Your

daughter plainly, as far as looks are concerned. But she's the nervous type like Jerry."

It was hard to accept the calm assumption that Nan Horner knew Jerome as well as his wife did, if not better, and Marcia stiffened inwardly.

"Laurie has a good deal of vitality," she said quietly. "She's interested in everything there is to be interested in."

Nan Horner had a disconcertingly frank way of staring that made Marcia uncomfortable. She stared again now, as if Marcia were some sort of oddity.

"So you're his wife," she said flatly, as if the fact were too astonishing to be accepted. "Oh, well, it's none of my business. If you have everything you need, I'll run along. Whistle if you want me. 'Bye, Laurie. Good night, Mrs. Talbot."

She took one hand out of her pocket for a casual wave and walked out of the room, while Sumie-san and Yasuko-san followed her, chattering in Japanese.

She mustn't let this outspoken woman disturb her, Marcia thought. It certainly wasn't any of Nan Horner's business what Jerome's wife was like, and the woman had acknowledged the fact.

Laurie came spinning back from a final inspection of the room. "It will be fun to live here! Can we explore the rest of the house now? It's so queer and different."

Marcia smiled at her exuberant child. "There'll be time for exploring tomorrow. Let's see how the fire is coming in your father's room and get ourselves settled."

"You're tired, aren't you?" Laurie said kindly, and Marcia squeezed the little girl to her. She was bone tired, weary to her very fingertips, yet she knew the cause was not the long flight across the ocean, or the train trip from Tokyo—it was an emotional weariness. She had been keyed up in anticipation for so long. All her forces had been gathered to meet whatever might happen when she came face to face with Jerome. Now there was nothing more to anticipate until Jerome himself appeared on the scene, and all the strength had gone out of her in a limp wave. There seemed to be no telling when she would see Jerome now. How odd it sounded to base his return on the full moon. There was something behind that remark she didn't understand, but she had no energy to puzzle over it now.

She and Laurie left the big room that would probably never be warmed by its single fire, and crossed the wide chill hallway, scuffing along in slippers that would not scratch or soil the beautifully polished floors.

Sumie-san bowed them into Jerome's bedroom with a wide smile that dimpled her plump cheeks. She had shed her padded coat and wore a patterned blue kimono, with short white *tabi* on her feet.

The bedroom was smaller than the drawing room, though still of old-fashioned, high-ceilinged proportions. A fire roared and snapped and a portable electric heater had been turned on. At least it was a more comfortable room, though a bit on the austere side, like Jerome.

The big double bed, well heaped with blankets, looked comfortable. Several pieces of modern cane furniture, of attractive Japanese design, were set about. The low chairs had runners connecting the legs so that they would not cut into floors or mattings. Jerome's big walnut desk was set near a window and there was a huge, well-filled bookcase against one wall. A bedside table held still more books, and a lamp with a cylindrical parchment shade. This, at least, was a lived-in room.

Laurie had gone to stand in fascination at the head of the bed and Marcia, sensing her stillness, turned to see what had caught her attention. In the center of the plain beige wall above the bed hung a Japanese mask, shadowy in the flickering light. It had been carved from dark red cherry wood with a skill that brought out every detail of expression in the face that looked down on them. Here and there touches of paint etched the red of the mouth, or the white gleam of teeth, the white of the eyes, but the forehead, the high cheekbones, the curved chin, were all highlighted in the polish of natural wood and seemed almost alive as firelight played over them.

"It's a demon, isn't it?" Laurie asked in a whisper, as if those long-lobed ears might hear.

Marcia knew what she meant. The face was utterly evil in its expression. The brows and eye sockets were set at an exaggerated slant with the eyeballs turning eerily down. The white above the eyeballs gave them a wild look of fury. The bushy black eyebrows were of real hair and black strands of hair hung from the chin. The nose was chiseled, but broad at the base, with wide, flaring nostrils which added a look of scorn and disdain. The mouth snarled, with lips apart, drawing menacingly down at the corners. Yet there were none of the conventional touches here of the demon mask. No fangs, no popping eyeballs, or other distortions. This was the face of a man—proud, intelligent, dangerous, wicked.

"I suppose it is a sort of demon," Marcia said, not

liking to think the artist had intended it as the face of a man.

"Anyway it's awfully spooky," Laurie said and turned her back on it uneasily. "I like the picture over the mantel better," she added. "That's nice, isn't it?"

Wearily Marcia sat down in a rocker before the fire and looked up at the Japanese print. The picture presented a snow scene in which two figures were walking under a snow-covered Japanese umbrella. The man was clad in a long black robe, showing gold and red only where the lower folds opened over a patterned kimono. A high black hood covered his head and one hand clasped the umbrella shaft just above the delicate hand of his companion. The girl in the picture was gowned all in white, except for the black and gold obi about her waist and the scarlet lining of kimono sleeves. A white cloth draped her head in soft folds, framing her face. Both figures wore high wooden *geta* which raised their feet above the snowy ground.

"Who do you think they are?" Laurie asked, always ready to make up stories.

Marcia recalled something she had read about the significance of a man and woman under an umbrella in a Japanese print. It was a symbol commonly used and meant that the two were lovers. The faces were typically expressionless, but there was a solicitous air in the man's manner as he bent toward the girl, a seeming shyness in her downcast look.

"Probably they're two sweethearts out walking together," Marcia said, and wondered at Jerome's sentimental choice of picture for his wall.

Sumie-san came in to set up a small table for them near the fire, and brought their meal on a red lacquered tray. The food was served in attractive blue-patterned dishes, a sprig of pine needles with a tiny cone attached gracing one corner of the tray. Marcia touched it and smiled her appreciation at the little maid. Sumie-san giggled in delight and hid her mouth with her kimono sleeve. Probably she had run out in the snow to fetch this twig fresh from the garden. She hovered over them as they ate and filled their cups with hot tea. Even Laurie drank a little tea, since there was no fresh milk on hand, and the food warmed and heartened both mother and daughter.

When they had eaten and the things were cleared away, they began to unpack what they would need for the night. Sumie-san came in again and explained with gestures that a bath had been prepared and was now *atsui*. Since Nan Horner had vouched for them, Sumie-san seemed to accept their presence cheerfully. She bore Laurie away to introduce her to the attractions of a Japanese bath, leaving Marcia alone for a little while.

Marcia undressed and put on a quilted blue robe. Then she moved slowly about the room, looking for something of Jerome, something to reassure her, to put her in touch with him again. The disappointment of this arrival, the big cold house, the appearance of Nan Horner, had all seemed to cut her off from Jerome, to point to a stranger. Urgently she began to seek in this room the man she knew and loved.

Book titles revealed his ruling absorption in science and there were various books about Japan as well. One volume she pulled out was a treatise on abnormal psychology and for some reason she glanced uneasily at the mask above the bed.

Its brooding presence ruled the room. The glaring eyes saw every corner, the unholy snarl seemed to mock whatever man might build of worth. The thing was undoubtedly a work of art, but how could Jerome bear to have it scowling down at him from the wall day in and day out? But then this was the sort of macabre humor he had begun to enjoy in late years. Here she had found something of him she did not want to remember.

An unfathomable distance seemed to lie between the two extremes of the mask and the gentle snow scene of two young lovers. How were they compatible? she puzzled. Until she knew, she felt she would have little understanding of the man Jerome Talbot had become, and that was a frightening thought—to come all these miles to confront a stranger.

Across the room against a wall that lay in shadow, another picture caught her eye. She picked up a shaded lamp nearby so that she could see it more clearly. This was a framed photograph, grimly realistic in its subject —a picture of shattered buildings left from a bombing. Broken walls and tumbled bricks spread ruin in all directions, with one half-destroyed building dominating the scene. This structure was taller than the other ruins and had once been a concrete building several stories high. It was still crowned by the naked girders of an open dome. In one corner of the picture a word was printed and Marcia bent to read it. The word was HIROSHIMA.

She set the lamp back on its table, remembering how terribly Jerome had been disturbed by what he had seen and heard in Hiroshima when he went to Japan in the early days of the Occupation. He had written so much home to her father, and he had felt, as her father had felt, that he himself had been instrumental in that cruel devastation. He had allowed himself to be worn down by a sense of the human guilt in which he believed he played a part. The long, non-atomic bombing of Tokyo must have been almost as devastating—what difference did it make to the people who died? Yet he had not been as troubled by that.

Strangely, it was this picture of Hiroshima which brought Jerome closer to her. She could understand his wanting to remember, to be continually reminded in a world which so easily forgot. Pity for his self-torture welled up in her and she went to sit before the fire, thinking of him intently, searching back through the years.

She was still sitting there when Laurie came back from her bath, flushed and rosy-warm, to snuggle happily into the big bed. According to Laurie there was nothing more fun than a Japanese bath. Marcia dropped a kiss on each sleepy eyelid and followed Sumie-san down chill hallways to the bathroom.

It was a big room, steamy and warm, with a slatted wooden floor around a huge sunken tub. Shallow steps led down into the water. By means of gestures, and accompanying giggles of amusement, Sumie-san made it clear that one washed thoroughly with soap and cloth, sitting on a low wooden stool. Then suds were rinsed away before the bather stepped down into the neck-deep tub of clean hot water. She also offered to stay for back-scrubbing assistance, but Marcia shooed her away and performed her ablutions alone.

When at length she lowered herself by degrees into the water, she found it certainly *atsui,* but not unbearable. Resting on a ledge with the water lapping about her neck, she let the heat soak away her weariness and worry and lull her into a state as sleepy as Laurie's. There was a big American bath towel with which to pat herself dry and then she bundled into her robe and ran back down the hall to the bedroom where the fire was sinking to darkened embers.

Laurie was sound asleep, brown braids flung across the pillow. But there had been a change in the room. Before Laurie had fallen asleep, she had stood on the bed to hang her plaid muffler over the mask on the wall. A good idea, Marcia thought wryly.

When she had turned off the lights, she went to the window to look out upon the white expanse of garden. Big snowflakes fell softly into a silent world. Beyond the bamboo fence the city of Kyoto lay invisible and Marcia could not be sure it was really there. She put on her nightgown and crept into bed beside the small, warm body of her sleeping daughter.

Far away, from some distant street, came the sound of three haunting notes played on a bamboo flute. Always the same three notes, wandering on through the night, with long silences between. Snow whispered at the window as she fell asleep.

FOUR

It was strange the way a bright new morning could dispel the concerns and the gloom of such a night. In the morning Marcia awoke to a resurgence of hope and courage. The snow had ceased to fall and pale sunshine brightened the windows. Beside her Laurie still slept as Marcia lay quietly beneath warm covers, letting new buoyancy flow through her.

Last night weariness and disappointment had made her fearful and suspicious. This morning she was rested and her depression of the night before seemed foolish. What did it matter that Jerome was not here to greet her? *She* was here in his home, ready to be part of his life as she had never been allowed to be part of it before. When he had written that disturbing letter he had been far away from her, but now, soon, she would see him, speak to him, touch him, and she knew with all confidence that she could bring him back to her, help him dispel whatever dark witchery held him in Japan. No matter what his self-torture, his self-blame stemmed from, it could not stand before her loving devotion.

Now she could remember Nan Horner with less rancor. It was natural that Jerome would have friends, and undoubtedly a woman of such obvious assurance and capability would take it upon herself to aid him if she could. But to regard her in a possible romantic light as a person who might hold him to Japan, was nonsense. Remembering the surge of antagonism she had felt toward the woman the night before, Marcia winced in distaste. She had never been jealous and possessive, and she must not again allow weariness and momentary depression to betray her. Jealousy was ugly, destructive, and she would have none of it. The mere act of dismissing the emotion gave her a sense of virtue and confidence.

When Sumie-san and Yasuko-san tiptoed in to light the fire and find out about breakfast, Marcia sat up in bed and smiled at them brightly. Laurie stirred and yawned and looked about her with wakening interest.

Breakfast would be served here, where it was warm, whenever she liked, Yasuko-san indicated. They might have a fine Japanese dish called *hamu-ando-egu,* which set Laurie burrowing into her pillow to hide her laughter. Marcia noted Sumie-san's observant glance at the plaid shrouded mask and thought the little maid caught her eye with understanding.

When the tray came there was toast for breakfast and a couple of juicy tangerines, to say nothing of a six ounce bottle of pasteurized milk for Laurie. The ham and eggs were definitely international, and the world seemed far less hostile than it had last night. Over the mantel the lady in white hovered dreamily and her black-clad companion held the umbrella solicitiously over her head. Hiroshima hung in a shadowy corner where it could be forgotten for the moment.

After breakfast Laurie was eager to get into coat and snow pants and go out to play in the unfamiliar snow of the garden. Sumie-san set to work at once on the guest room into which they would be moved. Marcia felt she would be glad to leave Jerome's room with its strange contrasts and unanswered questions. That room was not Jerome as she knew him.

Shortly after nine o'clock Nan Horner appeared briefly. Marcia went out to the entryway to speak to her, since she didn't want to take off her shoes and come in.

"You're invited to lunch at my house," Nan said firmly. "Twelve-thirty will be fine. I'll send my Isa-san to fetch you. I've a couple of appointments downtown this morning, but I'll look for you both at lunch. No need to ask whether you slept well. You look like a different woman this morning. Be seeing you."

And off she went abruptly and breezily, giving Marcia no chance to answer. She and Laurie would go, of course, Marcia assured herself, thrusting back a twinge of resentment at the other woman's highhanded manner. It would be good to talk to another American, especially one who had known Jerome in recent months.

Marcia had flung on a coat to go to the door and now she walked curiously the length of the hall to the drafty stairway at the rear. This might be as good a time as any to have a look at this Japanese villa which her husband had made into his home.

The stairs were foreign in style and wide, taking a square turn to the right at a landing halfway up. The uncarpeted steps were made of the same cypress wood with its silver-gray tone that had been used for flooring in the rest of the house. Nowhere had the wood been marred with varnish or paint, and the gleam of the natural wood was pleasing.

On the second floor the stairs ended in a tiny pocket of hall, with sliding Japanese doors all about. She slipped one door open, nearly putting an unwary finger through a paper pane, and looked into a Japanese room. The floor was covered with those squares of thick, springy matting, marked off with black tape which Marcia had read were called *tatami*. She stepped out of her slippers and crossed the matting to another sliding screen on the opposite side. Here was a second room, opening beyond onto a wooden gallery that seemed to run all around this upstairs area. Window-less wooden shutters, sliding in grooves like the doors, closed off the outer world and little daylight seeped into this upstairs gloom.

The bare floor of the gallery felt cold as glass beneath her stockinged feet. She did not go back for her slippers, however, but followed the gallery around to the front of the house. The outside shutters slid easily at her touch and she moved one a few inches so that she could look out. Now she could see the way in which the house was placed in relation to the hillside. This gallery overlooked the stepping stones of the front entrance and faced downhill. The house had been placed in a garden area, with its back toward the uphill side. The entrance gate of the Minato family, where she had gone last night, was around to the left. She could not see it from where she stood, but now at least she could see Kyoto. She thrust the shutter back still further and stepped eagerly into the opening.

The morning sun shone on a glittering white world of snow-crusted roof tops spread out below. The gray tiles of eaves made geometrical markings beneath the burden of snow. The green of pine trees and the occasional red of a shrine made exclamation points of color in the black and white scene. Kyoto was a vast, spreading, hilly city, surrounded by the serried flanks of snowy mountains. The voice of Kyoto came to her in the distant murmur of traffic, in the sound of horns, and of a temple bell booming, low and deep. But here on this hillside the snow hush lay upon houses and street and it was very still. Marcia breathed deeply and found an exhilaration in the air. How eager she was to know Japan, how ready to love it as Jerome must love it.

She slid the shutter back into place and followed the gallery around to the other side of the house. There she opened another shutter and looked down on the garden where Laurie was playing. This side garden was far larger than the narrow one which led to the front door. It held an ice-filmed fishpond with a tiny bridge over it, a stone lantern, capped with snow, small pine trees, and brown shrubbery. In a corner near the fence a plum tree spread dark branches, its lovely, deep pink blossoms just opening against the snow. However, all this perfection of arrangement had been spoiled by a high bamboo fence with pointed spikes along the top which cut across the center of the garden and separated it from the rest of the garden at the rear.

From her vantage point Marcia could look down into both gardens and as she watched, two Japanese children came out in the snow beyond the bamboo fence. The boy, who was older than Laurie, and a bit larger, wore dark trousers and a dark jacket, under which sweaters padded him into a roly-poly figure. The little girl might be about six. She wore a quilted kimono and she too was padded into barrel shape. Both children had round rosy cheeks and the girl's hair was cut in straight bangs across her forehead and a straight bob all around. The boy wore a black, visored cap, with his black hair showing beneath.

Thinking in terms of playmates for Laurie, Marcia regarded both children with interest. But there was a closed gate between the two gardens and Laurie could not see the neighbor children through the tight bamboo fence. At the moment, however, Laurie was in no need of companionship. As Marcia watched, she rolled one snowball after another in her mittened hands and flung them exuberantly in all directions—at a stone lantern, at a pine tree, even at her mother, when she saw her standing on the veranda above. And finally, she flung one over the fence into the next garden.

The snowball landed *squish* on the little girl's head and she stared at her brother in astonishment to see if he were playing some trick. The boy had seen the snowball come sailing over the fence and he looked in that direction, clearly puzzled. Neither child had glanced up at the other section of the house where Marcia stood watching.

Laurie sent her second snowball soaring high over

the fence and the boy hesitated no longer. With an impish grin, he rolled a good-sized ball of his own and hurled it back at the unseen assailant. It swooped over Laurie's head and she looked up at her mother.

"There's somebody over there!" she shouted.

Marcia laughed and nodded. Laurie ran in a streak for the gate and tried to pull it open, but when she found it firmly locked, she clambered to its top where she could look over into the rear garden.

The tableau was an amusing one: the American child climbing precariously to the top of the gate, gazing with interest at the two astonished Japanese children on the other side.

"Hello!" Laurie called.

The boy made a face at her. "Harro!" he echoed with cheerful mockery, while his padded little sister stared with eyes like bright currants in her round face. In a moment, Marcia was sure, the children would have taken matters into their own hands and broken past both fence and language barrier. But a sudden interference thwarted them.

From the other house came a Japanese woman in a dark blue kimono, running deftly through the snow on her *geta,* and took the two children by the hand. She saw Laurie clinging to the gate and shook her head at her, evidently forbidding her to climb over. When she turned and started back for the house with the children, Marcia decided to speak.

"Good morning," she called down to the trio.

The woman was young and very pretty, Marcia saw as she looked down. She had the exquisite chiseling of features that is both feminine and Japanese. Her skin was the pale color typical of a well-born Japanese woman, and the darkness of her eyes and brows contrasted with it attractively. But unlike the children, she did not smile up at Marcia in open friendliness.

She bowed politely in Marcia's direction and then swept the two children with her into the house. Marcia had the depressing feeling that she had been gently, courteously rebuffed. Plainly the young woman had not wanted her children to play with Laurie, nor had she wanted to give Marcia any friendly, neighborly greeting other than that demanded by good manners.

Laurie slid back to her own side in disappointment and began to roll snowballs again. There seemed no reason why she should not be allowed to play with the children next door, if they wanted to play with her. Perhaps Jerome had given some order that the children were not to be allowed on this side. Certainly he had taken special pains to seal off this part of the house from the rest.

Well, there was nothing to be done about the matter now. Before she closed the shutter, Marcia glanced down the gallery to the end and saw that a very un-Japanese door had been placed there. A door with a Yale lock. She went over and turned the knob gently. It was locked. That was natural enough, if Jerome rented out the other half of the house to tenants. There was no reason for the uneasiness that filled her, yet something of the foreboding she had felt the night before in this house returned to haunt her.

She closed the wooden shutter and retrieved her slippers. There was nothing more to be seen up here—just four bare Japanese rooms, the veranda running around three sides, and a ceiling-high partition cutting off this half of the house from the rest.

Thoughtfully she went downstairs and looked into the guest room next door to Jerome's bedroom, which Sumie-san was now tidying. The little maid had fastened back her kimono sleeves with purple bands to leave her arms free. Over her head she had tied a clean white cotton towel, and she looked workmanlike and busy.

The guest room was smaller than Jerome's and would therefore be easier to keep warm. The walls had been covered with a bamboo patterned wallpaper, now fading a little with age. Several pieces of comfortable, clean-looking cane furniture stood about. There was a low coffee table and small twin dressers of beige wood. This room had two beds, which would make for more comfortable sleeping, and there was a light beige scatter rug on the floor before each bed. The only pictures were two innocuous Japanese floral prints over the mantel. There were no disturbing details of any kind.

The morning passed quickly enough as she unpacked her suitcases and Laurie's and hung up their clothes in a wardrobe closet made of the same light-colored wood as the rest of the furniture in the room.

She called Laurie in to get her ready for lunch just before Nan's maid came for them. Isa-san arrived promptly at twelve-thirty and, unlike the servants in Jerome's house, she wore western dress—a neat blouse and skirt, with a western style cloth coat over them, and her hair was bobbed and waved. She spoke a little English and was happy to air it as she led them the short distance uphill.

Nan Horner's small house was in modified Japanese style, with one or two western rooms. Luncheon was served in a Japanese room where, to Laurie's delight, they sat on green silk cushions—*zabuton*—on the floor, centered around a brazier of charcoal which Nan called a *hibachi*.

"Japanese rooms are wonderful to live in, except in winter," Nan said. "But maybe that's what makes the Japanese a hardy race. I have a fireplace in my office, so I can keep fairly warm. In summer I set up a small table and chairs there on the veranda and have my meals practically in the garden."

Even now, the snowy garden seemed very close through the sliding glass doors that held away the outdoors. Winter sparrows hopped about in the snow feeding on crumbs which Nan had flung out to them, and snow-laden branches made a delicate pattern against the sky.

Marcia found herself studying Nan with more than a little interest. She found her a rather handsome, forthright woman of whom Jerome might well be fond. But to read anything more into the relationship would be foolish, Marcia assured herself, on guard now against the rancor she had felt the previous evening.

"I hope this is our last snowfall," Nan said. "It's nearly March and the camellias will be out soon. Spring comes quickly in Japan. You're lucky to be here for the spring season."

"I know," Marcia said. "I've read so much about Japan—I'm looking forward to the flowers," and was relieved Nan seemed to take it for granted that she would stay.

Today Nan wore a full brown skirt and a burnt-orange cardigan. Her short hair had been brushed carelessly back and her face seemed more angular than ever beneath deepset dark eyes. She reclined with easy grace on a floor cushion, while Marcia's pencil-slim skirt made sitting on the floor more difficult.

"There are so few foreign houses available in Kyoto," Nan said. "Besides, Japan is my home and I'm used to the customs. Except for heating arrangements, I find them comfortable."

Isa-san knelt beside them, stirring the beef and vegetables of *sukiyaki* in a modern electric frying pan.

Marcia found the simplicity of the room restful and attractive. There were no furnishings other than the low lacquered table on which the meal was being served. In one corner was an indented alcove with a hanging scroll of painted plum blossoms, a graceful branch in the vase beneath it.

"That's the *tokonoma*—the alcove of honor," Nan said. "We had trouble with the Occupation people at first. They didn't know any better and they shocked the Japanese by using those alcoves for storage purposes and goodness knows what."

"Did you live in Japan before the war?" Marcia asked.

"I'm a B.I.J.," Nan told her. "Born in Japan. My father ran an export business for many years out here. I grew up in the business, so to speak, and when my parents died before the war, I went right on with his work. When I saw trouble coming, I returned to relatives I'd visited a few times in the States. But I came out again right after the war ended and I'm back in exporting now. At first the Occupation used me as an interpreter." She gave Marcia a level glance. "That's how I met Jerry Talbot. I was assigned to the group he was working with in Hiroshima."

"Then you really did know him from the time he first came to Japan," Marcia said.

The *sukiyaki* was ready now, and Isa-san served it over rice in small bowls. Marcia and Laurie had both practiced with chopsticks a few times in San Francisco, so they ate as Nan did, though with considerably less skill.

"When you dine in real Japanese style," Nan said, "the rice comes last. But Americans like it with the meat and vegetables."

Throughout the meal Nan Horner seemed friendly enough. She kept the talk going, cheerfully, impersonally, encouraging Laurie to talk about her school and the things she liked to do for fun. But all the while Marcia felt little warmth. She sensed that the other woman was performing a charitable duty, rather than welcoming Jerome's wife. Neither liking Marcia, nor disliking her, merely doing what needed to be done. In spite of her earlier resolution, Marcia's sense of uneasiness about Nan gradually returned.

When they had finished eating, their hostess got up agilely, tugged her skirt into line and thrust up the sleeves of her cardigan.

"For the summer months I like to get into a cotton *yukata* at home—that's the cool summer kimono—but Japanese dress is no good in wintertime unless you wear long flannel underwear, as of course the men do. Even under western business suits. It's not aesthetic, but it keeps them warm. Come along to my office where you can be more comfortable."

Marcia was glad to get up and stretch cramped legs. A narrow polished hall led to a room near the entrance. There a welcome fire burned in the grate and there was a desk, a sofa, and comfortable chairs. Over the mantel hung a New Hampshire snow scene and Nan nodded at it wryly.

"Just to remind me where I stem from. My parents came from New England, though I seem to have taken root out here. I like Japan and the Japanese. And of course Kyoto is the place in the world that I know best."

Laurie was drifting around the room looking at everything with her usual eager interest. Bookshelves lined one wall, crowded with the lore of Japan, and there were other shelves with art objects on them. Marcia picked up a small rounded vase with plump sides glazed in a soft dark red, a design of storks and leaves in white and green against the red.

"That's an old piece of cloisonné," Nan said. "Perfect of its kind. I like the way a thing has a right to exist in Japan merely because it's beautiful. It needs to serve no other purpose. Maybe there's a lesson for the rest of us in that. Not that the contemplation of beauty alone will move the world ahead. I don't hold for clinging only to the past in Japan. New generations must be served—but I hope they don't forget their heritage."

Marcia turned the plump little vase in her hands. It was a delight both to the eye and to the touch and she could imagine the artist's joy in such work.

"I envy you in a way," Nan said. "Seeing Japan for the first time. Seeing it with a fresh eye. But what made you take so long about coming?"

Startled by the sharp question, Marcia threw a hasty glance at Laurie. The child had carried a book of colored pictures over to the hearthrug and was studying it, paying no attention to her elders.

"The time never seemed right for coming until now," Marcia said quietly. "Laurie was in school and—"

"You've taken her out of school now, I suppose?" Nan's tone was dry. "Sit down over here where it's comfortable." She patted a big armchair and then dropped into a swivel chair behind the desk.

Marcia sat down without comment. She did not want to be quizzed by Nan Horner. Her reasons for not coming to Japan were too personal and private, and they were no fault of her own.

Nan removed the top of a small brass incense burner on her desk, dropped in a cone of incense, lighted it and replaced the top. Her fingers moved absently and a thoughtful frown creased her forehead.

"I used to wonder about you," she said, not looking at Marcia now. "After Jerry married you, that is. I used to wonder what sort of woman you were when you didn't come out here to be with him. It could have been arranged, I thought, if you had wanted to come."

At this direct attack, Marcia sat up suddenly. "That's not fair! You don't know anything about it."

"Don't I? Well, maybe not. But I thought he needed you and you weren't where you belonged as his wife."

This was outrageous meddling. Marcia checked the angry words that rose to her lips, but her answer was curt. "I always wanted to come," she said simply.

The scent of sandalwood drifted up from the brass burner in a thin blue ribbon of smoke. Nan sniffed it absently.

"If I had been his wife, I'd have come. I wouldn't

have let anything block me. I might as well say these things before Jerry gets here. They need to be said."

Marcia found that her lips had a sudden tendency to tremble and she tried to steady them. She mustn't let this woman's words upset her.

Nan glanced in her direction and her manner softened unexpectedly. "Never mind. Though you haven't said so, it's none of my business. And of course you were ridiculously young for him. And still are, for that matter."

"You sound like my mother," Marcia said. "How does any third person know what is right for a man and a woman?" Then she changed the subject firmly to make it clear that she would discuss Jerome no further with Nan Horner. "Tell me about the Japanese family that lives next door to us. Did you say Minato was the name? I saw two children outside this morning and a very pretty young woman who seemed to be their mother."

"That would be Chiyo. She's pretty all right, and she comes from a good family. It's a mystery how she ever came to marry Ichiro Minato. I suppose it was the war."

"What's wrong with him?" Marcia said.

"Ichiro grew up to be a soldier. The military government did a good job on him, and he doesn't know how to be anything else. Chiyo is like a doll—delicate and fragile. I'm not unsympathetic to Ichiro's problems. In fact, I'm rather sorry for him. But there's such a contrast between the two of them."

"She wasn't very friendly," Marcia commented. "She took her children into the house as if she didn't want them to play with Laurie. And she didn't return my greeting in a very friendly fashion."

Nan played with the top of the incense burner. "If I were you, I'd leave the family next door strictly alone. You'll find most Japanese eager to be courteous and friendly. They harbor no hard feelings and they don't expect us to. But this situation is out of the ordinary."

"In what way?" Marcia asked.

Nan got up from the desk and went over to see what Laurie was looking at. "Take my advice and stay away from the Minatos," she said, closing the subject. "What's that book you've found, Laurie?"

Marcia knew that a door had been shut in her face. Now she felt more curious than ever about the Minatos. And especially about the lovely Chiyo.

Laurie had risen from the hearth and was showing the book she had found to Nan. It was a book of masks.

"I was looking for that horrid face that hangs on the wall in Daddy's room," Laurie said. "Do you think it might be in this book?"

"It's a mask of dark cherry wood," Marcia explained. "It seemed such an evil-looking thing that we covered it up for the night."

Nan laughed wryly. "I know the one you mean. In fact, I found that mask for Jerry. It's not an original, but it's a very good copy. It represents the villain from an old tragedy. He was not, as you might surmise, a very nice fellow. But he's not in that book, Laurie."

The sound of the bell at the gate tinkled through the house and Isa-san came bowing in to announce a visitor. "Yamada-san," she said. Nan seemed to hesitate for a moment, then she told the maid to show the visitor in.

"You'll like my friend Yamada-san," Nan said. "He is a gentleman of the old school. And a publisher of some of the best literature appearing in Japan today."

Yamada-san appeared in the study door, a small, elderly figure in a dark gray western suit. He was bald except for a ring of gray hair around the back of his skull, his face and head the color of old ivory, with heavy gray eyebrows bushed above keen, sparkling eyes. Yamada-san's was a venerable, kindly, intelligent face. He bowed low in the doorway, and then came in to shake Nan's hand in the western manner.

Nan introduced him and it seemed to Marcia that the name "Talbot" made him cast a penetrating look, immediately hidden by lowered lids.

Again there were bows all round, and Marcia found herself bowing too, as one did so easily in Japan. Yamada-san produced a flat box which he handed to Nan. It was of rough-textured navy blue cardboard, open along one side, with a white label pasted upon it. Marcia saw that it served as a cover for a square red book, gold-lettered along the spine. As Nan slid it from the box her expression seemed a little sad.

"So it's ready," she said. "And very handsome too. You've done a beautiful job with this, Yamada-san. Thank you for bringing it to me. This is my copy?"

"Is for you," Yamada-san said, bowing benevolently.

Nan seemed touched. "Thank you. I appreciate this. Please sit down. Isa-san is bringing tea."

The publisher seated himself, clearly pleased by Nan's reaction. As Nan slipped the book back into its box, Marcia held out her hand.

"May I see it?" she asked.

"You won't be able to make much sense of it," Nan warned. "It's all in Japanese."

The leaves were creamy and rough-textured, with three lines of Japanese characters running vertically down each page.

"There seems to be very little printing," Marcia said, and held the book open so Laurie could look at it too.

"That's because it's poetry," Nan explained. "The form is very simple and traditional. An exact number of syllables is required. I read it in manuscript and tried my hand at translating a few of the poems. Though I've lost the proper syllable form in these translations. Perhaps I can give you a sample—an approximation, at least." She took the book back. "Here is one:

> " 'Pine trees twist their limbs
> On the bare hillside—
> Samurai fighting.' "

"What's the name of the book?" Laurie asked, fascinated by the strange brushwork.

"It's called *The Moonflower,* after the title poem. At least that's what we would call it. The Japanese call the plant *yu gao. Gao* is the word for our morning glory, and *yu* means evening. Here's the poem:

> " 'Ghost white spirit flower
> Open to the moon;
> Death comes at dawn.' "

"Of course there isn't any rhyming. That doesn't matter in Japanese. It's the symbolic picture, the delicacy of the thought that is considered important. Am I right, Yamada-san?"

The venerable head nodded in dignity. "Many fine thoughts about death here," he said, leaning over to tap the pages with a forefinger. "Very noble, very sad."

Nan slipped the book back into its case with an air of finality and laid it on the desk. Marcia had the feeling that her hostess wanted to see the publisher alone, and when Isa-san came in with a bamboo-handled teapot and little cups on a lacquered tray, Marcia rose and said that she and Laurie must get back to the house.

Nan offered no objection, but saw them to the door, while Yamada-san sipped his tea and waited. When they had their coats on, Marcia held out her hand to Nan.

"Thank you for inviting us for lunch."

"Jerry will be home soon," Nan said. "He's sure to be along any day now because of—"

"The full moon?" Marcia said. "What did you mean by that exactly?"

Laurie had her galoshes on and she ran ahead into the yard. Nan put her hand suddenly on Marcia's shoulder.

"Listen to me, please, Mrs. Talbot. You've come to Japan too late. The wisest thing for you to do now is turn right around and go home. Go home before Jerry even knows you're here. Believe me, that's the only answer. It's too late for anything else."

Marcia stared at her in complete astonishment. Did this woman actually think that having come all this way, she would give up and go back? But before she could find words of protest, Nan held out her hand in a formal good-by. There was nothing to do but follow

Laurie to the gate, where Isa-san came to bow them out.

They walked home along the snowy lane between bamboo fences, while the tiled eaves of stepping-stone houses, each a level lower than its uphill neighbor, seemed to march down the hill beside them. They went in through their own gate and took off their shoes and galoshes.

In the entryway stood a man's pair of shoes and Marcia's heart began to thud. Laurie squealed with excitement at the sight of the shoes and darted into the hallway. Jerome stood near the foot of the stairs, with Marcia's cable in his hands, while Sumie-san and Yasuko-san hovered about him in eager welcome.

FIVE

THE DIM HALLWAY SEEMED AN ENDLESS LENGTH AS Marcia moved toward her husband. The moment was here, but she was no longer keyed up in preparation for it. She was suddenly frightened. Always she had pictured herself running eagerly into his arms, and now she could not. She had told herself that she would know the answer to her coming the moment she saw his face, and now she did not.

Jerome Talbot motioned the servants away with a careless gesture. His leanness, as always, made his height appear greater than it was, and his face seemed even thinner than Marcia remembered. His eyes were the same, though—hollow-set and dark, with vital fires burning in their depths. There were new lines about the mouth, a feathering of gray at the temples that caught at her heart. Because he was older than she was, she had always dreaded any sign of his aging. Love for him rushed through her in a wave of longing, yet now he regarded her somberly, without welcome, and she could not move toward him.

It was Laurie who broke the cold awkwardness of the moment. To Laurie this was her adored and fascinating father, and she did not take time to look for any difference in him. In an instant she had catapulted the length of the hall and hurled herself into his arms. He swung her up automatically and planted a kiss on her cheek, then set her down again. She folded both arms about one of his and clung to him in an ecstasy of affection.

"Are you surprised?" she cried. "We did send you that cable, only you didn't get it in time. But I think a surprise is nicer, anyway. Don't you think so, Daddy?"

Marcia felt her throat constrict. She knew so well how Laurie felt. The child had flung herself upon him in an outpouring of affection, as if by the fervor of her devotion she could force from him the affection she longed for in return. The temptation to imitate her daughter was strong, but Marcia held herself firmly in check.

Once he had greeted Laurie, Jerome seemed hardly to notice the child. He said evenly that he was indeed surprised, and waited for Marcia to speak. Somehow she managed to go to him quietly and lift her face for his kiss. He hesitated just a moment before brushing her cheek lightly with his lips. His restraint cut her further and it took all her will to suppress the tremor in her voice as she spoke.

"Hello, Jerome," she said.

The winged black brows she had once loved to trace with her fingers lifted sardonically, and his lips, straight, yet faintly sensual, curved in a mirthless smile. "Didn't you get my letter?"

She glanced at Laurie and shook her head in warning. Laurie knew nothing of the contents of that letter.

"I got it," she said. "And that's why I'm here."

"I see." He withdrew his arm from Laurie's fervent clasp. "If you'll excuse me now—I've had a long trip. I'd like a bath, and then I've some work waiting for me."

Quickly Marcia turned, glad of something to do for him. "I'll tell Sumie-san. Would you like something hot to drink? Have you had lunch—" She broke off because she had begun to sound like Laurie.

He shook his head. "Sumie-san knows what I want. It's not necessary for you to trouble yourself being wifely. If you'll excuse me."

"But, Daddy!" Laurie wailed.

"Hush, darling," Marcia said. "Not now. Your father is tired."

He crossed the hall to his bedroom and the door closed behind him. All the bubbling ferment subsided in Laurie and she looked completely bereft. Yet she tried to hide her hurt behind a grave young dignity.

"I guess he's tired. He'll feel better after a while, won't he? Is it all right if I go outside and play again?"

"Why don't you build yourself a snowman?" Marcia suggested. "That's something you could never do in California."

Laurie agreed that this was a good idea, and went outside rather meekly. Watching her go, a quiet anger began to stir in Marcia. She went into the bedroom she shared with Laurie and sat before the fire Sumie-san had lighted, staring into the red curlings of flame.

So this was the way he intended to be—withdrawn and cold and strange. But why? What had she done? The last time he had gone to Japan, he had parted from her lovingly enough. In the years she had known him she had glimpsed this cold side at times, though never before had it been directed toward her and Laurie. But as the stirring of indignation died, she began to feel shocked and sore and bewildered.

For more than an hour she sat before the fire, tense with listening. She heard him when he went down the hall to the bath. Heard him as he returned to his room. There was a long silence. Then he opened the door again, and she went out into the hall to find him putting on his coat.

"You're going out?" she asked evenly. "I hoped we might talk a little, get acquainted again."

He regarded her remotely. "I believe I said everything I wanted to say in my letter. You've made a foolish move in coming out here, Marcia. The only sensible thing you can do is turn around and go home."

"That's what Nan Horner said," she told him. "But it's not something I mean to do. I can't give everything up so easily without even understanding why."

Something flickered in his eyes and was gone before she could read it. "So you've met Nan?" he said.

"Sumie-san went for her last night when we got here," Marcia explained. "She came down and cleared things up. Then she invited us over for lunch today."

"I see." He moved toward the door uneasily, as though he was increasingly eager to escape. "I must go out now. Don't expect me for dinner."

He went into the entry hall to put on his shoes, and she watched him go out through the garden. Somehow she had not expected this—that he would leave the house so quickly, still cold and remote, with no word of kindness to her, or even of explanation. Never in the years she had known him had he been deliberately unkind, and this new attitude shocked and dismayed her to a frightening degree. For the first time she could almost believe in the words of his letter; words she had rejected so fiercely until now.

She was close to tears and despair and she fought back the weakness. She had not come all this distance to give up at Jerome's first unkind look. If she meant to fight for their marriage she would have to find more courage and endurance in herself than this.

Doggedly she put on her coat and galoshes and went into the side garden to join Laurie, who greeted her with pleasure. Together they rolled a huge snowball to make the base of a snowman. But she knew they were both pretending. Pretending there was, for the moment, no Jerome Talbot in their lives to wound and torment them.

Already the sun melted the surface and they had to dig into shaded corners for snow that was still firm. The physical effort of working with her hands, with her body, was a release for Marcia.

Once, as they worked at their lopsided snowman, she glanced up at the big Japanese villa behind them. Toward the rear of the upper gallery in the adjoining apartment, a section of wooden doors had slid open. A man stood in the aperture, staring down at them. It was the Japanese man she had seen upon her arrival the night before, Ichiro Minato. He did not blink or turn his eyes away when she caught his look upon her, but continued to stare at her stolidly. His expression was neither one of interest nor indifference. He stared as a stone image might have stared and there was no telling what thought went on behind his unwavering gaze.

"The inscrutable Oriental," Marcia thought dryly, and wondered if the cliché were really true.

Since she couldn't bring herself to stare as he did, she turned back to her play with Laurie. Later, when she glanced at the gallery again, the shutter was closed and only the house watched her.

Dinner that evening was a lonely affair. Sumie-san served it in a big gloomy dining room, heavy with mahogany furniture out of the past. There was a huge sideboard and a Victorian chandelier, a long table and stiff, high-backed chairs. Marcia wondered if the Japanese family which had once occupied this house had ever used this dining room, or if it had been kept as a foreign curiosity, more for show than for use. Certainly the rich, wine-red carpet revealed little sign of wear, though time had faded it. There was no fireplace here, and with only an electric heater burning, it was a chilly room. They ate hurriedly, grateful for the hot noodle soup Yasuko-san had made for them.

Afterwards the evening seemed endless. Unlike Laurie, Marcia could not settle down to look at pictures in a magazine. Her immediate problem was too urgent. When Laurie was in bed, she went into the drawing room, to sit huddled before the fire, wondering where Jerome had gone and when he would be back. In the dark, chilly room anguish lay heavily upon her spirit. Who were his friends in Kyoto? To whom had she turned so quickly upon coming back from his trip? Was it only his work at the laboratory that had drawn him away? She knew so little about him that she had no way of knowing.

The ringing telephone startled her. She listened while Sumie-san went to answer it, not expecting it to be for her. But the maid came to call her and when she picked up the receiver she heard Alan Cobb's voice. She had hardly thought of him since they had parted at the station the previous day. It was as if, since then, she had been projected into another world which had little relation to any other life she had ever known.

"Did you have any trouble finding your address?" he asked.

It was difficult to put aside her aching concern and dissemble casually.

"No, not really," she managed. "The driver took me to the wrong entrance first, but it was the right house." She sensed a lameness in her words and added an explanation, lest he suspect that something was wrong. "My husband was away and hadn't received my cable. But he came home today."

"Fine," Alan said. "I was sorry to leave you on your own yesterday. You looked a bit scared. But I had an idea you'd land on your feet. How is Laurie?"

His voice was relaxed, his words unhurried and he began to seem like a link with the ordinary everyday world outside the depressing atmosphere of this house. To keep him there on the wire and stave off the wave of anxiety that would return when she hung up, she told him about Laurie playing in her first snow, and a little about this picturesque house, although she did not give him its more gloomy details.

"You won't forget that I want to meet your husband?" he reminded her.

She had forgotten and she was sure Jerome would be indifferent to the idea, but she did not confess these things. She would try to arrange a meeting before long, she promised and let it go at that.

"How do you like the college?" she asked him, still wanting to hold to this thread of sound that stood between her and the dark thoughts that waited to engulf her.

"It's too soon to tell, but at least it's going to be interesting," he said. "I have my first class tomorrow. And they fixed me up in western-style living quarters. Everyone has been anxious to make me comfortable. It's a bit overwhelming."

They talked for a little while longer. He reminded her that he wanted to take Laurie on a sight-seeing trip one of these days when the weather improved, and then they hung up. She stood for a moment in the hallway near the foot of the stairs, aware of the brooding silence of the house, of the empty rooms above and the locked door cutting off the gallery upstairs. With silence, the house came into its own again. How muted and secret it seemed, how strangely hostile to her presence. Shivering, she hurried back to the fire in the drawing room and sat upon the hearthrug as Laurie liked to do, getting as close to the blaze as she could to warm the chilled core of her.

It was while she sat there that the strange music began—if it could be called music. Someone was playing melancholy minor notes on an Oriental stringed instrument, with an accompanying drumbeat and chanting in the background. She rose and walked around the room, trying to tell where the music came from. It was not drifting in from the street, but seemed to come from the rooms beyond the partition. There was a wailing monotony to it that wore upon her nerves and made her restless. It was not music which permitted escape and there was no shutting out the strange rhythm. When a woman's voice began to sing plaintively in Japanese, the sense of sadness, of mournful despair, was deepened. Then song and music stopped abruptly, and the ensuing silence seemed to ring with the sound, as if the rhythm of that strange drum were going on and on inside Marcia's head.

It was late when she gave up her vigil before the fire and went across the hall to the room where Laurie slept. Just as she was about to turn the doorknob softly so as not to waken her daughter, Jerome came into the house. She did not want to face him now, when her courage had long since ebbed, but she was not quick enough to escape before he saw her standing there.

"Wait a moment, Marcia," he said, and his voice was surprisingly gentle.

She paused, alert to the change in his tone and manner. He took off his coat, unwound the wool scarf from about his neck and then went to look in the drawing room.

"There are still some embers," he said. "If I poke them up, will you join me here for a few minutes?"

She followed him into the room, still uncertain, and stood beside the grate while he stirred up the fire and added coal from the bucket. Once he looked at her with the old, bright smile she remembered.

"Don't be angry with me," he said. "Though I can't say I'd blame you. That wasn't much of a welcome, was it? But you took me by surprise and I didn't know how to deal with the situation when I found you here."

"I know," she said. "I'm sorry," and longed to go to him easily in the old way and be held and comforted.

He tossed the poker aside with a clatter and stood up, tall and lean before her. Lightly he put his two hands on her shoulders and bent to kiss her cheek. The faint odor of his pipe tobacco reached her, familiar and unsettling. She held very still beneath the touch of his lips, knowing that this was not the time to turn to him in response.

"I don't know how to manage this gracefully any more than I did before," he said. "But I've had time to think a little."

Near the hearth there was an old leather chair, shabby and cracked, and he pulled it up for her, lowering her into it. She drew up her feet beneath her body and curled back in the depths of the chair, while Jerome stood beside the marble mantel, his face in shadow as he studied her. Behind him a tall mirror reflected the dark saturnine shape of his head.

"I've never wanted to hurt you, Marcia," he said at length. "Or to hurt Laurie either."

She was silent, waiting.

"I don't think you should have come out here," he went on. "But since you are here, why not make the best of it for a few weeks? See a bit of Japan, and help Laurie to get something from the experience. This house is your home, of course. Do anything you like to make yourself comfortable in it."

The implication was clear. She was to entertain herself for a vacation period and then go home and forget about Jerome Talbot. Forget that she had ever had a husband or a marriage! She looked up at him mutely and knew her eyes had brimmed with tears.

With a visible effort he suppressed the return of impatience. "You've always thought life a lot simpler than it is, Marcia. Sometimes it's necessary to accept the fact that there can be a—a sea change. It's something that can happen to anyone. My road took another direction from yours."

"I would have come with you," she said.

Again there was a stiffening in him, a withdrawal. "Will you accept the terms and stay for a while?" he asked.

She blinked her eyes against the bright flames in the grate, blinded by the shimmer of tears. If she accepted, or appeared to accept, she could at least remain in Japan. For the moment that was all she asked—to remain, to be near him.

"I'd like to stay," she said softly.

He bent to take her hands in his. "I will like having you here. Will you believe that, my dear? I think no one has laughed in this house for a very long while. Once I liked to hear you laugh, Marcia."

She smiled at him tremulously and hope stirred in her again. This was all she asked for the moment—that he not be indifferent to her, that she be granted time to win him back. Once he began to remember, then perhaps—

"That's better," he said and touched one corner of her mouth with his forefinger. "I want you to have fun while you're here. You've met Nan Horner and you'll meet other people through her. I don't go in much for Kyoto's social life. But you might have a party some night, if you like, invite some people in for dinner."

She nodded brightly. If this was the role he wanted her to play, then she would play it with all her heart.

When he had walked beside her to her door and said good night, he turned out the hall light and went into his own room. For a long moment she stood there in the thick darkness, remembering times when he would not have left her alone like this. In a trembling wave the longing for him swept through her, engulfed her. She wanted him with a hunger that startled her and left her shaken. This was worse than being across an ocean from him, to have him here in the next room and to be unable to go to him.

All about her the house was alien, cold and dark. Somewhere in its depths sounded the single quick spat of a Japanese drum, as if someone had struck it accidentally in putting it away.

SIX

IN THE NEXT FEW DAYS FEBRUARY GAVE WAY TO MARCH. Snow still lay upon the mountain tops, but it was gone from the roofs and streets of Kyoto, and the first stirrings of spring were moving upward from the islands to the south.

Within the Japanese villa nothing had changed and Jerome remained courteous, but remote. The pattern of his days was uncertain, Marcia discovered. Sometimes he worked at the laboratory—or so she supposed —but there was something strange about that.

When he had first come to Japan, he had invested a portion of his private capital in collaboration with two or three Japanese scientists working actively in the study of nuclear energy. He had written to Marcia's father about this work with excitement and elation. She had supposed that it was a continuation of the research and experiments he had been conducting in the States before the war, work in which her father had inspired his initial interest. Papers began to appear in scientific journals, written by Jerome Talbot in Japan. There had been some newspaper publicity about this "experiment in Kyoto," but the news had gradually died out, there were no more papers, and Jerome had ceased to mention his work in his letters home. Now he seemed to have lost all that early purpose and drive, and he blocked any effort on her part to inquire into his work.

All this troubled her. She remembered him as a man dedicated to science, indifferent to all else so long as no one interfered with his working pattern. Now there seemed to be no pattern in the sense that she remembered, and she discerned in him a suffering she could not reach or understand. There were days when he shut himself in his room and came out only for meals. There were evenings when he left the house altogether, without indicating his plans, so that she did not know where he went.

Yet in spite of her deep concern, she was not wholly unhappy in this new life. He was not completely indifferent to her and more than once she had caught that flicker in his eyes that she could not read. All she asked for the moment was to stay, to be near him, to be given enough time to work out her own purpose in coming here. The conviction was strong in her that if only she could stay long enough she could reach him again. He could not help but remember the sweetness of the past, just as she remembered.

In the meantime, there was the enchantment of Japan outside her door and she turned to it eagerly.

Jerome was kind to Laurie in a somewhat absent-minded manner, and once he brought home a pretty flowered kimono for her, so that she could dress up like a Japanese girl. When Laurie put it on, she provoked smiling consternation in Sumie-san. No Japanese lady would fold her kimono with the right side over the left in the western manner. A kimono was worn that way, Sumie-san pointed out, only in death. So Laurie and Marcia learned the elementary rule of closing a kimono with the left side over the right.

Another time Jerome brought home tickets to a series of three Kabuki plays, given as usual in one long continuous performance that lasted most of the day. She hoped he would take her, but when he did not offer to, she and Laurie went with Nan Horner.

Kabuki had been an exciting experience. Nowhere in the States had Marcia seen such beauty of scenery and costume. The pantomime was clear enough to understand, and while the speech-making was sometimes lengthy, there was also plenty of action, and dramatic entrances and exits over a platform from the stage through the audience. Nan said most Japanese couldn't understand the words either, since the antique court tongue was spoken in most Kabuki plays, but of course everyone knew the stories.

On other occasions Marcia and Laurie went exploring on foot, with a map of Kyoto to guide them. Marcia quickly grew fond of this gray Japanese city, with its surprising flashes of brilliant color and its friendly people. Jerome had made his home here, and for that very reason her interest was sharp, her curiosity high. Whatever she did, wherever she went, she found herself searching beneath the surface for the answers to her troubled questions.

To please Jerome she even planned a dinner party, as he had suggested. She had told him about Alan Cobb, and about Alan's desire to meet Jerome Talbot, with whom he shared mutual friends. Jerome shrugged off the Brewsters almost resentfully, but agreed without objection to having Cobb over for dinner. Marcia invited Nan Horner too and found herself looking forward to the evening. Perhaps a gathering of this sort would be good for Jerome, since he spent too much time alone.

One morning a few days before the dinner she awoke to a feeling of spring in the air. Laurie went outside to play right after breakfast. She was an enterprising child when it came to amusing herself, with an ability to make up games and fill her world with make-believe when this was necessary. But Marcia knew she longed for a playmate. Once Marcia had asked Jerome about the family next door and whether Laurie might not play with the children there. He had been oddly noncommittal. It was never wise to start running back and forth between neighbors, he said.

She had let the matter go. But this morning when she went out on the narrow lower veranda to see what Laurie was doing, she found that the gate between the two sections was open and a Japanese gardener was working back and forth between the separated gardens. Marcia paused on the veranda at sight of the little tableau being enacted near the gate.

Laurie stood beside the fishpond, as still as if she sought to capture a bird. In one hand she held her favorite doll, dangling it by one arm as if she held a fishing pole and bait. Indeed, that was really what it was, for through the open gate, moving one cautious step at a time, came the roly-poly Japanese girl, bright-eyed and solemn and intent. All her small being was focused on the extended doll and it was clearly a bait she found irresistible.

Neither Marcia nor Laurie moved, though once Laurie rolled her eyes drolly in her mother's direction. Step by step the bright-eyed child in the flowered kimono came with outstretched arms toward the doll. She almost had it in her plump little hands when the child's mother came out of the house next door. Chiyo Minato, running in tiny, pigeon-toed steps, hurried through the gate to catch her baby up in her arms. The little girl cried softly in disappointment and her mother hushed and soothed her.

The interruption was too much for Marcia to accept. She went down the side steps into the garden to face the other woman, forgetting the language barrier that lay between them.

"Please let her stay and play with my daughter," she begged. "Laurie is lonely. She only wants to play with your little girl, and she won't hurt her."

The young Japanese woman looked a little like a doll herself. Her dark blue kimono was patterned today with pink blossoms, and from the white folds of the under kimono showing at the V of the neck, her neck and head rose gracefully. Her black hair was drawn smoothly into a chignon at the nape of her neck. These days most younger Japanese women wore their hair like any American woman, but this girl's hair was long and straight. Her delicate features were as lovely as Marcia had remembered and they were as expressionless as those of any face in a Japanese print.

"You don't understand me, do you?" Marcia said

helplessly. "Oh, dear! *Chotto matte, kudasai*—wait a minute, please." That was one phrase she had picked up, at least. The woman hesitated and Marcia dashed into the house to get Sumie-san, who spoke and understood a bit more English than she had been willing to reveal on Marcia's arrival.

But by the time she had drawn Sumie-san from her housework and brought her into the garden, Chiyo Minato and her child had vanished and the gate was closed again between the two houses. Laurie sat on a rock holding the doll, tears of disappointment in her eyes.

"Why did she have to be so mean?" Laurie wailed. "I wouldn't hurt her little girl. I'd have let Tomiko play with my doll. Why did she take her away?"

At a loss, Marcia turned to Sumie-san. "Why next door baby-san no can play here?"

Sumie-san shook her head and murmured something about a fox.

"What fox?" Marcia asked. "What are you talking about?"

Sumie-san cast an uneasy look at the house behind them, as if someone might be listening. "Fox very bad spirit. Fox comes inside rady. Makes very bad thing."

A "rady," of course, was a "lady," but that didn't seem to clarify the matter.

"Never mind, Sumie-san," Marcia told her and sent the little maid back to the house. "It's no use, Laurie. I don't think Sumie-san really accepts the difference between make-believe and reality. I'm afraid you'll have to give up any idea of playing with the children next door."

That evening she told Jerome about the incident.

"What did Sumie-san mean about a fox getting inside a woman? And what has that to do with little Tomiko and Laurie?"

Jerome shook his head in irritation. "If you get started on foxes turning into women, and the other way around, you'll never know where you are in Japan. Pay no attention to Sumie-san's nonsense. But keep Laurie in her own garden. I've already said I don't want any neighborly mixing with the people next door."

She had to leave it at that, but she still felt the ruling was unreasonable. Though it was true that the man, Minato-san, seemed to behave oddly on occasion. Yesterday when she and Laurie had gone for a walk along the hill, he had come to his gate and stared at them solemnly, just as he had once done from the gallery. Other Japanese neighbors were curious and inquisitive —that was to be expected—but with Minato-san she sensed something more. Animosity, perhaps?

She had given him a polite bow and said, *"O-hayo gozai-masu,"* but he hadn't batted an eye, or returned her "good morning." She was tempted to mention his behavior to Jerome. But any reference to the people in the other half of the house seemed to disturb him, and she knew he would give her no explanation.

The incident had made her wonder about Ichiro Minato and what he did for a living. He always seemed to be about the place, often a bit red in the face, as if he enjoyed his *saké*. He appeared to have no steady occupation of any kind. Why did Jerome keep them on as tenants if the family were undesirable? she wondered. Her curiosity about Chiyo had been given little to feed on, but she wondered about her and wished she might break past the language barrier.

As the night of the dinner approached, Marcia found herself looking forward to it eagerly, almost cheerfully. There had been a time when Jerome had been proud of his wife as a person and as a woman. He had thought her pretty and liked the way she dressed and carried herself. These things had seemed important to him and part of his affection for her. So on the night of this dinner she would dress for him in the smoky blue that was his favorite color—a sheer wool that she knew was becoming and which he had not seen her wear. Somehow she must be new and different and exciting for him. If only she could break through his guard. More and more she had the feeling that it was a guard held up deliberately to conceal some gentler emotion behind.

On the afternoon of the dinner, Marcia decided that she must certainly brighten the mahogany-dark dining room with flowers, and she sent Sumie-san out to see what she might find that would be suitable. But when the little maid returned she brought with her a curious assortment that left Marcia baffled and helpless.

There were a few unopened buds, some pods and dried leaves and a variety of twigs and branches. To please Sumie-san Marcia tried to set them up as a centerpiece, but Japanese flower arrangement was beyond her. They both ended in helpless laughter over Marcia's inability to deal with such ingredients.

They were laughing together when Jerome walked into the dining room.

"Just look!" Marcia cried in despair, waving a hand at her incongruous efforts. "Can you ask Sumie-san to do something with this stuff? When I ask her, she just shakes her head."

Jerome regarded the table in dry amusement. "Japanese flower arrangement isn't intended for centerpieces. The flowing line is important, not the mass and color that the Occidental sees in flowers. The Japanese regards a flower arrangement as something to set against a wall and view from the proper angle."

"I don't think Sumie-san went to a flower shop at all," Marcia said. "I believe she just gathered this stuff up in the garden. I can handle flowers, but how can anyone possibly—"

A look that might have been one of malice crossed Jerome's face. "You're right, of course. The efficient western woman often finds herself at a loss in the Orient, and far less clever than she thought. Let me see if I can get you some help," he added, and went out of the room.

His look had made her uneasy and she wished she had said nothing to him about a centerpiece. But now she had no choice, so she sent Sumie-san back to her dusting and waited for him to return.

He was back very quickly and she saw with surprise that he had brought with him the young Japanese woman from next door.

"You can relax now," he said, faintly derisive. "This is Mrs. Minato and she will take care of everything."

Chiyo Minato made Marcia a low, polite bow and murmured a greeting in Japanese. She gave the effort at table decoration a glance which did not reveal what she thought of it, then gathered up the commonplace materials and began to work her own magic. Jerome lingered in the room, watching as if he were enjoying himself in some enigmatic way.

How strange, Marcia thought, that he had asked Mrs. Minato to help after all his talk about avoiding the people next door.

Chiyo removed the materials to the sideboard, making a charming picture as her small dimpled hands moved with graceful assurance. Jerome watched her with obvious appreciation and suddenly, beside all this Japanese daintiness, Marcia began to feel downright awkward and ungainly. The comparison was absurd, she told herself, but nevertheless she moved to the other side of the room so that the difference between herself and Chiyo would not be so clearly emphasized in Jerome's eyes.

When Chiyo had completed the arrangement, she stood back to view it critically. The result was an idealized, formalized version of nature. Now Marcia could see the grace of line in dry twigs, the beauty of a perfect leaf, the promise of a tight-folded bud.

Chiyo bowed again to Marcia and spoke in Japanese.

"She says it is very poor," Jerome translated. "She feels that one should not hurry this sort of creative work. It should be conceived first in the mind, then with the hands."

"I think it's beautiful," Marcia said sincerely. "I could never have managed it myself. Please thank her for me."

"She understands you well enough," Jerome said. "I'm glad you are able to appreciate her artistry."

The barb in his words was clear and suddenly Marcia knew that he had brought Chiyo here deliberately to give his wife this feeling of unhappy contrast.

Mrs. Minato murmured again in Japanese, but she did not look at Marcia as she bowed herself out of the room. Jerome went with her to the door and Marcia let them go. Why had he wanted to hurt her in so petty a way?

She was still staring thoughtfully at the floral arrangement when Sumie-san returned to admire Chiyo's handiwork.

"Naisu, naisu," Sumie-san murmured. *"Kirei desu, ne?"*

Marcia nodded solemnly. "Yes, it is nice—very pretty. But I still have no centerpiece." She looked about the dark, depressing room and moved abruptly in revolt. The Occidental woman was not, after all, wholly lacking in imagination and ingenuity. "Come with me," she told Sumie-san. "We're going to the flower shop."

They put on their coats and went out together. Near the corner they caught a cruising taxi and Sumie-san gave directions.

The flower shop was a tiny one, tucked in among other shops, with flowers everywhere in buckets and vases, and all amazingly cheap. A Japanese woman was choosing one of this and two of that, and the proprietor seemed astonished when Marcia bought armfuls of gladiolas and dahlias and peonies. At least she felt among old friends here, with all the familiar American flowers available, though in a variety of types she had never seen before.

Twenty minutes later they were home again, their arms filled with blooms. Sumie-san unearthed two huge vases in a storeroom and Marcia filled them with lavish masses of color. She set them on the floor in opposite corners of the dining room. Then with a handful of blossoms and a shallow dish she contrived a flat arrangement for the center of the table.

It was late when she stood back to survey her handiwork. The room had brightened considerably. The masses of color counteracted the dark emphasis of mahogany and the room seemed more cheerful. But when she turned to the sideboard and looked again at Chiyo's lovely arrangement, she knew that she had painted with a calcimine brush, while Chiyo had achieved the delicate line of true art.

As she dressed for dinner, she found that the pleasure she had anticipated in wearing the blue dress was dampened. The dress showed off her dark hair, and she had never before minded being tall and slim. But now she felt oversized and ungainly.

Impatiently she fastened her earrings. There was no need for such self-doubt. Mrs. Minato was lovely, of course, but if as Jerome's wife she resented every look of admiration he turned toward another woman, she would have an unhappy time of it. She gave her hair a last smoothing, approved her reflection and turned away from the mirror.

Jerome was still dressing, so she slipped a coat over her shoulders and went into the garden for a few breaths of clear, sparkling air. There were stars out tonight, and a big moon rising. She watched its rim come up behind the black lace tracery of a pine tree and remembered Nan Horner's curious remark about the full moon, and her evasiveness when Marcia had questioned her further. The moon had been full for several days now and nothing had happened that seemed to have any unusual significance. As far as she could tell, Jerome appeared to have taken no notice of it. He had gone out in the evening several times, but that was not unusual.

Marcia took one last deep breath of pine-scented air and then turned back toward the house. As she did so, she caught the faint click of a sliding shutter being closed upstairs in the other part of the house. But though she stood for a moment looking up at the second floor, she saw no one and heard no further sound.

Yet she had the feeling that someone stood behind the slit of a nearly closed wooden door, watching her. Was it Minato-san again? But he never troubled to conceal his interest in staring at her, never bothered to hide. Was the secret watcher of whom she was so intensely conscious the pretty Chiyo?

There was no way of knowing and Marcia went inside uneasily.

In the big drawing room Jerome was prodding the fire, adding more coal from the bucket. She hesitated at the door, wondering if he would greet her with the same faintly malicious look she had seen in his face earlier. He set the coal bucket down and turned toward her absently, wiping his hands on a handkerchief.

She crossed the room quickly to stand close beside him, feeling oddly young and a little tremulous, like a girl dressed up for her first beau. As she waited in silence, standing before him as she used to do in the past when she hoped for his approval of something new she was wearing, she could not keep the love and yearning out of her eyes. His lean dark face was expressionless as he looked at her, his straight mouth unsmiling. Yet there was no malice now, and for an instant his eyes softened as he spoke a phrase she remembered from the early days of their marriage.

"Such a pretty thing," he said and touched her hair with light, quick fingers.

She longed to move naturally into his arms, to lift her face for his kiss, but she did not dare, and the unwelcome sound of the bell at the front gate shattered the moment.

Nan Horner was the first to arrive and Marcia went out to greet her. Nan removed her shoes in the entryway, put on slippers and came breezily into the house. Laurie, her hair newly brushed and braided by Sumie-san, came running to join them. By special permission she was to stay up for the company, having promised that she would not ask too many questions.

In the drawing room Jerome greeted Nan in friendly fashion, knew her taste in drinks and automatically supplied her with bourbon and water. Nan seemed elaborately casual, and perhaps a little prickly in her responses to him.

"It's high time you brought your wife and daughter out to Japan," she said, sounding as though she enjoyed prodding him.

He did not rise to the bait. "This is only a short visit," he told her quietly. "Marcia wants Laurie to grow up at home and I agree with her plans."

"Nonsense," Nan said, settling her angular frame into a befringed velvet chair. "It will do the child good to have a look at how other people live." She took one foot from its loose slipper and wriggled her toes comfortably. "If I had my way, travel would be compulsory for the entire human population."

"I suppose that's why you stick so closely to Japan?" Jerome said.

Nan gave him a steady look in which there was some meaning Marcia could not catch. Then she turned to Laurie. "Brought you something," she said. "A *presento,* as we say out here."

Laurie left the footstool upon which she had been sitting in prim good behavior, and took the small package Nan held out. She glanced at her mother for permission to open her present, and when Marcia nodded, she slipped off the red and white Japanese string.

"What's this?" she asked, holding up an oddly folded bit of paper that had been stuck beneath the string.

"That's called a *noshi,*" Nan said. "It's a symbol of the fish and it's part of every gift in Japan. Symbol of good luck and all that sort of thing."

"Oh, look!" Laurie cried, unfolding the tissue. "It's a little mask!"

She held it up and Marcia saw that it was a miniature plaster mask—the reddish-tinted face of a small amusing demon with fangs and puffed-out cheeks and goggle eyes. But somehow this mask was only funny and not like the carved face in Jerome's bedroom.

"You were interested in my book of masks," Nan said, "so I thought you might like a little one for yourself."

Laurie was clearly delighted. She thanked Nan and returned to her hassock, turning the little mask about in her hands, so that firelight and shadow gave it varied expressions.

The bell sounded again and Sumie-san ushered Alan Cobb into the room. Marcia had almost forgotten how he looked, but now his thick sandy hair and the gray eyes which smiled so readily seemed quickly familiar again. After these days of Jerome's tense, nervous presence, Alan Cobb seemed surprisingly relaxed, his hands resting quietly in repose when he was not using them, his movements calm, as though an inner sureness ruled him. She sensed, however, that he watched Jerome with a certain guarded interest.

Jerome shook hands with Alan cordially enough, though Marcia was aware of his lack of any real concern for this man who was a stranger to him. He had never made new friends easily.

They settled about the fire in the least uncomfortable chairs, while Marcia explained to Jerome and Nan that Alan Cobb had come to teach in a Kyoto college.

"How do you like working with a class of Japanese boys?" Nan asked.

Alan accepted a glass from Jerome and held it up to the fire, studying the glow of amber. "I'm going to like it. I've been given a surprisingly warm welcome."

"Why should it be surprising?" Nan asked directly. "They're eager for American teachers out here."

"I know," Alan said. "But a few resentments would be natural, I should think, even at this late date."

"Not when you know the Japanese," Jerome broke in. "Not when you understand how the majority of the people felt about the war. I don't mean the soldiers, I mean the people. When you're riding a fast express which collides with another express and a great many people are killed, you don't blame the passengers on the other train. You blame the engineers and the railroad companies."

"But if the passengers chose the engineers?" Marcia began. "If the company is responsible to the people?"

Nan took a drink from her glass and shook her head. "That wasn't exactly the case in Japan. It's easy to say that any people ought to be responsible for their leaders. But this was still a feudal country, even though the feudal form was supposedly done away with. The passengers hadn't the slightest notion of how to control the engineers, or run the train. They trusted in whatever leaders were in power. There were forward thinking, liberal statesmen, of course, but the militarists opposed them, and even assassinated many of them over the years. The general populace was accustomed to doing what the ruling powers dictated, and had been so accustomed since ancient times. Democracy's a concept that came in with the Americans and it will take a good many years to develop roots."

"I suppose all that's true," Alan said. "But since there's still the residue of an emotional reaction in me, I wonder why it shouldn't exist in them? I keep wondering if some fellow who is smiling at me in so friendly a fashion was at the other end of a gun during the war. Of course I don't feel that way about the students in school—they're too young. They only remember the bombs."

"You were in the war?" Jerome asked.

Alan sipped his drink, studying Jerome as if he measured him in some way, expecting something in him which he had not found. "In a way," he said, and let the matter drop. He had not mentioned his friends, the Brewsters, and Marcia wondered why.

Sumie-san came to announce dinner and Marcia led the way to the long dark dining room, brightened with its flash of flower color and the lighted candles on the table. On the sideboard Chiyo's arrangement caught Nan's eye and she asked at once who had made it.

"Mrs. Minato, from next door," Marcia said.

Nan nodded thoughtfully, her eyes on Marcia for a searching instant. Whatever the situation next door, Marcia thought, Nan knew all about it, that was clear.

When she had seated her guests, she hurried into an account of her failure in trying to create a flower arrangement with the things Chiyo had used so gracefully. She made the story lightly amusing, so that Nan would think nothing of Chiyo's coming into help, and she avoided Jerome's eyes. When she turned to Alan to inquire about his class, she felt as though she had skated successfully over some rather thin ice.

"Are you having any language difficulties?" she asked.

He grinned. "That's putting it mildly. I wanted to use an interpreter, but the authorities won't have that. They insist that these boys have taken English in school and they understand it. But it's pretty difficult. They want to run before they can walk and deal with complicated, subtle ideas before they have any comprehension of essentials. Everything must be said very slowly and repeated over and over. Even then I can't be sure how much I've got across. The worst of it is they won't ask questions or challenge anything I say."

"Of course not," Nan said. "Asking questions is considered impolite. If you can break down that hurdle you'll really be accomplishing something. It's the thing that maddens every foreign teacher who comes here. Without questions, how can we have individual thinking? And goodness knows individual thinking is what Japan needs. All through lower school these kids have been taught that proper behavior consists in being exactly like everyone else. Japan is a country of ritual. You're supposed to accept what is laid down without question."

Alan grinned wryly. "I'm not so sure that isn't the trend in America these days too."

The soup was steaming hot and the chill of the room set the guests to eating gratefully. During a momentary break in the talk a sound stole through the silence, startling Marcia. It was the musical strumming in a minor key which she had heard before. Again the lovely, gentle voice began to sing plaintively.

Nan looked sharply at Jerome, but if he had heard, he gave no sign that he was aware of the sounds coming from the wing beyond the partition. Yet Marcia had the strange feeling that he listened intently with an inner ear. He went through the motions of eating, of passing the plate of saltines, the celery and olives, but she sensed that he was no longer really listening to the conversation.

It was Nan who seemed most aware of the need for carrying their attention away from the music.

"Alan Cobb?" she repeated the name thoughtfully. "Sounds familiar somehow. Any reason why I should know your name?"

"He writes books," Laurie put in. "He's famous. Reporters and people met him at the airport in Tokyo."

Alan shook a chiding finger at her. "Thanks for the build-up, but you shouldn't put me in a spot like that. Makes me self-conscious."

"Any book that's been published in Japan?" Nan asked.

"It wasn't a very good book," Alan said shortly. "I'm

trying to live it down by writing another. Something that will hit what we might call a more positive note."

What had his first book been about that he always shrugged it aside so quickly? Marcia wondered.

"I'm all for the positive note." Nan smiled. "How do you propose to achieve this miracle in today's world?"

He didn't seem to mind her faintly taunting manner. "It's not as hard as you think," he said good-naturedly. "All I do is look for people who have lived through some sort of difficult experience and come out of it having, presumably, learned something."

He glanced at his host, but Jerome had an absent look in his eyes, and Marcia knew that he still listened to the distant singing and strumming. Alan dropped the topic at once and Marcia made an effort to change the subject.

"How is Yamada-san, Nan? I enjoyed meeting him so much."

Jerome's attention was suddenly arrested. "Where did you meet Yamada-san?" he asked Marcia.

"She met him at my house," Nan put in a bit abruptly. "He came in to bring me a copy of a book he has just published." She looked away from Jerome. "A book called *The Moonflower.*"

"Nan translated a couple of the poems for me," Marcia said. "They were strange, but rather lovely."

A faint color had risen in Jerome's cheeks and he stared at Nan as if he disapproved of her intensely. If Nan noted his expression, she ignored it and went on calmly, explaining.

"Yamada-san merely happened to drop in," she said. "I didn't expect him. I'm glad Marcia had a chance to meet him—he's as fine a Japanese gentleman as I know. His only son was killed during the war and he carries a deep grief behind that serene exterior. Yamada-san is thoroughly old samurai stock. Poor dear."

"Why poor dear?" Marcia asked.

"Because of his wife. Mrs. Yamada has *demokurashii* between her teeth and refuses to be a proper Japanese wife. Democracy's a big thing in Japan today. She no longer walks behind her husband, she votes and makes speeches to other Japanese women. It's all pretty bewildering to Yamada-san, who finds himself being reproached by the husbands of ladies his wife is influencing. To his way of thinking a regrettable new day is dawning in Japan."

Jerome, who appeared to be paying little attention to the talk, suddenly fixed Alan with a look that seemed oddly antagonistic. "Marcia tells me you know the Brewsters in Washington."

Alan nodded casually. "I did an article about Mark Brewster for a scientific journal some years ago. We've kept in touch ever since and I look him up whenever I'm in Washington. You stand pretty high with him, as you probably know."

"He's inclined to overrate people," Jerome said shortly.

"I doubt that," said Alan, but the words had no ring of flattery in them and it was Jerome who looked away.

Marcia had the curious feeling that under the casual words there had been a crossing of swords and that Alan had somehow drawn blood, though he did not look happy about it.

There was a moment's awkward silence. Then, just

as Nan started to speak, Sumie-san hurried in. She said something in Japanese to Jerome, sounding upset, and Marcia caught the name "Minato-san."

Jerome put his napkin beside his plate and pushed his chair back. But before he could rise Ichiro Minato came to the doorway of the room and there was agitation in his manner. The ugly scar that cut down from his scalp across his forehead looked red and angry and there were runnels of sweat streaking his face.

"I'm sorry," Jerome said. "A crisis has apparently arisen next door. Will you excuse me, please?" Without a word to Minato he stood up and went out of the room. The Japanese man remained in the doorway a moment longer, his eyes moving from one to another at the table, as if he had a special interest in this gathering.

"*Komban wa,* Minato-san," Nan said. He repeated the good evening greeting and bowed to her. His gaze rested briefly on Alan Cobb, and moved on to Marcia, for whom he had a long, slow stare. Then he turned with almost military precision and followed Jerome out of the room.

"That one's been a soldier," Alan Cobb said.

Nan nodded. "Yes indeed. And a nasty fighter, I imagine. Trouble is, he doesn't take kindly to doing anything else. Jerry got him a good job up north in Hokkaido last year, but his wife wouldn't go up there and he only stuck it for two months before he came trotting home."

"Perhaps he didn't want to leave his wife," Alan said.

"I gather that was the basic idea," Nan agreed. "I'm not unsympathetic to Ichiro, but I wish he'd find some positive answer to his problems. I feel as sorry for Chiyo as I do for him."

Did the pretty Chiyo want to be rid of her husband, Marcia wondered. But she did not ask the question. It came too uncomfortably near her personal concern.

"He gives me an uncomfortable feeling," Marcia said. "I keep thinking he's watching me for some reason—as if he were waiting for something. But he doesn't say anything. He just stares."

"You'll have to get used to being stared at here," Nan warned her. "In Tokyo westerners are less of an odd breed. But there aren't too many of us in Kyoto, and you can't blame people for being curious."

Over the excellent steak they talked about various aspects of Japan. Time ran along and Jerome did not return. The music and singing had stopped and there was a distant murmur of voices speaking in Japanese.

"Do you suppose someone is ill?" Marcia asked Nan uneasily. "What do you think has happened?"

Nan shrugged without answering and Marcia felt that she knew more than she was willing to put into words.

"Maybe it's the fox woman," Laurie said in sudden inspiration and Nan stared at her in something like dismay.

"What do you mean—fox woman?" Nan asked.

"Sumie-san says there's a fox that gets into the Japanese lady next door and that's a bad thing. What does she mean?"

Nan recovered herself quickly. "You'll meet foxes around every turn in Japan. The fox is supposed to be an evil and mischievous spirit who bewitches the unwary and can take on the human form when it gets a chance. As a matter of fact the Japanese are a bit mixed up about the fox god by now. There's a marvelous little *inari* shrine near my house that I'll have to show you, Laurie. The fox was the messenger of the gods and is always connected with the harvest gods and business transactions. But sometimes this connection is forgotten and the fox is placated as a god in itself. A naughty god who can do great harm if he becomes angry with you."

Laurie knew when she was being put off and would have asked another question if Sumie-san hadn't come in just then. This time she brought with her the little Japanese boy from next door. He removed his cap from his head and bowed politely, reporting to Nan in Japanese. It seemed that "Tarbot-san" would not be able to return for dinner and had sent his apologies. Nan asked the boy a question or two, and he answered. But when the child had gone, she did not explain what he had said.

All Marcia's hope and pleasure in the evening died. Why had Jerome gone next door? What was happening in this house that was being kept from her?

When they left the table and returned to the huge drawing room, Nan went to one tall window and looked out into the night.

"Of course," she said, as if to herself. "O Tsuki-sama is ruling the skies tonight."

"Who's O Tsuki-sama?" Laurie asked.

"My favorite Japanese goddess," Nan said. "The goddess Moon. There are said to be ten thousand ways to look at the moon and there are moon-viewing ceremonies held at certain times of the year. The moon belongs to all those who are lonely and despairing.

There's a dangerous beauty about moonlight which is never to be wholly trusted." She broke off, laughing. "There—I didn't expect to make a speech!"

Marcia could not join in her laughter. She did not like this strange talk about the moon. Clearly there was a meaning here which Nan had tried to gloss over.

Outside the garden lay silver and black in the moonlight, and in the wing beyond the partition all was quiet. An ominous dread hung heavily upon Marcia's spirit. Time seemed to be slipping away from her, carrying her always farther from Jerome. Outwardly she strove to play the role of hostess for the rest of the evening, but inwardly her worry mounted. She could feel nothing but relief when the evening came to an end and she no longer needed to pretend that her thoughts were upon her guests.

After Nan and Alan left, Marcia stayed up, waiting for Jerome. Her feeling of apprehension had increased, and she was tense with anxiety when he finally came in. She knew at once by the closed look of his face that he would tell her nothing. He made no explanation, no apology, though he was clearly under some strain.

"Go to bed," he said curtly. "You mustn't wait for me. This doesn't concern you."

She longed to tell him that everything which touched Jerome Talbot concerned her, that she wanted only to help, whatever the problem might be. But she dared not put her feeling into words while his guard was so plainly raised against her.

Silently she went into her own room and got into bed. But now, though the uneasiness did not leave her, and the sting of his words, shutting her out, still hurt, another thought returned to give her faint comfort. She recalled that moment before Nan had arrived when there had been a softening in his manner. She could not forget the touch of his fingers on her hair, or the bitter sweetness of the words, "Such a pretty thing," that were an echo from happier days. Because of that moment the gulf between them did not seem quite so painfully wide, though for the moment she did not know how to bridge it. She must be patient, she told herself, she must try to understand. Somehow she must keep faith with her love and refuse to let happenings which she could not comprehend defeat her and send her home too soon. As long as there were moments when she was able to reach Jerome, she could afford to be patient. Time and patience—these were everything.

SEVEN

ONE WINDY MARCH NIGHT WHEN JEROME WAS READING in his room and Laurie long asleep, Marcia went upstairs, troubled and lonely, to wander through the dark, empty house. The air was softer tonight, with the promise of spring, and already green things had begun to grow. She was not cold in her nightgown and silk robe, and she slid back a shutter on the front gallery and stood for a long while watching the lights of Kyoto flicker in the wind. A great plain of spreading lights crisscrossed the valley, with the dark arms of the mountains reaching all about.

The night sounds were familiar now. She knew the *tofu* seller's horn, and the three-note flute melody, haunting and lonely, of the *sobaya-san,* who carried about his own little soup kitchen and sold hot buckwheat noodles. There was the omnipresent clatter of *geta* up and down the street—that scraping sound of wooden clogs which would remind her forever of Japan.

She closed the shutters on their tracks and went idly around the veranda corner to the side of the house overlooking the bamboo fence. The moon was thinning now, but the lights from the house next door fell upon the garden and she stood for a little while looking down upon the ordered formality of shrubbery and stone lantern and fishpond.

On the far side of the rear garden grew a huge camphor tree, its great roots fantastically exposed above the ground. She had noted the beautiful tree before by daylight, but now something about it puzzled her. Something white stood in its shadow—something she could not place. Not a stone lantern—there was none there. And this outline seemed soft and draped.

As she watched, puzzled, the object moved, drifting soundlessly across the garden toward the fence. Marcia's breath caught in her throat. The ghostly movement was scarcely like that of a woman walking, but she realized that the drapery fell in the soft lines of a white kimono, and that a woman did indeed move down there in the garden. Her head too was draped in white that hung about her invisible face like a soft hood.

There was no reason, of course, why Chiyo should not wander in the garden late at night, yet somehow the woman's movements seemed odd and strange. As Marcia watched a man came quickly into the garden and she recognized the stocky figure of Minato-san. He went at once to the woman and spoke to her in low tones. She turned obediently at his words and started back across the garden, walking at his side. But before she reached the house, she glanced upward in Marcia's direction. She must have seen the American woman standing there in the aperture left by the opened shutter, for she halted, the white hood tilted a little as if she stared upward, studying Marcia. Her face still lay in shadow, but Marcia had the unnerving sense of an urgent gaze reaching out to her across the dark garden.

Minato spoke again, but the woman did not stir. Her entire being seemed frozen into vigilance. Before Marcia could draw back from the strange, penetrating look, she heard a step on the veranda behind her and suddenly Jerome's hand lay upon her arm, pulling her back into shadow. With his other hand he slid the wooden shutter across, hiding her from the view of the garden.

"But why—" she began, and his grasp on her arm tightened, silencing her.

"Hush!" he warned and drew her quietly toward the dark stairs. He struck a match to light her down the upper flight and she saw his face in the flicker of light —tense and white and angry above the silk collar of his dark dressing gown.

"I'm sorry," she said unhappily when they reached the lower hall. "But I don't see why you should worry about Mrs. Minato seeing me."

The anger seemed to fall away from him and leave a strange sadness behind.

"Why can't you let well enough alone?" he said. "Why don't you take Laurie and go home?"

He seemed so disturbed, so weary, that she hardly knew him. When he turned from her and went to the door of his room, she followed him helplessly, longing to offer assurance, to offer anything except her promise to go home. When he did not close the door against her, she followed him tentatively into the room.

In the lamplight she glanced at the carved cherry wood mask above his bed. The eyes with their rolling eyeballs were as she remembered, the curved mouth as evil. She went closer to the bed, staring at the mask.

"Why do you keep it there?" she asked. "It's frighteningly ugly."

He propped himself on a corner of his desk, one leg swinging, and gazed sardonically at the mask.

"It suits my taste," he said. "I keep it there to remind me of what men are like."

"What men are like?" she repeated in bewilderment. "I've never known anyone as wicked as that."

He raised a dark winged eyebrow. "You, my dear, have always been a romantic. Perhaps it's time you grew up. My friend up there was carved by an artist who saw into men's souls. He didn't create an imitation of pretty exteriors. He drew the inner man. The inner core of—everyman."

But she couldn't accept his cynicism. "Do you think my father was like that?"

Jerome's dark face softened a little. "Your father was never like other men. But he couldn't face what men were doing to the world."

She moved toward him quietly, driven by her need to reach past the barrier he set between them. "My father hoped for great things from you. You were the most brilliant of all his bright young men. What are you doing with what he gave you?"

If she had hoped to touch him on the quick, she saw at once that she had failed. He made a sound of exasperation, as if she were a stupid child.

"Listen to me carefully," he said, and his voice was cold. "The man your father knew, the man you knew as a bride, no longer exists. That is the thing you have to face and accept. It's not something that happened by my own choice. It's not something I have done purposely to hurt and disappoint you. It has happened. It is. The man I am today is someone you don't know. If you want a portrait of him, look up there!"

She would not look at the mask again. Her mouth tightened, and the slender line of her jaw grew firm in the expression he had once called stubborn. He reached out with a quick gesture and turned off the lamp, leaving only the fire to light the room.

"There," he said. "That's the way he shows his colors best. Look at him now, Marcia!"

His will compelled her and she stared reluctantly at the wall above the bed. The high carved cheekbones glinted red in the fire glow, the eyes seemed to glimmer with a wicked light that mocked all mankind.

But she would not be swayed by a carved bit of wood hung on the wall. She recognized its spell, but she knew spells that were surely stronger.

"You're being theatrical," she said deliberately. "You've always had a taste for dramatic trappings. But you can't frighten me away with stage settings, Jerome. You're needed at home. I don't mean just personally by Laurie and me. I mean that your work is needed in your own country. Why must you stay in Japan?"

He left the desk and ranged restlessly about the darkened room. "You're as persistent as ever, aren't you? And as quick as any woman to slide away from the true question. It doesn't matter where I work or what I do. It's only a matter of time before that fellow up there comes to the fore and men begin to destroy themselves. We're already at it."

There was a greater sickness in him than she had known. Her arms ached to go out to him, to comfort and heal him. But he did not want her comfort and she could feel her shoulders drooping a little in discouragement and despair. Whatever she said to him led only to a blind alley, to questions he would not answer. Yet there was something more she must ask. The thing she feared most of all because the answer meant finality. The thing she had been pushing away ever since she had come to Japan.

"Is it because you've fallen in love with someone else that you want to be rid of me? Is there someone you care about here in Japan?"

She could not look at him now, but stood like a child, with her long brown braid hanging over her shoulder and her eyes frightened and downcast, her body stiffened against the blow that might come.

"The eternal female!" He laughed mockingly and the sound shocked her. "In the end all vast discussions boil themselves down to the personal and particular. He-loves-me-he-loves-me-not. Do you really think it's as simple as that?"

She put her hands to her face to hide the tears she knew would come. She had no answer for him now, but stood defenseless with her head bent. She felt his nearness before he touched her braid, put his hands lightly on her shoulders.

"If you mean do I want to marry someone else, then the answer is no. Marriage is not for me. It was wrong for me the first time, but I wasn't honest enough to face up to the fact. It would have been better to hurt you then, instead of now."

She tried to turn away, wanting only to escape the pain of his words, wanting only to hide her love and her longing from his eyes. But now his hands held her firmly where she was, his fingers pressing into her shoulders. He shook her, almost roughly, and her head fell back so that she looked up into the dark flame in his eyes.

"Do you think I've forgotten?" he demanded. "Do you think I haven't been reminded a hundred times of a saner, sweeter life since you've been under this roof? Do you think I haven't been tormented, knowing you were here in the next room and that for your own sake I mustn't touch you?"

She stared at him in blank astonishment and suddenly he bent his head and kissed the hollow of her throat in the way she remembered. Now the flame touched her too and she made no effort to resist the sudden importunities of his hands, his body. This was Jerome whom she loved, and nothing else mattered. If he came back to her now, perhaps she could hold him, never let him go again.

A shower of embers fell in the grate and in the flare of light the face on the wall seemed to smile in abominable mirth.

She knew at once where she was when she opened her eyes the next morning. She turned eagerly in the bed to seek again the warmth of Jerome's body lying next to her. But the bed was empty, her husband gone. The coal fire burned in the grate and she knew she must get up and go to Laurie's room before the child wakened and missed her.

But a drowsiness and languor held her, and the sweetness of immediate memory. He had not been impervious to her after all. His feeling for her was not dead, and that was all that mattered. Now he would surely let her stay and the strains between them would be lessened, a new life would begin. She did not understand as yet what bonds held him here, but if she stayed and put all her efforts into helping him, perhaps they would weaken and fall away. Perhaps now there would be some healing for him in her arms, in her love.

She sat up in bed and turned her head to look at the mask. In the cool gray light of early morning, it was only carven wood, its features frozen in the form the artist's knife had given them. She could put away from her for the moment the knowledge that a man had wielded the knife, a brain had guided the hand; that it was the creation of a man who knew the depths of human evil.

She pulled her knees up beneath her chin, waking herself slowly, comfortably to action. A moment more and she would hop out of bed and into her robe. She would go to see if Jerome was at breakfast and join him in a cup of coffee. Her arms stretched wide above her head and a tingling ran all through her body. Today she was alive as she had not been for a long while.

Casually her eyes rested on the Japanese print over the mantel—the picture of the two young lovers, the man dressed in black, the woman in her graceful white robes, the white hood draped over her head. And suddenly she stiffened, remembering. What had happened later had almost wiped out the earlier occurrence. It came back to her sharply now—the moment when she had stood at the gallery rail upstairs and watched that strange, white-garbed figure move softly across the garden.

She examined the print again, seeking in the pictured figure the woman whom Ichiro Minato had led back into the house last night. Was that why Jerome had chosen this particular picture—because it reminded him, too, of the woman in white? She studied the stylized features of the girl for any resemblance to the lovely Chiyo, but the faces in the print were lifeless, as if individuality of character were something deliberately shunned by the artist.

What change could have come over Chiyo, causing her to stop and stare in so strange a way? Was she at the root of whatever trouble existed next door? And how deeply was Jerome concerned?

But with the memory of last night still warm upon her she did not want to think about Chiyo Minato.

The sound of Jerome's step in the hallway reached her and she quickly propped a pillow behind her so that she could sit up in bed. Her dark braid swung over her shoulder and she let it stay, remembering how Jerome had once liked the novelty of a girl with long hair. She did not wait for his greeting when he came into the room.

"Good morning, darling," she said, not trying to keep the lilt from her voice. "I meant to get up and have coffee with you, but I suppose I'm too late."

"I've had breakfast," he said and came gravely toward her across the room.

She opened her arms to him, free now of all restraint. But he did not come to her in the way she expected. He took her hands in his, not ungently, and sat on the bed beside her, still grave and unsmiling.

"Marcia," he said, "you must take Laurie and leave Japan as soon as you can arrange to go."

She stared at him in astonishment and dismay. "But, darling—" she began.

"What happened last night mustn't be repeated." His tone was cool and remote. "I don't particularly like myself for letting it happen."

His words cut cruelly into her mood of gaiety. She pulled her hands from his and drew the bed covers high, huddling beneath them, staring at him with wide shocked eyes. He turned from her and went to his desk, picked up his wallet and pipe, made the automatic motions of a man leaving for work. But they were hurried motions that indicated his wish to escape quickly from her wounded look.

"We'll talk about details later," he said. "As soon as you set the day I'll see about getting your plane ticket." His entire being had closed against her. She let him go without a word. When she heard the sound of the front gate closing, she slipped out of bed and into her robe. She found that her teeth were chattering, though the room was warm, and that she felt almost ill with the shock of her reaction.

Yet nothing of her resolution had wavered. Her will clung tenaciously to its original purpose.

"I will not leave," she told the mask on the wall, as if it were a real thing that could hear her. "I don't know what you are driving him toward, but you can't drive me away. He needs me and I love him and I'm going to stay."

As she turned from the mask, her eye was caught by

the familiar look of a book on the bed table. She picked it up and saw that it was the same volume of Japanese poetry which Mr. Yamada had brought to Nan Horner: *The Moonflower*. So he had given Jerome a copy too.

She ruffled through the pages and saw that someone had written English script here and there beneath the Japanese characters in an effort to translate the poetry. Nan Horner, perhaps? The handwriting was not Jerome's, and while he spoke some Japanese, she did not believe that he could read the characters.

A few lines drew her attention and she paused to read them.

> "Azalea petals bright in the sun;
>   Black as earth
>   Beneath the moon."

Japanese literature so often took a gloomy turn, delighting in symbols of despair, she thought. Here was another:

> "Searing white light,
>   Wild burst of sound,
>   The world dies in flame."

Bombs had never fallen on Kyoto, but all except the very young remembered the time of the bombs in Japan. This poet had seen them fall. A man or a woman? She must remember to ask Nan Horner sometime. She replaced the book on the table and drew her robe more tightly about her to shut out the unreasonable chill.

Perhaps a hot bath would help. Sumie-san said the

bath was ready and Marcia went into the steaming bathroom to soak neck deep in hot water. She was beginning to feel like the Japanese about hot baths. As she soaked, her resolution not to be driven away strengthened. If anything, Jerome had proved his need of her to a much greater extent than before. He had spoken last night of a sweeter, saner life, which surely meant that he did not find much of satisfaction and sanity in his present pattern of life. Something was tearing at him, destroying him, and she must stay and fight it at his side. By the time she had toweled herself dry, her courage was intact again.

When the phone rang after breakfast, Sumie-san answered and carried on the usual *"Moshi-moshi"* conversation that was the inevitable "hello" in Japan. Then she came to summon Marcia.

Alan Cobb was on the wire.

"Something's come up," he said. "A young friend has offered to act as guide and take me through Nijo Castle this afternoon. I wondered if Laurie would like to go."

"Laurie would love it," she told him readily. "You're good to think of her."

"Fine," he said. "Will it be all right if we stop by for her around two?"

"Yes, of course—" Marcia hesitated. Sitting around this gloomy house waiting for Jerome to come home was a depressing prospect. "Would you mind if I came too?" she asked. "I'd love to see Nijo Castle."

He said that of course he would be delighted, and when he'd hung up, she went to the side veranda to tell Laurie about the invitation. The little girl knelt beside the goldfish pond feeding the darting fish some powdered concoction which Yasuko-san had supplied. Beside her stood little Tomiko from next door. The gate between the two gardens was open and the two children were happily absorbed in the goldfish feeding. For once no Japanese woman darted out of the next house to snatch up her child as if Laurie might harm her. Perhaps Chiyo was becoming more accustomed to her new neighbors. Or perhaps she had heard they would soon be leaving.

EIGHT

ALAN COBB CAME FOR THEM THAT AFTERNOON IN ONE of Kyoto's busy little taxicabs. Yoji, Alan's guide, proved to be a young student in his teens, friendly and eager to practice his English. He wore dark trousers, buttoned jacket and visored cap that all students wore. Laurie, Marcia and Alan got into the back seat, while Yoji sat up in front beside the driver.

Once more Marcia was aware of Alan's relaxed and easy air, which carried about it, nevertheless, a sense of certainty and confidence. Where Jerome had a tendency to flicker like a flame, shifting from brilliance to gloom and back again, Alan seemed to burn with a more even fire, with a steadiness and strength at the core that she found herself responding to, as she had on the trip to Kyoto. He was a man far from easily read, however, for all his smiling, open manner.

"Did the trouble next door clear up?" he asked,

when Marcia was settled in the cab and Yoji had been introduced.

She did not look at him. "I don't know. Jerome didn't talk about it when he came home."

"Nan wouldn't talk either," he said cheerfully. "I tried to pump her when I took her home that evening."

She was not deceived by his casual air. "Why are you so interested in my husband?" she asked him directly.

"The answer to that isn't altogether simple," he said. "I could give you several reasons. My book. Mark Brewster's interest in him. My own knowledge of his work." He seemed to hesitate.

"There's still another reason, isn't there?" she prompted.

"Perhaps an adding up of all these," he said and turned from the subject to draw Yoji out, encouraging him to talk.

Yoji's "l's"—that nonexistent letter in the Japanese vocabulary—gave him trouble when he tried to express his longing for knowledge about America. He turned around in the front seat and fixed Marcia with an interested look.

"Prease you rive in San Francisco?" he asked.

Marcia explained that she lived just across the bay in Berkeley, and Yoji sighed in vast yearning. It was clear that he wanted, more than anything else in the world, to visit America. Alan said most of the boys in his class had wistful dreams along this line.

"There's not much opportunity for a boy like Yoji in Japan right now," Alan said. "I suppose there are a hundred college graduates for every job, and the pay is low. It's hard for them to make any except arranged marriages. Yet our notions about love are becoming popular in Japan, thanks to books and the movies. There have been a lot of hopeless romances, even suicides."

Yoji listened earnestly, but Marcia suspected that he had caught little of this.

The day was bright and not too cold and the streets of Kyoto thronged with people. Mostly one saw western dress, the young women looking trim and smart as any Tokyo girl in their American-style skirts and sweaters.

Laurie loved the little open-front shops, with all the goods displayed on traylike shelves that tilted toward the street, so that the passer-by could see the merchandise at a glance. The shops were wonderfully neat in their arrangement of goods, but you often had to step over mud puddles to enter them. Dust was clearly a problem and the owners of small stands and shops were constantly dousing the ground thereabout with pails of water.

Marcia could see the upward curving tiled roofs and white towers of Nijo Castle rising above lower buildings before the cab pulled up at the main gate. A moat still barred the way to high, slanting stone walls surrounding the castle, and tiled eaves rose in sharp points against the sky. Alan purchased their tickets and Laurie was delighted with the delicate drawing of Nijo Castle printed in pale green on her souvenir stub.

As they walked over the bridge and through the gateway, Yoji took upon himself the duties of a guide, telling them about the castle. Across the courtyard rose a great inner palace with elaborately carved and decorated eaves, and Yoji led the way toward it.

Laurie, never having been near a castle of any description before, kept Yoji busy with her questions. Others were visiting the castles today as well, and Marcia glimpsed a few American faces.

They left their shoes at the entrance and stepped into the slippers provided. The floors were of the beautiful, unvarnished wood that was usual in Japan, always polished to a soft luster.

Wide corridors led past the palace rooms. Without any furnishings, these rooms seemed surprisingly bare to the western eye, and after a time monotonous. But the sliding screens that formed their walls were handsomely painted with scenes of mountains and sea, cherry blossoms and pine trees, and the ceilings were lavishly designed and often painted in gold leaf. All about Marcia sensed serenity and beauty. One could understand the formality of Japan in such a setting, where ritual was everything and no man must break the pattern. In ritual lay security and little need to think for oneself. It was probably a good thing that the new Japan was breaking away from stultifying form to some extent. Yet the old had the dignity of beauty and assurance.

Laurie tried tiptoeing along the "nightingale floor" of a corridor that led to the shogun's rooms, and it squeaked beneath her feet, meant to warn of the approach of one who came stealthily and therefore could have no good intent.

Released from the depressing atmosphere of Jerome's house, Marcia felt almost gay. Despair was for those who accepted its rule and today she would have none of it. She sensed that Alan watched her with a questioning look, but she did not know what he questioned, nor particularly care. It was enough to be light-hearted for the moment and free of any immediate strain.

In the main room of the castle life-size figures of the shogun and his attendant lords had been set up, looking startlingly alive in their elaborate silk robes. They were placed in the positions they might have taken for some important function—the shogun on the slightly raised platform at the back, the others in descending rank leading away from him.

Yoji, with the typical Japanese affection for children, had become Laurie's willing companion, and when she drew him away to view the garden paralleling a corridor, Marcia stood beside Alan, studying the room and figures.

"I keep noticing the differences between Japan and the Philippines," Alan said. "Here you never get away from a sense of history behind everything you see. A civilized sort of history that's missing in the jungle past of the Philippines."

She glanced at him, a little curious. "I remember you said during the trip that you'd lived in the Orient as a child. Was your father stationed in the Philippines?"

He nodded. "Manila, most of the time. We lived on Military Plaza and I went to the American School in Manila as a boy."

"What was it like in Manila?" she asked as they walked on to view the next room.

A slow smile curved his mouth. "What I remember is made up of bits and pieces. The papaya trees with their big, fingered leaves. The heat. The houseboy who went barefoot because he had only recently come down from the mountains. The American public library inside the Spanish walled city, and how hot the cement sidewalks were when I walked there in the afternoon to get books to read. And of course I remember Manila Bay and the sunsets over Corregidor."

"Have you ever gone back?" she asked. "I mean since the war ended?"

For an instant he hesitated, then shook his head. "So much of what I remember has been bombed out of existence. I'm not sure I want to go back."

She sensed something behind his words that held her off—a turning away, the same sort of withdrawal she had felt in him before.

They walked on toward the place where Yoji and Laurie stood gazing out at the lovely garden.

The sudden swaying movement of the floor beneath her feet startled Marcia. All about them the doors and screens of the palace rattled and shook. A nearby American woman gave a nervous squeal and clutched at her husband. In the garden the leaves of an ancient camphor tree rustled as if shaken by a mighty hand. Marcia, as a girl from the San Francisco Bay area, knew what had happened.

"Earthquake," Alan said, and took her arm lightly. "Not a bad one, I think."

It had lasted no more than seconds before the earth was quiet again. Yoji had taken Laurie by the hand and turned back to join them. He was grinning as if something funny had occurred and Laurie's eyes were dancing with excitement.

"That was a Japanese earthquake!" she cried. "Did you see the way the tree out there shook all its leaves?"

"Very smarr size eart'-quake," Yoji said apologetically. "Catfish moving whiskers."

He explained the legend of the huge catfish which lived at the core of the earth. When it twitched its whiskers the land felt a tremor. But when it really wriggled its tail then a great earthquake shook Japan.

"It's when the ground goes up and down that you'd better start running," Alan said. "I gather that a slight sideways movement isn't considered serious."

When they had completed their tour of the castle, Yoji left them at the gate, having promised to do an errand for his mother. Alan suggested that they take a cab downtown and walk through the shopping section. Marcia was happy to agree. She had no desire to hurry back to the dark Japanese villa that was becoming for her a haunted place filled with unanswered questions and the presence of a man who had turned into a stranger.

They got out of the cab at Sanjo Bridge—bridge number three—and walked along a narrow sidewalk on Kawaramachi, a shopping and theater street. Laurie paused in delight before the windows of a doll shop, where Japanese court ladies and gentlemen in samurai costume posed, cunningly executed and dressed to the last detail. Inside were glass show cases and wall cases filled with dolls of every description. Laurie led the way in and stopped entranced before a group of character dolls representing a Japanese family. A little girl doll, with the plump rosy cheeks and solemn dark eyes that one saw everywhere in Japan, seemed to hold out her arms to Laurie.

"This one looks just like Tomiko!" Laurie cried. "Oh, Mommy—"

"My treat," Alan said, smiling, and raised a finger toward the store attendant.

Marcia tried to protest, for the dolls were expensive, but Alan paid no attention.

"I can't think of any better way to spend some of my Japanese royalties," he said. "Are you sure that's the one you want, Laurie?"

There was no need to ask. Girl and doll appeared to have fallen in love with each other.

The doll was carried away and packed in a box, tied handsomely in figured tissue and colored paper ribbon. Since this was intended as a *presento,* the little paper fish symbol was again tucked beneath the string.

Laurie hugged the box to her in delight as the store keeper bowed them politely to the door.

Alan looked as pleased as Laurie over the purchase and shook his head smilingly at Marcia.

"Bachelor's prerogative," he said.

They wandered on past camera stores, tiny eating shops where congealed-looking plastic imitations in glass cases showed the food that was being served inside. There were American type drugstores, and amazingly beautiful Japanese candy stores, where the confections within were like something freshly picked from a flower garden.

The next store to draw them inside was Maruzen Bookstore, which had the look from the doorway of any big American bookshop. It was a busy place, with Japanese at every counter, some of them merely reading, as if this were a library. For the most part the Japanese books were bound in paper, with colorful pictures on the covers.

Laurie found a table of books for children and began

to leaf through those which had pictures in them, while Alan paused to examine a standing row of volumes, suddenly exclaiming as he drew out a book printed in Japanese characters.

"My book," he said dryly to Marcia. "I didn't expect they'd still have it around."

The cover picture on the paper volume arrested Marcia's attention. It showed a fierce looking Japanese soldier in modern uniform, with a long curved sword dangling from his belt. In the background rose the tower of a building that looked Spanish, and there were a few palm trees nearby. That Spanish architecture, the tropical foliage, the Japanese soldier—did they stand for Manila? she wondered.

She looked at the man beside her, startled. "You weren't able to leave the Philippines before the war, were you?"

"No," he said quietly, "we were caught. My father died in the fighting there and my mother and I didn't get out in time."

Marcia touched the pictured Spanish tower with her finger. "Santo Tomas?" she said.

He nodded. "I was interned there for four years."

He made the statement simply and she offered no sympathetic response, sensing that he would reject it. "This is the story of your imprisonment, then? What did you call it?"

"It's not a title I'm proud of, any more than I'm proud of the book. It's called *The Tin Sword*. That's a phrase that grew up in Japan among those who disliked Bushido, the way of the samurai, and didn't want to see modern Japanese carrying the sword of the warrior. It's an angry title, I'm afraid, just as it's an angry book."

"Why shouldn't it be angry?" Marcia asked. "You must have had plenty of reason."

"It was the wrong kind of anger." Alan was almost curt. "It was against the wrong thing."

There were questions she wanted to ask. Why, under such circumstances, had he wished to come to Japan? And how did he feel now about the country and the people? But Laurie returned just then and Marcia postponed her questions.

"Would you mind if I bought your book?" she asked Alan.

"I won't object," he said, but he did not look altogether pleased as she made the purchase.

As they went out to the street again, there seemed a certain restraint upon him, as if finding the book had turned his thoughts to matters he wanted to forget.

NINE

WHEN SHE GOT HOME MARCIA TOOK ALAN'S BOOK INTO her room and put it away in a drawer. Somehow she did not want Jerome to see it. If it had been written in a vein of which Alan himself no longer approved, she did not want Jerome scoffing at it, or perhaps even growing indignant over the title. Perhaps she would show it to Nan Horner and ask her to translate a little of it.

At dinner that night Jerome seemed unusually cheerful and pleasant. The feeling of well-being and release which the afternoon had engendered continued in Marcia. Jerome showed more interest in Laurie than he had done since her arrival, and when she brought the doll she had named "Tomi" after Tomiko, to the table to show her father, he admired it and listened to the account she gave him of their day.

"I'm glad you're getting around a bit," he told Marcia. "It would be a shame to leave Japan without seeing more of it. You must arrange a trip to Nara, and to some of the other beauty spots of Japan."

She agreed that she would like to see some of these places, and did not argue with his assurance that all was settled and she would shortly go home to the States.

Basking in the light of her father's rare attention, Laurie told him about Nijo Castle, and now, inevitably, the fact came out that Alan Cobb had spent the years of the war in a Japanese prison camp in Manila.

"Santo Tomas?" Jerome's brows went up in surprise. "I wonder why he didn't mention it when he was here the other night?"

"I don't think he likes to talk about it," Marcia said.

Jerome's interest in the subject of Alan apparently lapsed quickly and he did not pursue the matter. After dinner, he sent Laurie off to the bedroom to play with her new doll and asked Marcia almost formally to come into the drawing room for a talk.

The big room seemed gloomier than ever tonight. The wind had risen, blowing down from the mountains, and it seemed to circle the house, setting its ancient joints to creaking. Jerome closed the door and came to stand beside the fireplace. Superficially, his manner was pleasant, as it had been all through dinner, but it seemed to Marcia that his eyes were a little wary. Her feeling of gentle gaiety which had persisted from the afternoon began to ebb in the face of his watchful attention.

"Have you done the thinking I asked you to?" he said. "Have you decided how soon you can return to the States?"

She curled herself into the worn leather chair and clasped her hands about her knees. Only the firelight moved in the room, sending wavering shadows up the walls. This was the moment when she must let him know clearly that she could not accept his decision to send her home. How much easier it would be, she thought with longing, if she could talk to him with her head against his shoulder in the old way.

"Sit down here," she pleaded, gesturing to the hassock near her chair.

For a moment his eyes softened and he looked as if he might do as she asked. Then he stiffened, suddenly alert and listening. His attention had shifted to something outside the room. To the wind, perhaps, whining at the windows, whispering around the eaves. Upstairs something creaked as if there were someone there who tiptoed stealthily.

"So we have nightingale floors like Nijo Castle?" she said, keeping her tone light.

"Listen!" Jerome said and tensed to the furtive sound.

The soft, stealthy creaking began again. It might be footsteps, or it might be only the wind blowing about an old wooden house. Marcia held her breath in suddenly fearful listening. Jerome strode to the hall door and opened it softly, then stood listening again. He went toward the stairs.

The room seemed vast and empty without him, filled with dark corners and recesses and shadowy movement. The clock on the mantel was running now and it spoke loudly in the silence, as she waited for Jerome to return. For a little while she could hear him moving about upstairs, then he came down again.

"This house has played tricks like that on me before," he said ruefully. "Of course no one can come through from the other half of the house. I'm the only one who holds a key."

"Why should anyone want to?" Marcia asked. The softening in him had vanished and he was far away from her again.

"I don't trust Minato any farther than I can see him," he told her. "He is a leftover from the war and a misfit. He drinks too much and he has developed a grudge against me."

He drummed idly on the marble mantel, while Marcia waited for him to go on. What lay behind such a grudge, she wondered. Chiyo, perhaps? If Jerome were interested in Chiyo—that would surely disturb Ichiro. Marcia turned in quick revulsion from the thought. Jerome had never been a person whose motives were simply understood. There were complexities in him and this might be something far less simple than Chiyo's possible attraction for him.

Nevertheless, she put her question into words. "Why has he a grudge against you?"

His fingers paused in their drumming. "That's not your concern. I merely want to impress it upon you that during whatever time you remain in this house you are to be on guard against Minato. Don't speak to him. If he ever approaches you, get away from him quickly. He has a background of violence from the war."

He was alarming her now. "What about Laurie?" she asked. "Would he hurt Laurie?"

He started to speak and she was sure he meant to deny this, but he broke off the words, watching her warily again. "He might, at that," he said. "I don't know. The point is that we can take no chances. The sooner you're out of this house for good, the better. It may not be a safe place for either you or Laurie."

Was he merely trying to frighten her, using any weapon which came to his hand?

"Why don't you ask him to move out, if that's the way you feel about him?"

"That's easier said than done." His sigh was one of exasperation—with her, not with Minato. "When are you leaving, Marcia?"

There was no hope now that he would soften again. She sat up very straight in her chair, putting both feet on the floor, bracing herself a little. "I'm not going home. I want to stay here as your wife until you are ready to come home. After last night I can't believe the things you wrote in that letter."

The flame that always burned deep in his eyes seemed to leap to angry life and his brows drew down, as his face darkened.

"You can't stay here," he said harshly. "You're tampering with things you can't possibly understand. Go back to the States where you belong. Japan is not for you."

She slid out of the chair and went close to him. "Last night you wanted me. Why is it different now?"

The anger in his eyes frightened her and for just an instant she feared he might strike her. Then he pushed roughly, furiously past her and went out of the room. A few moments later he had left the house and the shadowy room seemed to crowd in upon her, thrusting at her with hateful, alien hands. It was as if it were repeating Jerome's words, "Get out! Go home!"

She turned out the lights and fled from the dim fire glow. In the wide hallway, she stood for a moment listening, but the wind sounds disguised the familiar and created new creakings and whisperings, so that all the house seemed alive with strange portent. At night the servants retired to their own quarters unless they were summoned and the main part of the house stood hollow and empty except for herself and Laurie. For a moment she thought of going upstairs and looking about, trying that door into the other half of the house, just to make certain no one was there and that the door was locked. But such an exploration seemed foolish when Jerome had looked upstairs only a short while before and had found nothing wrong. It was even possible that his own anxiety had been staged to frighten her into leaving.

The front door locked automatically and Jerome had closed it when he went out. Fortunately this half of the house had been westernized, with regular doors and windows so that it was not necessary to shut themselves in behind sliding wooden *amado,* as was the case in Japanese houses. The truly Japanese house was singularly easy to burglarize. But this one should not be.

Nevertheless, she did not hesitate long in the dim hallway, but hurried to join Laurie in the cozier warmth of the bedroom they shared. The little girl sat on a low stool by the fire, with a chair pulled up close to hold her dolls and the miniature mask Nan had given her.

She smiled at her mother. "Will you play with me tonight, Mommy?"

Marcia was grateful for Laurie's cheerful, outgoing nature. She sat on the rug beside her daughter and they made up stories between them, as they played with the dolls for an hour or so, until it was Laurie's bedtime. When the child was asleep, Marcia sat on beside the fire, not reading—just waiting for the sound of Jerome's return. How long could she play this waiting game? How long could she stay here in the face of his determination to have her leave? What home could there be for her in staying? And yet, and yet, last night . . .

The memory should have warmed her, but now she shivered and gave up her watch beside the dying fire. He had never stayed out this late before. Where did he go on such occasions? Who were his friends? How very little she knew about the man who was her husband.

Before she turned off the lights in the bedroom, she opened the door into the hall and listened once more to the moaning wind sounds, the creakings. But though ghostly footsteps seemed to rustle along the galleries above, nothing came down the wide dark stairs. Far away, in the other part of the house, someone was playing a samisen again, and singing to the music. How forlorn and melancholy Oriental melody sounded to the western ear. And what a paradox the Japanese were. Underlying their literature, their painting, their music, was so often a note of tragedy. In the arts tragedy seemed only a step away most of the time, and in life too, as Alan had said. There was frequent mention of suicide in the papers, often among young people thwarted in love and unable to accept the old ways their parents set down for them.

Only last week a young couple had jumped into the flames of Mihara volcano on the island of Oshima—as so many hundreds had done before them. When life thwarted them, they gave themselves so readily back to the gods. Yet always in the streets, or among the Japanese one met, there was friendliness and apparent good cheer. In Japan one never heard harsh words or raised voices. Courtesy and good manners were the rule, with no resentment shown toward a recent enemy. All this made it hard to understand how such a people could be brutal in war, or given so readily to tragedy in their personal lives.

She closed the door and wished vainly that she had some way in which to lock it. Tonight, for the first time in Japan, she did not feel safe and secure. She had not been really afraid before, even on her first night here, before Jerome had returned, but tonight—perhaps because of his words about Minato, because of his search upstairs, and because Jerome himself had gone out of the house, she felt uneasy and fearful. How far removed was her present mood from the happy one of the afternoon she had spent with Alan Cobb.

Before she got into bed, she went to the window and looked out into the windy night. She could see the tops of pine trees, black against the cloud strewn sky. There was something about Japanese pines that made them like no others. They were truly the pines of Japanese prints, their trunks twisted, their foliage falling into layered, delicate patterns. A thin moon crescent rode the clouds and she felt a sense of relief that at least there was no full moon tonight.

Earlier Sumie-san had brought a hot water bottle for her bed, and her cold feet sought it for comfort as she burrowed beneath blanket and quilt.

The samisen was silent now and Marcia lay staring into the dark, listening for Jerome, wondering why he did not come back. At length, in spite of herself, her eyelids grew heavy and she drowsed a little, pulled herself awake and drowsed again.

It might have been close to three in the morning when she came suddenly wide awake, with all drowsiness banished and all her senses alert. She did not know whether or not Jerome had returned, but the sound which had startled her awake was not that of his key in the door. It was the same sound she had heard earlier in the evening—a wind-wrought sound of creaking upstairs that sounded like soft footsteps.

So light they were, so faint, that she would have heard nothing if the gallery floor had not creaked as if beneath some weight. It was the wind again, she told herself and listened for the night sounds outdoors. But the wind had died down and the night beyond the window had a misty look as if fog were rising in the garden. Yet still the faint, light creaking sounded from the floors above. No—now it was on the stairs. As if light spirit feet trod the polished wood, descending with the barest whisper of sound.

She tried to think of Jerome's assurance that only he held a key to that upstairs door. But the creaking was no longer on the stairs, it drifted faintly across the hall and was suddenly arrested in silence. Where had the sound stopped? Midway in the hall? No, it had come closer than that. If someone had really come into this part of the house and down the stairs, he was poised now just outside her door, listening surely for any sound within.

She thought of screaming and did not dare. To scream was to announce dangerous knowledge of the intruder's presence. If Jerome were still away, who would come to help her? Two frightened women in the servants' quarters? No, it was better to lie in frozen silence, stiff and quiet, pretending to sleep, even though her eyes stared into the thick darkness of the room. Darkness that gave way, even as she watched, to a shaded sliver of light as her door opened softly. The sliver widened and a suffused radiance entered the room.

Only in pretended sleep lay some possibility of safety for Laurie and herself. Marcia closed her eyes, tried to breathe naturally and not in frightened gasps. If only Laurie did not hear the intruder, if only she stayed asleep.

She could sense the light through her closed eyelids now, as it advanced into the room, grew more concentrated as it approached her bed. What was intended? Was she to be stabbed as she slept? Smothered? Someone stood beside her bed, holding a lantern high so that the light fell upon her face. An unfamiliar scent reached her, the scent of some sweet night flower in a woman's perfume. It was a woman, not a man who stood beside her bed.

She opened her eyes a slit, even though the fluttering of her lids must be evident to the person who stood there. In the lantern light she saw the smooth white silk of a kimono. She let her gaze widen, travel upward to the brilliant scarlet of a gold-embroidered obi and to a pale hand that held something long and slim and shining. For a single, horrified instant Marcia thought it was a knife. Then the woman made a sudden movement with her hand, flicked open an ivory fan, and raised it to her face.

Marcia stared upward, dazzled by the light, trying to

seek past it to the face of the woman in white. But a draping of cloth covered her head and left her face shadowy behind the fan. Whoever it was wanted to conceal her identity.

"Who are you?" Marcia murmured softly. "What do you want?"

The shrouded head bent gently in a bow, and the softest of voices spoke to her. *"Gomen nasai,"* the woman said and Marcia knew the words meant "Excuse me." The lantern was lowered and the woman turned away. Softly she padded across the room in her white *tabi* and went out the door. Marcia lay with every muscle tensed, listening to the creaking journey in reverse . . . across the hall, up the stairs, along an upstairs gallery. Then the night was silent and mist drifted thick against the window panes.

A cold reaction of terror flooded through her. She fumbled for the lamp beside the bed and then flung back the covers. Laurie lay quietly asleep. All the house was still when she opened the door and listened. No wind creaked against wooden timbers. On all sides the emptiness, the loneliness, seemed to press upon her until she could not endure it. What if that figure in white returned, what if . . . With a faint sob she rushed toward Jerome's door and opened it.

"Jerome!" she whispered urgently to the silence. "Jerome, are you there?"

A creaking of his bed answered her as he sat up, and she clung to the door for a moment in a trembling rush of relief.

"What is it?" he said, and turned on the light. "What's the matter?"

That fearful moment when the woman in white had

stood beside her bed was still petrifyingly real in Marcia's mind, and she did not hesitate. She flung herself across the room and into her husband's arms. For a moment her teeth chattered so hard that she could not speak clearly and he held her gently, smoothed back the hair from her damp forehead as if she had been a child.

"You're all right now," he said kindly. "You must have had a bad dream."

Love for him welled up in her, painfully sweet. Held like this with her cheek against his chest, she could hear the sure, steady beat of his heart. But tonight there was no quickening of response in him, and after a moment he put her gently out of his arms.

"Here," he said, "get this blanket around you. You're clammy cold."

She sat on the edge of his bed, huddled in the blanket, missing his arms, longing to slip beneath the covers and get as close to him for warmth and comfort as she could. But he sat up beside her and rubbed her hands briskly in his big warm ones. Gradually the chattering stopped and she could speak.

"Someone came downstairs from the other part of the house," she whispered. "Someone came into my room."

She felt the stiffening that ran through his body. "Nonsense, Marcia. The door upstairs is locked. No one could come through."

She nodded vehemently. "Yes—someone did! A woman dressed in white. She was carrying a lantern and she stood beside my bed and looked at me. When I opened my eyes, she put a fan in front of her face so that I couldn't recognize her. Was it Chiyo? Is there something—wrong with Chiyo?"

Jerome put an arm about her shoulders and held her still. Quietly he insisted that what she had imagined was impossible. He had dreams like this sometimes too —when for a little while the dream seemed to spill over into reality, so that it was difficult to know where one ceased and the other began. That was all that had happened to her—a disturbing dream.

She clung to him helplessly, repeating . . . until gradually as his soothing words went on, she began to doubt herself. Was it possible? Had the things that had happened in this house built themselves up in her subconscious mind until they had spilled over into an extraordinarily vivid dream?

"You must go to bed now and get some sleep," he told her. "Come, I'll take you back to your room."

She longed to say, "Let me stay here. Don't send me away!" But she was thoroughly awake now and the terror was fading, giving way to the restraint that lay upon her where Jerome was concerned. There was nothing else to do but let him take her back to her room.

There he tucked her in and bent to kiss her lightly. "Leave the light on," he said. "You'll feel better that way. Call out if you want me. You'll be all right now and everything will look more sensible in the morning."

When he had gone she lay still and tense again, listening. Had it really been a dream? Was that possible? Or was there still a faint fragrance, a little like sweet cloves, hovering in the room? She breathed deeply, trying to catch the scent, but with her very effort it eluded her and she could no longer be sure that she smelled anything alien in the room.

She lay for a long while, going futilely over the experience in her mind. It did not seem to be slipping away from her like a dream. She could remember everything that had happened with the utmost clarity and now one detail returned to tantalize her more than all the rest—one strange, incongruous touch that she had been only half aware of at the time. The woman's white silk kimono had been folded across in the western manner, right side over left. But in Japan such a fold was used only in death.

TEN

THE NEXT DAY SEEMED LONGER THAN ANY OTHER
Marcia had spent in this house. Jerome left early in the
morning and did not return all day.

Once in the late morning, driven by loneliness, she
decided upon a gesture she had never dared make before, lest it annoy her husband. She would find a pre-
text to call him at the laboratory. Just to hear the
sound of his voice, to talk to him for a few moments,
would break the heavy silence that pressed in about
her. Last night when she had been so frightened he
had not been unkind. Surely he would not mind, even
though he had always disliked interruptions.

It was not easy to extract the laboratory number
from Sumie-san and get her to put through the call.
The little maid put repeated obstacles in her way, but
Marcia was insistent, and with much shaking of her

head, Sumie-san gave the operator the number. Then she handed the phone silently to Marcia.

The signal in Marcia's ear rang on and on, but no one answered and, when she finally hung up, she had the feeling that Sumie-san had known very well that no one would answer. Jerome either did not answer his phone, or he was not at the lab at all. Of course any number of reasons might call him from his work, and there was no need to make something in her imagination of so slight a matter. Yet a feeling of uneasiness beset her.

During the afternoon Nan Horner dropped in casually. As she grew accustomed to Nan, all Marcia's early resentment of her had faded, and today her breezy, matter-of-fact presence was especially welcome. Marcia greeted her warmly, sent Sumie-san for tea and led Nan into the drawing room.

Vigilance over the children next door had lessened and Laurie was outside playing with Tomiko, so Marcia and Nan could be alone.

Nan was not one to beat about the bush. Teacup in hand, she came directly to the point. "Just wanted to see how you were doing. That young man I met here the other night—Alan Cobb—came in one evening to borrow some books on Japan. While he was there he told me about your outing to Nijo Castle. He said you looked a bit peaked and he thought you might either be coming down with something, or in a state of worry."

"I'm all right," Marcia said steadily.

Nan, brown as autumn leaves today in her tweedy suit, reddish brown scarf and brown walking shoes, regarded her with a frank and thoughtful stare.

"If you ask me, you are looking a bit under the weather. And I know Jerry's not apt to see what's right under his nose. Sure you're feeling all right? Newcomers usually get the collywobbles sooner or later. But once you get over them, you'll be fine."

"There's really nothing wrong with my health," Marcia said with an effort.

Nan gave her a long steady look and then set her teacup aside. "You know, I was prepared to dislike you when you turned up here as Jerry's long-absent wife. I didn't think I'd have any patience with you, or sympathy for you."

"You needn't feel sorry for me," Marcia said.

"It's not that I'm sorry for you," Nan went on. "It's more that I've begun to have a certain admiration for you. You came out here in the face of Jerry's objections and I suspect that if it had been up to you, you'd have come a whole lot sooner."

She got up and strode the length of the big chilly drawing room, then back again. Marcia watched her in silence.

"Now that you're here, what are you going to do?" Nan asked.

"I'm going to stay," Marcia said. "I want to stay until Jerome is ready to come home with me."

Nan whistled softly and then bent to run a forefinger along Marcia's chin. "Hm! Alan's right about you. There's something to the way you set that small jaw. He said you had what it took to land on your feet."

"What does he know about me?" Marcia asked, feeling suddenly prickly. "Why should he discuss me with you?"

"There's no law about not discussing one's friends,"

Nan said mildly. "I suppose we all do it, so don't ask to be excepted. In your case, we do it because you've somehow got under our skins and we don't like to see you trampled on and hurt."

Marcia stiffened. "No one's trampling on me. I think there's something terribly wrong in Jerome's life. Perhaps I'm the one who can help him. Sometimes I think he knows that—though he'd hate to admit it."

"Perhaps you're right." Nan opened her oversized leather handbag and took out cigarettes. Marcia refused the extended packet, but Nan lit one for herself, puffing absently.

"This morning," Marcia said, "I tried to phone Jerome at the laboratory. I couldn't get an answer, and Sumie-san behaved in such an odd way about the call. As though she knew I wouldn't find him there."

Nan shrugged. "He was probably out on some errand. Perhaps she knew about it."

"Then why didn't she say so?"

"You are getting jittery," Nan said.

Marcia brushed that aside. "Is he ever there? Does he do anything at all with his work any more?"

"What you need," said Nan calmly, "is a bit more social life than you get in this mausoleum. I'm planning a little dinner later on, after cherry blossom time. To honor publication of *The Moonflower*. Just a small party for Yamada-san and a few friends of Haruka Setsu."

It was clear that Nan did not mean to discuss Jerome's absence from the laboratory.

"Haruka Setsu?" Marcia asked.

"The woman who wrote the poems," Nan said, and it seemed to Marcia that a speculative look had come into her eyes. "You might tell Jerry what I've planned, since you'll both be invited. I haven't seen him for a week or so."

The need to talk to someone who was a friend surged up in Marcia. Today Nan seemed unexpectedly sympathetic and understanding. Marcia let her words come in a little rush.

"Last night Jerry was angry with me because I refused to go back to the States, and he went out of the house and didn't come home until very late at night." She paused and caught her breath. "Nan, do you know where he goes?"

Nan blew two smoke rings and followed their floating course with an absorbed interest before she spoke. "If you're going to stay here, my girl, don't ask questions. Just try to be what he wants you to be, and get him to go home with you. There's a slim chance that he might. But not if you go excavating for old problems and troubles. There are some things he'd turn you out for—and make no mistake about it."

"But you could tell me," Marcia persisted. "You know whatever there is to know. Don't you?"

The sympathy went out of Nan's eyes and the muscles of her face seemed to tighten.

"There's one thing you might as well understand," she said. "Jerry is an old friend of mine. He was a friend long before he married you. Whether you like it or not, I've been sorry for you. I've wanted to help you out. But my loyalties lie first of all with Jerry Talbot. What he wants you to know, he will tell you. So don't come to me with your questions."

Bright color burned in Marcia's cheeks at the rebuff, but her gaze did not leave Nan's face. "Last night someone came through from the other side of the house into this part."

Nan's hand halted in the act of flicking ash into a tray and the ash fell unheeded to the carpet. "Yes?" she said.

"It was a woman in a white kimono carrying a lantern. She came into my room and stood beside my bed looking down at me."

"What happened then?" Nan asked. She turned away from Marcia's look and ground out the cigarette with an almost angry gesture.

"Nothing, really. I asked who she was and what she wanted. I don't know whether she understood me or not. She said, '*Gomen nasai*,' and went away."

"And did you see who it was?"

Marcia had the feeling that Nan was waiting for some special answer, but she had no idea what it was. "The woman had a white drape over her head. It could have been Chiyo. But I don't think so."

Nan seemed oddly relieved. She came back to Marcia and put her hands on her shoulders. "Listen to me. Don't tell Jerome about this. Don't mention that this woman came into the house. It will only make things more difficult."

"I've already told him," Marcia said. "I was too frightened to lie there shivering after she left. I went to his room and told him right away."

"I see. And what did he say?"

"That I'd dreamed the whole thing," Marcia admitted.

"Perhaps you did. It's possible, isn't it?"

Marcia regarded her steadily. "You know it's not. I won't be frightened and confused like this. I won't let

Jerome make me doubt my own senses. Or you. There must be another woman besides Chiyo in the Minato household. I saw a woman in the garden once before and she stared at me in the strangest way until Minato-san took her inside. If there is another woman, you might as well tell me who she is."

Nan hesitated as if she sought for words, then, abruptly, she seemed to make up her mind. "I suppose there's no harm in your knowing. She's a penniless relative. Chiyo is wholeheartedly attached to her because of what they went through together during the war. They were bombed out of their home and lost not only all their possessions, but every other member of the family as well. Family ties are very strong in Japan, and Chiyo and this cousin—she's about ten years older than Chiyo—are all there are left. Chiyo was young enough to make a recovery from the experience. The older girl grew more and more—well, melancholy. The whole thing is very sad."

"Is she dangerous?" Marcia asked. "Chiyo's cousin, I mean?"

"I—I don't imagine so," Nan said, but she sounded oddly uneasy.

"Nan—will you tell me the truth about one thing? For Jerome's own sake I need to know. Has he been having an affair with Chiyo Minato? Is that why Minato has a grudge against him? Is that why Jerome won't put the family out of the house? Why he doesn't want me here?"

Nan looked abruptly at her watch. "Glory be! I'm already ten minutes late for my appointment. Got to run, girl. Thanks for the tea."

Marcia followed her to the door and Nan turned

back for a moment as she stepped into her shoes. "I've told you where my loyalties lie. There are some questions you must see I can't answer, or even discuss. You'd better save them for Jerry. But that's one I wouldn't ask him, if I were you."

She was off as breezily as she had come, and Marcia found that she had been left with more unanswered questions than ever. Was this "melancholy" cousin mad? Was insanity the answer to the mystery that seemed to shroud the house beyond the dividing wall? Why should everyone be so secretive about it?

Jerome came home at dinner time as calmly as though he had never stamped out the house yesterday, or been away most of the night. He seemed quite cheerful, as if he had come to some conclusion, or made a decision. At dinner he once more bent his interested attention on Laurie and Marcia ached a little over the way the child held out her heart to him. One ought to be able to do that with confidence to any father, but Marcia had no faith in Jerome's whims. He could hurt Laurie all the more if he took something of her love before he turned away from her in boredom.

At the dinner table Marcia told him of Nan's visit and that a party was planned to celebrate the publication of Haruka Setsu's book. Jerome turned a quick look of surprise upon her at the news, but he made no comment other than that he would talk to Nan about it.

The matter of the phone call had continued to trouble Marcia and she saw no reason why she should not ask Jerome about it directly.

"I tried to call you at the laboratory today," she said casually. "But I suppose you were out at the time."

He made no effort to be evasive. "I'm more likely to be out than in. There's not much use in trying to get me there."

"But weren't you working there with some Japanese in the beginning? Isn't anyone there these days?"

"Only the spiders and mice," Jerome said wryly. "And they can't answer the telephone, or make the mess of things that the scientists have. My Japanese friends dropped out of the picture long ago. We decided to follow different roads."

"What road are you following?" Marcia asked.

He regarded her coolly. "That, my dear, is my affair. I'm sure you will be happier here if you will stop behaving like Pandora."

Once more she had come up against a blank wall, with no way through and no way over.

After dinner he suggested that Laurie come for a walk with him along the hill, and when she ran eagerly to get her coat, he spoke casually to Marcia.

"Let's say that you stay a month or so. Through the cherry blossoms, at least. Then we'll re-examine the situation and see where we stand. Will you agree to that?"

It was more than she had expected after last evening. "Yes, yes, of course," she said quickly.

He smiled at her. "All over the bad dream?" But before she could answer, Laurie came dashing back, stuffing her arms into the sleeves of her coat.

"At least this will give me some chance to get acquainted with my daughter," Jerome said, still smiling at Marcia disarmingly over the child's head.

They went out together and not even Laurie thought of inviting her mother to go along. Marcia tried to be pleased over this new interest in Laurie on Jerome's part. It was foolish, she told herself, to feel uncomfortable about it, but she was worried about so many things concerning Jerome these days.

The remark he had made about mice and spiders taking over the laboratory, his admission that he no longer went there regularly, continued to haunt her. This aspect made her worry more than a merely personal matter. Jerome Talbot had been a man to reckon with in the world of science. She had often heard him spoken of with respect by friends of her father and she was well aware of the larger picture he had once filled. Now, clearly by his own wish, he was being forgotten. Forgotten, not by reason of failure, but because of his own lack of willingness to contribute. At home there might have been some pressure put upon him, since the country could not afford the waste of a man like Jerome. Out here they could not reach him and perhaps they had given up trying.

As the days ran along the camellias bloomed and faded and the trees unfurled the green banners of spring. The air was tinged with bright warmth and the time of the flowers was approaching. In her loneliness Marcia turned to the solace of burgeoning beauty and took Japan to her heart, as so many had done before her.

Already, in the southernmost island of Kyushu, cherry blossoms were blooming, and the excitement of spring was moving slowly northward through the islands of Japan. There were days when it was possible to throw open doors and windows to the warmth, and in Japanese houses the sliding doors stood open to the gardens.

In these days of early April Laurie seemed ecstatically alive. Jerome took her about with him often, and a closer relationship appeared to be growing between them. Yet it seemed to Marcia that there was a nervous eagerness about the child that was not altogether reassuring.

One afternoon Marcia missed Laurie and received no answer when she called her. The child was in none of the downstairs rooms, nor was she out in the garden, and Marcia went upstairs for a glimpse next door, to see if she might be there. Instead, she found Laurie on an upstairs gallery.

She sat curled in a corner, the sliding doors open beside her. Laurie, however, was wasting no time on the view. There were tears streaking her cheeks and she held something in her hands that seemed to give her cause for grief.

"Is something the matter?" Marcia asked gently. "What's troubling you?"

When she saw her mother, Laurie jumped to her feet and put her hands behind her back. The tears dried on her cheeks and she looked almost defiant. Since rebellion had never been part of Laurie's nature, Marcia was taken aback.

"What is it?" she asked. "Is something wrong?"

With a swift, explosive movement, Laurie took one hand from behind her back and hurled something far out into the side garden. The small dark object went sailing over shrubbery and through the trees, to drop out of sight on the far side of the garden. There was defiance in the way she faced her mother.

"What was it you threw away?" Marcia asked, suppressing her own sense of alarm.

"Nothing," Laurie said and would not meet her eyes.

Marcia held out a hand to her daughter. "Never mind, if you don't want to tell me. But I can't very well help you if you won't tell me about it."

Laurie shook her head so vehemently that her braids flew over her shoulders. "There isn't anything the matter," she said and slipped away to run ahead downstairs.

Laurie had escaped her as she had never done before, and Marcia tried to tell herself that this was no more than a sign of growing up, that all mothers had the same problem. But she remained troubled out of all reason, and that evening, when Laurie had gone for a walk with her father, Marcia searched the garden. But the shrubbery was thick and she found nothing that Laurie might have cast away.

With the coming of spring, the delicacy and beauty of the garden revealed itself more and more, and as the days grew warmer Marcia began to take a special pleasure in sitting outside where she could read and savor the loveliness around her at the same time. No matter how troubled she might be, the garden always lifted her spirits and brought her a quiet happiness on its own account.

There were no flower beds. What flowers there were would present themselves in season on bush and tree, but there was an appreciation evident for the individual object, whether wood, or stone, or growing thing. The small pine tree beside the stone lantern had been carefully trained to complete a picture. The stepping stones in a curving line that led from house to fishpond, had long ago been lovingly chosen for texture, shape and color. The arch of the little red lacquer bridge curving over the pond added to the pleasing sense of balance. Everywhere the green of grass and brown of earth were contrasted to the best possible effect and the whole had been created by an artist of his craft. Only the bamboo fence cutting obstinately through what had been intended as one property, was harshly out of keeping with the rest. But Marcia could turn her back on that and enjoy what remained of the picture. There was so much for an American to learn from Japan. Perhaps western ways were aiding Japan to get back on her feet, but Japanese ways would always enrich the foreigner.

Both Sumie-san and Yasuko-san were delighted by Marcia's pleasure in the garden and her willingness to savor its varied detail. They went out of their way to point out its individual beauties as it grew into spring, and Marcia enjoyed their interest. She was learning that Japanese servants were far more a part of the family than they were cook and maid. It was wise to thank them after each meal and show special appreciation for their efforts. They seemed genuinely happy to have her as a member of the family, once they were sure that she would not come between them and their loyalty to Jerome, or interfere with their little services to him. Laurie's presence pleased them, and often Yasuko-san or Sumie-san would take her along on shopping trips. Laurie was quickly picking up words and phrases in Japanese, outstripping her mother in that respect. She could manage a bit of talk to Tomiko by now when the child came over to play.

Marcia's questions about the Minatos remained un-answered and she caught no further glimpses of the woman in white. Even Chiyo seemed to keep out of sight and there had been no opportunity for Marcia to break through the tantalizing barrier between the two houses.

Then one day early in April, something happened which shed a new and surprising light on the family next door. Minato-san had brought home some tiny turtles for his children, and little Tomiko had given one of them to Laurie. On this particular morning the two girls were playing happily with their turtles near the edge of the fishpond, while Marcia sat on the veranda steps watching.

In through the gate from the other house swaggered the boy, Taro. He was somewhat bigger and older than Laurie, and he had all the confidence of the young Japanese male in the presence of lowly females. For a few moments he stood watching the girls, making what were plainly teasing remarks in Japanese. Laurie looked up, smiling uncertainly, and he made a face at her. Then, with calm assurance, he leaned over his little sister, picked up her turtles and tossed them into the fishpond. Tomiko's face puckered and tears came into her eyes. But when she tugged at Taro's sleeve, pleading with him to recapture her pets, Taro thrust out his hand roughly and pushed her down on the grass.

Tomiko burst into tears, but Laurie, always one to hate injustice and despise a bully, hurled herself suddenly into action. Taro had turned his back and was swaggering toward the gate, when Laurie went after him. She catapulted herself into the middle of his back with a force that knocked the wind out of the boy. He stumbled and she was upon him like a fury, pummeling and pushing, until he collapsed, alarmed by what was happening to him. When she had him face down Laurie sat herself astride his back and banged his head into the earth.

"You're mean!" Laurie shouted. "You're just a mean old Japanese boy!"

Marcia watched in mingled dismay and amusement. Taro was getting exactly what he deserved. But when he let out a yell of anguish, she supposed she must go to his rescue.

She stood up, but Taro's yells had brought help from the other house. Before Marcia could move to his aid, Chiyo Minato ran through the gate with her kimono flapping open at the knees in a most un-Japanese and unladylike fashion. She rushed to the two children and pulled Laurie off Taro's back.

"What are you doing?" she cried in English, shaking her excitedly. "What are you doing to my son?"

For just an instant Marcia was too startled to move. That the delicately Japanese Chiyo should suddenly make a western-style dash across the garden with her kimono flying and burst into words in an accent that was completely American, was too astonishing to be grasped.

But now Laurie was crying too, though more in indignation than anything else, and Marcia went quickly toward the little group.

ELEVEN

"I'M SORRY IF LAURIE HURT TARO," MARCIA TOLD Chiyo, "but I'm afraid your son was in the wrong. He was rough with his little sister, and he threw their turtles into the fishpond."

At the sight of Marcia, Chiyo seemed to freeze into her familiar pattern. She regarded her with a blank lack of understanding, but the mask had been donned too late and the words Chiyo had spoken could not be unsaid.

"You know English, don't you, Mrs. Minato?" Marcia said curiously. "And you speak it without the accent of a person who learns it as a foreign language. Are you a Nisei?"

Chiyo turned away from her, not answering for a moment. She wiped Taro's tears and comforted the weeping Tomiko. Laurie was brushing herself off indignantly and still muttering. It took a good deal to make the gentle Laurie angry, but when she lost her temper, she did it in a large way.

"He thinks that because he's a boy, he can do anything he likes and we girls have to take it," she cried. "But that's not the way we do in America. I don't like boys who tease."

Taro threw her a last doubtful look and darted for the safety of his own house.

"He won't bother us any more," Laurie told Tomiko. "Let's see if we can fish those turtles out of the pond. See, there's one swimming over to a rock on this side."

Chiyo watched the girls go back to their play, and then turned reluctantly to Marcia. "I don't speak English much any more. Sometimes it comes out when I least expect it."

Chiyo's face was the much-admired melon seed shape, long and oval, her skin very white, her eyes faintly tilted and as dark as any eyes could be. She looked so lovely and delicate, so very Japanese in her gray kimono with the white bamboo pattern, that the words she was speaking seemed all the more incongruous. A hundred questions and doubts were surging up in Marcia's mind. If this girl spoke English so well, it was even more likely she should interest an American who was a long way from home.

A painful flare of jealousy swept through Marcia, bringing with it a curiosity that sickened her a little. To want to know . . . everything. And yet to realize that by knowing she might inflict unbearable pain on herself was a shaking experience. Still she managed to smile at Chiyo. No matter what the result might be, this was an opportunity she could not let pass.

"Won't you come in the house for a little while and talk to me?" she said. "The cat's out of the bag now. You can't put it back."

There was a tremulous look about Chiyo's mouth, as if she were not far from tears.

"I—I must not come in—" she began, but Marcia touched one kimono sleeve lightly.

"Please come. There will be no one there but me. Sumie-san will bring us tea."

After another moment of indecision Chiyo allowed herself to be persuaded. She stepped out of her *geta* at the entrance and moved across the polished floor in the modest pigeon-toed fashion of the proper Japanese lady. Marcia led her into the cozier bedroom, which she used much of the time now as a sitting room, in preference to the huge drawing room.

"We'll be more comfortable in here," she said. "Try this rocker, it's my favorite chair."

Chiyo sat down stiffly, her eyes downcast, her face expressionless. She was far from inner repose, Marcia suspected.

"You wear a kimono so gracefully," Marcia said. "So many Japanese have taken to western dress. But you ran just now as though you had grown up accustomed to our sort of clothes."

"My husband prefers the old ways," Chiyo said softly. While her speech was American in accent, it was faintly stilted, as though she had used English seldom in recent years. "I like the kimono," she added. "It reminds me that I am Japanese." She looked straight at Marcia. "I want to be only Japanese."

There was almost a challenge in her words and Marcia sought to reassure her. "Why not, if that's the way you prefer it? But you were American once?"

"American born," Chiyo said quickly. "A Nisei, with Japanese parents. We lived in San Francisco until I was eleven years old."

"I lived across the bay in Berkeley," Marcia said.

Chiyo nodded her smooth black head. "Yes, I know."

Sumie-san brought tea and set the tray on a low table between the two women. Her face showed nothing of the surprise she must have felt that their neighbor should have been invited into this house. Marcia could imagine what a buzz of discussion would go on in the kitchen when she returned.

There was silence while Marcia poured the green tea and passed the plate of salted *sembi* that were like small brown cocktail crackers. For all her outward calm, she felt keyed up, excited, yet wary at the same time. Chiyo must not guess how curious she was about her, how eager to thrust aside the curtain of mystery that hung between the two sides of the house. The unpleasant flare of jealousy she had thrust away. Or so she hoped.

"Could you speak Japanese when you first came here?" Marcia asked.

"Yes, of course." Chiyo sipped her tea. "It is my second language. I grew up speaking both English and Japanese as a child. But it was hard for me when I first came here. I was really an American child then. I didn't want to be Japanese. My parents had wanted for a long time to visit their homeland and they didn't want me to be wholly American. A few months before the war started, they brought me to Japan."

"It must have been painful to have your two countries at war," Marcia said.

"It was. Especially since I was neither all Japanese, nor entirely American. The other children thought I was strange. I could speak the language, and I looked Japanese, but I didn't know enough about Japanese ways and customs. My parents had become Americanized in many ways, and there was so much they hadn't taught me. I made mistakes."

"What sort of mistakes?"

Chiyo smiled a little sadly. "I didn't even know how to open a *shoji* properly. There is just one place to put your hands, and you must kneel first on one side, then on the other in just the right manner as you slide the door back. There are hundreds of exact customs like that which a Japanese girl must know, or else be considered badly brought up. But those were small things. I learned them in time."

With a sudden gesture that was more American than Japanese she set her teacup down.

"I must go now. I should not be here at all. My—my husband would not like it."

"Why should he mind?" Marcia asked directly.

Chiyo sat in silence, not answering. Though she had come into the house and had talked with only a little hesitation, there was no friendliness in her. She still held herself coolly aloof.

"Please wait, don't go so quickly," Marcia said. "There are so many things about this house that I don't understand. Why are we forbidden to have anything to do with each other? Why are our children not supposed to play together?"

Chiyo started to speak, hesitated, lowered her eyes. "You must ask your husband these things."

It was clear that direct questions would do Marcia no good if they concerned the life of this house.

"Then tell me about your first years here," Marcia said. "I want to understand what it was like."

Chiyo did not look at her as she began to speak. "My father was killed in the fighting in New Guinea, though he did not believe in the war. All the rest died at home—my mother and aunt, my brother and sister. Our home in Tokyo was destroyed. At the end the Japanese people no longer cared about winning or losing. They wanted only for the war to stop. It was so with me—I had no country. I had only suffering and loss."

Nothing could be said in the face of Chiyo's stark words.

"But you're happy again now with your husband and children?" Marcia said gently.

Chiyo bowed her head in silence and Marcia wondered how truly happy she was.

"What of your cousin?" Marcia asked. "She too has recovered from the war?"

There was a moment of silence. Then Chiyo spoke so softly Marcia could hardly catch the words.

"My cousin has suffered most of all. She will never recover. My cousin is—is ill."

Once more a door had been closed and Marcia sensed that it would not open again on this occasion. Nor had she any wish to prod further in the face of Chiyo's unhappy account.

Chiyo rose and bowed in the Japanese fashion. "*Arigato gozaimasu.* Thank you for the tea. I must go now." She went silently to the door and Marcia accompanied her into the hall. But before they reached the side veranda, Chiyo turned to her, suddenly earnest.

"It would be best for you to go home soon, Mrs. Talbot. Best to take your little girl and go back to America."

"My husband is here," Marcia said steadily. "I want to make my home with him."

Chiyo's face was expressionless, but it seemed to Marcia that anguish looked out of her eyes. Her tone was suddenly urgent. "If you stay something terrible may happen. You are not wanted here. You will only hurt the innocent if you remain."

For a moment the two women looked at each other and all semblance of friendship was gone. An unspoken enmity had sprung to life between them.

Chiyo bowed again, formally, stepped into her *geta* and hurried into the garden. At the fishpond she picked Tomiko up in her arms and bore her away through the gate, shut it firmly behind her.

Marcia looked after her, feeling a little ill with the mingling of emotions that swept through her. Though Jerome's name had not been spoken, something had come into the open. It was, Marcia thought, as if Jerome had stood there between them, claimed in some way by each woman, turning wholly to neither.

Laurie came toward her from the garden. "Why did she take Tomiko away? Is she mad because I pushed Taro down? But he was mean first. Why did he have to tease us and spoil our fun?"

Gently Marcia smoothed back the locks of hair that strayed loose about Laurie's forehead. "I suppose he wanted to tease you because a Japanese boy is like any other sort of boy—he thinks it's fun to tease little girls. Weren't you ever teased by boys at home?"

Laurie thought about this solemnly and managed a rueful grin. Marcia pressed her cheek against Laurie's for a moment. There was an aching in her to give Laurie more than she had, more of what she deserved. But even as she held her, Laurie pushed away.

"It's almost time for Daddy to come home. Is it all right if I walk a little way to meet him? He'll pick me up in the car and bring me back."

"Run along," Marcia said. "But watch out for the *bata-batas.*"

There were no sidewalks once you got off the main streets of Kyoto and the little three-wheeled trucks, which the Japanese had named for the noise they made, tore down the narrow lanes with their horns blaring and with little care for pedestrians. Strangely enough, no one ever seemed to get run over, and most Japanese walked calmly down the middle of the road unless forced aside by the immediate presence of traffic. Laurie promised to be careful and hurried away.

The servants always noted what happened around the house, and now Sumie-san was out in the garden with an improvised net attached to a length of bamboo pole that she used for stretching kimonos out to dry. Deftly she scooped and captured the two remaining turtles. She had set a small can of sand near an azalea bush while she fished, and now she drew it out and dropped the turtles into it. As she dried her hands on her apron, something in the garden seemed to catch her eye and she bent to retrieve it from under the bush. She turned it about curiously in her hands, then came across the stepping stones toward Marcia.

"Berongs Raurie-san," she said and held it out.

Marcia thanked her and took the small object, recognizing it at once. It was the little demon mask that Nan Horner had given Laurie when they had first come to Kyoto. Laurie must have carried it into the garden and forgotten it.

But as Marcia took the mask into the bedroom to put it among Laurie's things on the mantel, she remembered something. That azalea bush was on the far side of the garden. Laurie had flung something in that direction the other day. It must have been this little mask she had thrown away.

But why? What had prompted her action? She had loved the amusing little face when Nan gave it to her. Once Marcia had caught her in front of a mirror, puffing out her cheeks and scowling furiously in imitation of the mask and they had laughed together. So why had she changed her mind about it? What had she so wanted to conceal from her mother when she tossed the mask hurriedly away?

Marcia had a feeling that she should not question Laurie about this. It was better to let the incident fade out of her memory, if that was possible. Perhaps Laurie would accept the mask again and play with it, if her mother said nothing. On the mantelpiece sat the Japanese doll that Alan Cobb had given Laurie. The head with its Dutch cut black hair was propped against a mirror that reflected the doll's gay red and white kimono. Marcia set the mask beside the doll and left it there for Laurie to find.

She heard Jerome's car and a moment later Laurie came in the front door, while her father went to put the car away in the little garage that was set in a corner of the property. Laurie came into the room excitedly, full of news.

"Tomorrow's Sunday and we're going to see the cherry blossoms at Kiyomizu Temple!" she cried. "Just the three of us. You and me and Daddy. He's going to tell you about it at dinner."

Determinedly Marcia thrust away the shadow of Chiyo. If Jerome wanted to take them to Kiyomizu, that was a good sign. Whatever had happened in the past could not be undone, but there was still the present to fight for, and the future. Perhaps it was just as well that she and Chiyo had faced each other openly. The Japanese woman would know now that Jerome's wife did not mean to give up easily.

She had heard of Kiyomizu. Nan said it was one of the most beautiful and interesting of all the many temples in Kyoto. The cherry blossoms were opening everywhere now in their full glory. It was necessary to see them quickly before they reached the supreme moment of beauty and dropped from the trees full-blown. And to see them with Jerome—that was what she had come to Japan for!

Laurie noticed the mask on the mantel at once. She did not glance at her mother, but went quickly to pick it up and examine it.

"Sumie-san found it in the garden," Marcia said casually.

It was hard to know whether Laurie heard her or not. As her mother watched, the child took down the doll. Carefully she fitted the mask over the plump happy face and set the doll back on the mantel. The amusing little demon mask no longer seemed funny, for the innocence of the doll had vanished. The demon had a body now. It could caper about the world in human form. Some inner voice warned Marcia to let the matter alone, to give it no further emphasis by questioning. Laurie's face was strangely solemn as she turned from the masked doll. She did not look at her mother as she went to get ready for dinner.

TWELVE

THAT NIGHT MARCIA LAY AWAKE FOR A LONG TIME, thinking back through the years. There was no wind tonight and the creakings were only the normal ones heard in an elderly wooden house. Jerome slept in the next room and no sense of menace troubled her.

How clearly and achingly she could remember him as he had been after her father's death, when he had come back from Japan for the first time, and for the first time had seen her as a grown young woman plainly in love with him. For a little while he had turned to her as if the daughter of the man he had worshiped could answer some deep need in him. It was as if, in coming home, he had fled from something in Japan that he wanted never to see again, something he needed to forget. Or perhaps he fled from something in himself that left him fearful and touched with horror. Whatever he had felt, he had turned in those first days of their marriage to Marcia's eager gift of love as though it could hold away the ominous dark that encroached upon his being.

Marcia turned restlessly on her pillow, trying to understand, to fathom.

Chiyo—was it Chiyo?

Chiyo, the lovely and delicate and delightful. Chiyo, who would surely please the senses of any man. And she was American born, she could speak his own language. Yet Marcia had a feeling that there was something more, something less obvious which held Jerome to Japan. Chiyo, yes, but still something more than Chiyo.

Ichiro Minato was plainly a malcontent and not a particularly pleasant person. Yet he stayed on in this house. Why? What was the adherent that held these people together under the same roof? What part did the woman in the white kimono play and what was the nature of her illness?

At length Marcia slept and woke to find spring rain streaking the window panes, soaking the thirsty garden. Laurie was downcast until later in the morning, when the sun broke through and brought blue skies with it to bless the afternoon.

Sunday was not a day for the closing of business in Japan. A few offices might close, but most shops stayed open. Monday was the more popular closing day throughout the country. Nevertheless, holiday throngs seemed to be out that afternoon, because of the cherry blossoms. Jerome left the car at the foot of Teapot Hill, so they could walk up past the tiny, open-front shops. Kyoto pottery was famous and the shops were endlessly fascinating with their display of everything from tourist trash to the beautiful and unique. There were exquisite tea sets, dishes of every kind, colorful ceramic figures of gods and men and animals, doll shops and souvenir shops. And always, as they climbed the steep hill, the bright red pagoda that fronted the temple buildings rose above them, beckoning like a finger.

When they reached the stone steps leading up to the main entrance, Jerome chose instead to take them around to the side.

"The view is more unusual this way," he said. "We'll approach from the ravine below the temple walls."

He seemed interested and alive today, Marcia found to her joy. He was almost as vital and compelling as she remembered him from the old days, and she responded as eagerly as Laurie. Away from the dark Japanese villa she could be gay in the old way that had once appealed to Jerome and drawn him to her.

As they rounded a walk that approached from the low side, the full glory of the cherry blossoms burst upon them in pink and white clouds of bloom. The hillside seemed alive with color and Marcia could understand why the Japanese made something of a cult of cherry blossom viewing. All over Japan this month, wherever the trees bloomed, people thronged into the open to savor their beauty with a conscious appreciation and satisfaction. The throngs were out at Kiyomizu today, with more kimonos than usual in evidence among the ladies, since the kimono was more fitting for the ceremony of flower viewing. Cameras were busy around every turn and the temple steps seemed to be a favorite spot for groups to gather and be photographed.

Young Japanese women in trim blue uniforms led various tours about the temple grounds, and Marcia found it even more interesting to watch the people than to look at cherry blossoms and temples. Children were everywhere. To Laurie's delight they came upon some dozen or more little girls squatting on the earth with paper laid out before them as they painted the scene in water colors. Most of the pictures were very good, since the Japanese learned to paint as quickly as they learned to write with a brush. Indeed, the two media were similar.

Approaching the temple from the park that spread its walks and steps far below on this side, they had an impressive view. A great stone retaining wall, high as the wall of a castle, slanted upward, with the roofs of Kiyomizu rising in a cluster above the wall and spreading back along the hillside. Halfway to the rear the stone wall ended and a gigantic wooden platform supported the remaining buildings of the temple and held them in the air far above, on a level with those in front. The platform was supported by countless tree trunks, upended and tall as they had been in life, bound together by an open wooden cross structure. The Japanese, who had only wood to work with as an architectural medium, used it with imagination and never-ending beauty. The high platform overlooked the ravine, while steep, slanted roofs of ancient thatch rose in the background.

Near the hillside they found a broad bank of steps rising steeply to the level of the temples above. They climbed through the pervading shimmer of cherry blossoms, until they too could stand with the throngs on the platform and look down into the ravine and out over the roofs of Kyoto. All around them was the murmur of Japanese voices, and the sound of the stream below, the "clear water" that gave Kiyomizu its name.

"It's so beautiful it hurts," Laurie said softly and Marcia pressed her hand. Much of the beauty of this day and place was, for them, due to Jerome's presence, to his almost affectionate mood.

They circled the main temple buildings, climbed still higher beneath a stone torii and between two snarling stone dogs. Before a smaller building at the top level an elderly Japanese woman pulled the hempen bell rope and clapped her hands three times to attract the attention of the god. Then she bent her head in prayer with her palms together in the familiar gesture men of many faiths used when they prayed.

Beyond they found a small garden, a pond with an island in the center and a bridge leading to it. A large turtle sunned himself lazily on a rock and hardly troubled to pull in his head as they went by. Jerome found a low wall where they could sit alone, withdrawn from the visiting throngs. Afternoon sunlight poured over the scene, shining on temple roofs and stone lanterns, setting the cherry blossoms ashine with glowing light.

The moment seemed to brim with emotion and Marcia slipped her hand into Jerome's, leaned gently against his arm. His fingers closed about her own, but when she looked up at him, she saw that he was watching Laurie.

"Tell me," he said to his daughter, "do you know why the samurai chose the cherry blossom for his emblem?"

Laurie shook her head, and he went on, his tone

light, casual, yet with an awareness behind it, as if he watched for something.

"The cherry blossom falls at the peak of its beauty, instead of withering slowly like other flowers," he said. "The old samurai, the warrior, considered it a more noble thing to meet death at the peak of his career, at the crest of his powers, instead of growing old with his glorious days behind him."

Marcia looked about at the foaming sea of blossoms, and mused out loud. "That's all right for cherry blossoms and it sounds fine as a romantic tradition. But I hope the Japanese don't hold with that belief now."

"They did during the war," Jerome said. "There's a Japanese proverb, 'The cherry blossom is the best of flowers, the soldier is the best of men.' It's tradition to believe that, like the cherry blossom, the soldier is born to die at his peak. Japanese soldiers were trained to die. Perhaps that's one trouble with Ichiro Minato. He was trained to die and he didn't die. Now I suppose he feels dishonored, as if he had no right to be alive. Marcia, has he ever bothered you in any way? Minato, I mean?"

The sudden question surprised her. "He has never even spoken to me," she said. Somehow she did not want to mention the times when Minato-san had stared at her so strangely.

A blemish had fallen upon the day with this talk of death and soldiers. Marcia got up from the wall, hoping to turn the tide of Jerome's thoughts by moving away to something new. But he touched her arm lightly, arresting her, and she turned to look into his face again. The Lucifer look was alive in his eyes and she sensed in him a rising pitch of intensity that suddenly frightened her. She wanted nothing to spoil this lovely day, nothing to break the sense of companionship shared with him.

But he went on and she sensed a mockery in his voice she did not understand.

"You think this is all very beautiful, don't you?" he asked. "But let's put it to a test. Close your eyes for a moment and shut it out. Close your eyes, Laurie."

Marcia did not close her eyes. She stared at her husband, her anxiety increasing. But Laurie shut her eyes obediently, and stood waiting, unguarded and eager for whatever surprise might come.

"Can you hear the planes?" her father asked. "No— keep your eyes closed. They're planes out of the war years, Laurie. Perhaps planes out of the future. Can you hear them now?"

The excitement in Laurie matched his own as she responded to his make-believe. "Yes, I can hear them, Daddy. There are a lot of them coming. They're flying over the mountains to Kyoto."

"Listen then! Listen and you can hear the 'bombs away!' They're dropping now, straight as death. One hit and all Kiyomizu is gone—cherry blossoms and temples and human beings."

Shock brought Marcia alive. "Stop it!" she cried. "What are you doing?"

But it was already done. Excitement gave way to horror in Laurie's face. She opened her eyes and looked about her at a scene that had plainly changed before her vision, as if she saw smoking ruin, desolation and death.

The suddenness with which the world of cherry blossoms had crashed about them sickened Marcia.

The reversal of emotion was too sudden, too cruel. She put an arm about Laurie, seeking to erase the pain and bewilderment that suddenly gave her daughter's face the look of a grown woman.

"Don't believe him—he's only playing a game!" she cried, trying to keep her voice light with an amusement she could not feel. "No one has ever dropped a bomb on Kyoto, Laurie. No one wanted to destroy all this beauty and art. Kyoto is still old Japan."

Jerome paid no attention to her. "But it could happen, Laurie. It could happen any time. When you look at men you have to remember that. You have to remember what lies underneath. They can build beauty, but they can destroy it too. Don't trust so easily, Laurie. Don't give your heart so readily."

There was a new destructiveness in him, Marcia saw in dismay, a hateful, ugly thing that not only reached out to destroy others, but which cut inwards as well, destroying himself.

A hot tide of anger began to rise in Marcia. She must see him alone as quickly as possible and talk to him about the monstrous thing he had just done. Fortunately, Laurie was resilient and happy-natured. She would forget this moment shortly and be herself again. But could she, Laurie's mother, forget it? She felt bruised and sick, for all her anger.

Jerome seemed to read the indignation in her eyes and he smiled as if it pleased him, even though he pretended to apologize.

"I'm sorry, my dear. Perhaps I should keep my little imaginings to myself. Come along and let's enjoy the rest of the place. There's a dragon I'd like you to meet, Laurie."

But the bloom had gone out of the day. Laurie walked soberly beside her father as they moved toward the front gate of the temple. A fiercely scaled dragon reared its head in a fountain, but Laurie, who would have delighted earlier in so magnificent a bronze dragon, watched solemnly and did not smile. Visitors to the temple paused beside the fountain to catch water in a wooden dipper and rinse their mouths and palms so that they might go symbolically cleansed and purified into the grounds of this Buddhist temple.

"Let's go home," Laurie said finally, and this time she turned toward her mother. "My tummy feels shaky inside."

If there was anything Jerome did not enjoy it was the company of a sick child. He moved with alacrity to get them to the car and Marcia sat in the back seat, with Laurie's head on her lap. By the time they reached home, the little girl felt better, but she wanted no more than milk toast and fruit for supper, and by way of precaution Marcia tucked her into bed after she had eaten. Laurie asked to sit up and look at her books, so Marcia fixed a light for her, and piled the books she requested on the table beside her bed. Then she went in search of Jerome.

He was in his room and at her tap he called to her to come in. He seemed wryly amused at the sight of her, but he got up and drew a chair near the desk where he had been sitting.

"You're looking very much like a mother tonight," he said. "A ready-to-do-battle mother. I'm not sure the look becomes you."

"This isn't a joking matter," she said steadily. "I've tried to make allowances because you don't know very much about children. You haven't been around any American children for years, and you certainly aren't acquainted with your own daughter."

He sighed and tapped the papers on his desk. "If you don't mind, I'm not in the mood tonight for a lecture on fatherhood."

From where she sat she could see the carved mask on the wall and she tried to keep her gaze away from it. The rolling eyes and sneering mouth seemed to jeer at her, and they distracted her from what she wanted to say.

"You mustn't do frightening things like that to Laurie," she told him, stumbling a little over the words. "The most wonderful thing about her is her happy, confident nature. I don't want anything to spoil that."

He flung aside the pencil he had picked up, and now his face was alive with dark vitality. "I can see that the child has need of a father. Women always believe children should be protected to the point of unfitting them for life. What do you think is going to happen to Laurie's happy confidence, as you call it, when she finds out what is waiting for her away from your protection? You're making a weakling of her."

"She's only seven," Marcia told him indignantly. "And it isn't weak to be loving and warm. A child isn't wise enough at seven to know what to do with the ugly things in life. If you continue what you started today, the result may be disastrous for her."

"Are you wise enough at your age to know what to do with the ugly side of life?" he asked sardonically. "Have *you* ever grown up?"

Marcia stiffened. "It's you who haven't grown!" she cried heatedly. "It's you who are running away from the work you ought to be doing. You haven't been able to face what's ugly in life and find the good in it too. But I won't let you twist Laurie in the same way. I won't let her be alone with you again unless you give me your word to avoid tormenting her as you did today."

He laughed out loud, as though her words delighted him. "And how will you manage that if I choose to see her alone? Our daughter, my dear, is already nine-tenths on my side, no matter what I say to her. So how would you stop me? Though of course you could take her home, if you wanted to do that."

Her eyes widened as she stared at him. "Do you mean you would use Laurie cold-bloodedly, just to force me to go home?"

"I might," he said coolly. "Anyway, you can think it over."

She turned from him and walked to the door.

Outside in the dim hallway, she clasped her arms about herself to still her sudden shivering.

From kitchen and dining room came a clatter of dishes. All was quiet in Laurie's bedroom, but she could not go in there right now. She could not let Laurie see her face until she had found time to compose herself. Outside, the evening was still light. She caught up a jacket from the hall tree and let herself out the front door. She would walk for a while in the soft Japanese twilight, with only strangers to see her abroad —strangers who would not know how to read the trouble in a western face.

She turned uphill past Nan's house, following the narrow lane between bamboo fences, hurrying past Nan's so she would not be seen. Nan Horner was a friend of Jerome's and it was quite likely she would side with him.

As she walked she began to cry softly, the tears streaking her cheeks. She could let them come; it did not matter now. Though when she went back to the house there must be no helpless tears.

Some sort of small shrine blocked the way ahead. She saw a quiet, empty enclosure and moved toward it as to a haven where she could be completely alone until she had regained control of her emotions.

THIRTEEN

THE SHRINE WAS SET IN A TRIANGULAR PLOT AT A PLACE where the lane forked off in a V. A stone fence all around enclosed it like a small island, and the entrance at the point of the V was marked by two freshly painted, bright vermilion torii—the sign of a Shinto shrine, as Marcia had learned by now. These gates were formed by two upright columns of wood, with crossbars overhead. On either side of a paved walk the enclosure had been thickly planted with trees and shrubs. Somewhere off to the left side she could hear the murmur of a stream, and the wind sighed in tall pines.

The peace of the little shrine invited her and she stepped beneath the first torii, went between two stone lanterns and under the second vermilion gate. Ahead rose the small building of the shrine, set high on a concrete base, but in itself hardly larger than an oversized doll's house. Overhead a sloping tiled roof sheltered the shrine from the rain, though it stood open on all sides, the green of shrubbery crowding close.

As she followed the short, straight walk, she saw a trough of water on her left, with the usual wooden dipper waiting. Ahead, guarding the immediate approach to the shrine were two little stone foxes set on bases of field rocks cemented together, their heads turned as if to watch her, with alert ears cocked and pink tinted inside. The plumed tail of one curled high in a great brush behind him, the other's tail was broken. White vases of greenery graced the altar, but there was no image here, as there would be at a Buddhist temple. A thick hempen bell rope, crimson and white, hung ready to summon the god, and there were two more small porcelain foxes facing the altar.

She was glad she had found this shrine. She could stand here in the quiet, with only the drip of water in the trough and the sighing of the wind for company. She had run head-long from the house, from the frightening thing she had glimpsed in Jerome. If he meant to use Laurie against her in this cruel way, he would succeed in his purpose. She would have to take the child and go home.

Was this the answer she had flown the Pacific for? Was her determination to save their marriage a blind and foolish thing? The tears had dried on her cheeks, but the ache in her throat and in her heart went on.

"How can I stop loving him?" she thought miserably. "How can I learn to hate him so I may be free of him?"

That in itself was a disturbing thought. Never before had she wanted for even a moment to be free. Always she had believed that it was better to be Jerome's wife and have whatever he chose to give, than to have the whole of any other man. But here in this quiet place she had suddenly glimpsed herself in a new light, glimpsed herself as a woman caught in the spell of an enchantment from which she must certainly fight free.

The evening light was fading as the mountains cut off the sun and the little shrine grew cool and dusky. The two stone foxes, one with a cylinder in its mouth, the other a ball, stared at her curiously, as if wondering who she was and why she had come to this place. Stories of the fox god returned to her mind. The way of the fox, inhuman and wicked, was to take the guise of a human body and wreak evil in the world. But these little foxes seemed cheery beings who meant her no harm. She bowed to them politely and turned to go. As she did so, a shadow blocked the opening of the farthest torii.

A figure stood there shrouded in dusk. She could see that it was a man, though she could not make out his face as she moved toward the entrance to the shrine. She supposed it was some worshiper come to pray. He did not enter, however, but remained near the gate, watching her. For the most part, as she knew, the streets of Japan were safe to any woman. But there did exist the outcasts, the beggars, the thieves, and it was growing darker by the moment. There was no other way out—she must walk past the figure quickly and hurry home.

As she approached him, the man stepped full into her path, halting her, and now she saw his face. It was Ichiro Minato. Jerome's warnings about him returned to her mind, far from reassuring now, when she must walk directly past him in the dusk. The lane beyond stretched empty of passers-by. If he meant her any harm, there was no one to turn to for help.

"Good evening, Minato-san," she said, trying to sound casual and confident.

He bowed courteously enough. Then he took a step closer to her. "You come, *okusama*. You come."

"No," she said firmly. "I must go home now, home to Talbot-san."

Minato shook his head. "No Tarbot-san. You come."

And now he stepped so close that she could smell the odor of liquor and hear his heavy breathing. There was nothing to do but move quickly or be trapped in this deserted spot. She put out her hands and shoved him off balance, ran past him up the lane toward Nan's house. If she could reach Nan's she would be safe and Nan would come out and deal with Chiyo's drunken husband. She could not tell whether he followed or not because of the beat of her own running steps on the earth and the pounding of her heart in her ears.

Someone opened Nan's gate just as she reached it and she ran into the arms of Alan Cobb.

"Hello!" he said. "What's all this? Somebody chasing you?" He held her gently, his eyes kind and sympathetic. For a moment she was sharply aware of his breadth and height, and of the clean smell of good health that was a part of him. Then she drew away and looked over her shoulder in apprehension.

"It was that Minato who lives in the other half of our house. I think he followed me when I came out. He'd been drinking and . . ."

"There's no one coming now," Alan said. "Would you like me to look?"

"No," she said, and put up her hand to thrust back the pins in the loosened knot of her hair. "I don't want to make any trouble. Perhaps—perhaps I only imagined that he meant me some harm."

He fell into step beside her, transferring the books he carried to the other arm. "I have to confess that this soldier of Japan still disturbs me a little. Your friend Nan Horner has been lecturing me on the subject."

"What do you mean?" Marcia asked, glad to escape to a plane of casual conversation.

"Nan's a bit sorry for Minato-san. And I must say she gave me a new slant on the returning soldier. After the surrender he didn't come home a hero after all. He came home loathing himself for being alive, and expecting rejection and disgrace for being conquered. But his reception was even worse than he expected because by that time the Japanese people knew more about what had been perpetrated by their own soldiers and they were pretty sick about it. So a good many soldiers who had gone off expecting to die for Emperor and country, came home alive and found themselves scorned and repudiated."

"But that was so many years ago," Marcia said.

"Yes, and I suppose most of them have been absorbed into the community by now. But Minato's kind carries the mark of war. And I don't mean just that ugly scar down his forehead. I wonder how that happened? Did he get the other fellow—the one who almost got him?"

They had reached the house and Marcia wished she could keep him talking a while longer. The very casualness of his manner was something to bring her back to an everyday world.

"Won't you come in?" she invited. "Laurie would love to see you."

He shook his head. "Thanks. I'd like to. But I think I'd better come by appointment when I do. I've tried to call your husband at the lab a couple of times, but haven't been able to reach him. Nan says he's not often there."

"You wanted to talk to him about material for your book, didn't you?" she said, brushing quickly past the matter of the lab.

Once more his eyes seemed to question her in some way. "That's the reason I've given him and I suppose it's true enough. In part, at least."

"What do you mean?" she asked, puzzled. There had always been something odd about Alan's attitude toward Jerome.

It was as if he measured her for a moment. "I hate to see waste," he said. "I hate it as much as Mark Brewster does. Waste in particular of a man like Jerome Talbot."

Marcia was silent. Who knew better the waste of a man like Jerome than she?

Alan went on almost angrily. "There are so few qualified and so many needed. Why isn't he doing what needs to be done? What right has he to throw his genius away when it's wanted so desperately? Knowing that he's here, knowing what he has to give and that he's not giving it, is something I find hard to swallow. I can't sit back and say this is none of my business. The future is every man's business these days."

Everything he said was true and she could only agree soberly. "Sometimes I'm frightened," she confessed. "There's some torment driving him that I don't understand."

Alan opened the gate and came with her through the garden to her own entryway. As light from the house fell upon them, he saw her face and put out a finger to trace the smudges on her cheeks.

"Tears? Did Minato frighten you as much as that?"

"No," she said quickly. "That was nothing. I—I was anxious about Laurie. But what you said just now concerning waste—is there anything I could do? I want to help, Alan, if only I can find a way. So far I've failed at every turn."

"Perhaps it's too late," Alan said, "though I hate to accept that. Perhaps it's something you couldn't affect anyway. Don't eat your heart out over it." He smiled and held out his hand.

She gave her own into his and felt once more the warmth and strength that seemed to flow from the clasp of his fingers.

"I worry about you," he said surprisingly as he turned away.

She looked after him as he walked to the gate. How much did he know? How much had Nan told him of her personal problem? Somehow she would not mind his knowing.

As she went into the house to face Jerome, she felt less alone than she had been only a short while before.

She would tell Jerome about Minato at once, she decided, and let him determine what to do about what had happened. But when she tapped at Jerome's door there was no answer. Sumie-san came into the hall to say that she had stayed with Laurie when *danna-san* had gone out and Laurie was now asleep.

Marcia thanked her and went into her room. Laurie lay on her stomach, her braids flung over the coverlet.

How vulnerable a sleeping child looked, Marcia thought, and bent to kiss one warm, flushed cheek.

A book Laurie had been looking at lay open on the blanket. Picking it up, Marcia saw that it was a collection of Japanese fairy tales which Jerome had given the child. The stories were probably too difficult for her, though she had started to read when she was six.

Marcia sat down beside a lamp and began to skim idly through the book. What strange tales they were! One was of a beautifully gowned woman who appeared on the street like any woman, but when a man approached her she would turn toward him, faceless and horrible. It seemed that Japanese ghosts had neither faces nor feet, and by that means you could identify them. Another story was a melancholy tale of Yuki-onna, the white lady of the snows, who represented death to all who beheld her. There was also the usual sprinkling of demons and foxes, and the whole concoction was probably no worse than the Brothers Grimm, whose stories Laurie already adored. But with Laurie's new tendency toward nervousness, this sort of thing might just as well be put out of her reach for the time being.

Next door the playing of the samisen began again, and Marcia stiffened at the sound. She had grown to dread the music and the singing. The melancholy, monotonous strains wore upon her nerves, made the evil in this house, centered in that mask in Jerome's room, seem to come closer about the bed of her sleeping child.

When a light clatter sounded against the window pane of her room, she almost cried out in alarm. It wasn't raining. Had the wind blown a branch against the pane? But she did not think any tree stood close enough for that. She sat, utterly still and shivering, listening to the sounds of the night. Were those footsteps she heard in the garden? Had the meeting with Minato and these eerie Japanese tales disturbed her to the point of weird imaginings?

The spatter against the window sounded again and she sprang up and turned off the light. She recognized the sound now. Someone in the garden had thrown a handful of fine gravel at the window pane. Shielded by darkness, she pulled aside the curtain and peered into the night. She could see no one, nothing, yet she knew someone stood there waiting in the dark garden.

If it was Minato again, she surely need not fear him when a shout would bring help from his house as well as her own. Perhaps it was better to face him and try to find out what it was he wanted. Since her meeting with Alan she felt less afraid of Chiyo's husband, less lost in the loneliness into which the afternoon at Kiyomizu had plunged her. She slipped into her jacket and went to the entryway, where light threw a faint radiance into the garden.

"Who is there?" she called softly.

The sound of *geta* on stepping stones reached her and Minato, in his usual western slacks and shirt, but with his bare feet thrust into wooden clogs, stepped to the edge of the radiance and bowed to her.

This time he did not approach her and he fitted a stiff smile over the mask of his face, as if to be reassuring. The scar that ran down from his black hair to one eyebrow shone livid in the pale light.

"Prease, you come my house," he said and bowed to her again.

"But why?" she asked. "What do you want?"

He made a quick gesture, as if to hush her, and beckoned. Then he hurried away as if he expected her to follow, and moved toward the front gate. She was no longer afraid, but suddenly curious. She slipped on her shoes and followed him into the dim lane in front of the house.

He did not let her come near him this time, as if by the very distance between them he would reassure her. He moved ahead, picking up his *geta* lightly without scuffing the ground. At his own gate he paused and looked back to make sure she was following. Then he went through and out of sight, leaving the gate open behind him.

For a moment uncertainty held her and she wondered about the wisdom of following him as far as his own house. But the samisen still played. Upstairs lights burned. There were people there. At the far corner of the house, Minato waited for her and did not move until she stepped toward him. Then his shadowy figure flitted around the corner.

The gentle, singing voice upstairs seemed to draw her on. Was it Chiyo who sang so sadly?

Marcia followed Minato into the rear garden, and he beckoned her close to the side of the house, where the upper gallery made an overhang, and they were lost in shadow. By his gesture she knew she was meant to stop here and listen to whatever was going on upstairs.

As she realized his intention, distaste filled her. She had no wish to eavesdrop upon the affairs of those who lived in this part of the house. Not even if their affairs concerned her, as they very well might. But before she could escape, a woman laughed softly—a light splintering of sound. The music ceased and she heard Chiyo's voice speaking in Japanese, swiftly, sweetly. Marcia turned away, wanting to hear no more, but now Minato stepped into her path as he had done earlier that evening and there was a look of angry insistence on his face. Clearly he meant her to remain.

A man's voice answered Chiyo and while the language was Japanese the voice was Jerome's. She stood for a frozen moment listening and knew that this was the thing Minato intended her to hear. Then she pushed past Chiyo's husband and ran toward the front of the house and the open gate that led toward home. Minato made no effort to stop her or to follow. When she hurried through the gate and back to her own part of the house, he was nowhere in sight. Whatever his purpose, he had succeeded in his effort.

She went to her own room and undressed for bed in the quiet dark. Only the whisper of Laurie's breathing broke the silence. Now no sound of samisen drifted from the other house, but Marcia crept beneath the covers and put her hands over her ears as if to shut out the very memory of that music. Its melancholy notes were a part of her now, an aching sorrow of realization that ran through her body like physical pain. Now she was sure of the thing that until now had only tantalized her. It was Chiyo who held Jerome to Japan. Not merely in the past, but in the present. The happiness Marcia had felt at Kiyomizu, the feeling that Jerome had been, however briefly, hers again, had all been an illusion. Perhaps an illusion which he had built in her deliberately before he as deliberately destroyed it with his words to Laurie.

From the mantelpiece the Japanese doll watched her in the gloom, its rosy cheeks hidden behind the demon mask that Laurie had placed over the face.

FOURTEEN

In the days that followed, Marcia did not find it easy to come to a decision. It seemed a simple solution to go to Jerome and say, "You've won—I'm going home." Yet something held her back. There was a soreness, an aching in her that would not let her be, yet it was not wholly pain for her own loss and defeat. It was also because of Jerome himself. He too was suffering in some strange way, and over something she did not understand.

This feeling was increased one day when Jerome came through the house unexpectedly and found her in the garden, laughing out loud with Laurie over a game they were playing with a ball. It was not laughter that came from her heart, but Jerome could not know that. He stood on the veranda ledge watching, and Marcia turned to see the change in his face.

Laurie chased her ball across the garden and had to

hunt for it in the bushes. Slowly Marcia went toward
him, drawn by the sudden gentleness in him.

"I remember the way you used to laugh," he said.
"It was the thing that most appealed to me about you.
You don't laugh as much as you used to."

"No," she said, and looked up into his eyes.

He turned away and went into the house. Knowing
only that this moment of emotion must not be allowed
to slip away, she stepped out of her shoes and ran after
him in her stocking feet. There was no pretense in him
now, as there had been at Kiyomizu.

He went into his room and sat down at his desk,
leaned his head in his hands, and she followed him
there. Long ago he had suffered from severe headaches
and her fingers rubbing over his temples and at the
back of his neck had seemed to ease the pain. She came
up behind him and put her hands gently over his forehead, pressing her fingers at the places where the pain
used to come. He reached up and caught her hands in
his, held them against his cheek, then turned the palms
to kiss them lightly.

"Tell me how I can help," she pleaded. "You know
that's all I want—to help you."

He let her hands go abruptly. "There's nothing you
can do," he said and the stamp of the stranger was back
upon him.

But she could not give up at once.

"Have you deserted your work completely?" she
asked. "What has happened to all the things you meant
to do?"

"What happens to the things most of us mean to
do?" he said. "What, for instance, are you getting out
of life?"

"I'm not sure what I want any more," she said. "Except to help you."

There was no gentleness in him now. "You take too much upon yourself. When will you learn that I prefer my own way? No one can help anyone else."

There was nothing more she could say, and she left him sitting there. Yet she had not reached the moment of complete defeat. As these times of softening, of indecision, of inner struggle were revealed, she felt increasingly that something in him still reached out toward her and she could not bring herself to give up and turn away for the last time.

Kyoto seemed filled with Americans these days, here for the cherry festival and dances, and tourists poured in from all over Japan. The Japanese were great travelers and loved nothing better than to visit the noted places of their country. Sometimes it appeared to Marcia that they moved according to an established pattern, rather than out of any individual desire to satisfy a personal interest. A place, a sight, was known as "famous." Therefore one visited it and looked upon it at the prescribed moment of day or season. But one did not go wandering off in idle search of the unexpected beauty that might become peculiarly the possession of the beholder. Even in the enjoyment of beauty, ritual played an important part.

Jerome took time now to bear Laurie off with him and introduce her to the cherry festival sights. Marcia began to dread these excursions because as often as not Laurie came home in a nervous, high-strung mood that made her unlike herself.

Now and then Marcia wondered about Ichiro Minato and what he had hoped for in bringing her into his garden to listen that night. She had seen him only a few times since then and he had looked away as if he did not recognize her. How did he feel about what was happening? Did the Japanese take such matters differently? Or had Minato reached so wretched a depth of existence that he could no longer manage his own life in any way? Had he hoped that Jerome's wife might take stronger action than he had been able to take?

Jerome seemed to have no fear of him. He spoke to Minato curtly at times and in a tone he used to no other Japanese. Plainly he disliked the man and had only impatience for him, as if he were a buzzing fly that could not be brushed away. How much did Jerome underrate Minato? Marcia wondered. It might astonish her husband to know that the Japanese was sufficiently concerned with what was going on to have betrayed Jerome's presence in his house to Jerome's wife.

For a brief space of time the cherry blossoms brightened all Kyoto, shining white and pale pink among the gray tile roofs. They were at their most glorious, with enormous double blooms, in Maruyama Park. Then they dropped at their peak of splendor and were gone for another year. May brought azaleas, bright pink and flaming red; wisteria, lavender and sweetly scented, dripped from arbors; and great iris blooms opened. The moon waned and darkened and grew full again.

One afternoon Marcia took the Japanese copy of Alan's book out of her drawer and carried it up the hill to show Nan. But in the end it was not Alan's book they talked about that day. The time of the dinner Nan had mentioned was approaching; the dinner she was giving to honor publication of Haruka Setsu's book. Nan and Alan Cobb had struck up a friendship and Alan wanted to meet Yamada-san, so he was to be there, Nan said. But when she indicated that Ichiro and Chiyo Minato were being invited too, Marcia rebelled. How could she endure an evening of being polite to Chiyo, of pretending friendship toward her? How could Nan, who surely knew the truth, expect this of her?

"I think I'd better stay home with Laurie," she said evasively.

"Bring Laurie along." Nan was brisk. "Dinner at a Japanese eating house will be a new experience for her." She gave Marcia an appraising look. "You're certainly off your feed these days. What have you got against my little dinner?"

They were sitting once more in the western-style study in Nan's house. Nan had been showing her some priceless kimonos she had bought when the war had first ended and peeresses were eager to part with their treasures. There were other kimonos Nan had exported to the States in the conduct of her business, but these she had kept. Perhaps she would give them to a Japanese museum sometime, she said. She had not enjoyed this particular aspect of her work.

Marcia picked up a magenta colored ceremonial kimono and let the cool silk slip absently through her hands. "I don't think I have to tell you why I don't want to attend a dinner with the Minatos present," she said.

Nan pressed out one cigarette and reached for another. "You talk in riddles today. What am I supposed to know about the Minatos?"

"I don't want to be in the same room with Chiyo," Marcia said, miserable now. "It's hard enough to be under the same roof."

Nan made a slow business of lighting a fresh cigarette. Her eyes did not meet Marcia's as she spoke. "Chiyo is to be pitied, you know. She's in a difficult position. It won't help matters for you to dodge this dinner. I hope you'll reconsider." Nan waited, an air of persistence about her.

Suddenly the struggle seemed no longer worth the effort to Marcia. If she must, she could surely find the courage to endure Chiyo's company for an evening. Soon, very soon now, she must bring herself to take the final step and go home to the States. Then what happened at this dinner would no longer matter.

"All right," she said quietly. "I'll come."

Nan nodded her approval. But when Marcia rose and picked up Alan's book, she held out her hand.

"Mind if I keep that for a few days? There's someone I'd like to show it to."

"Keep it as long as you like," Marcia told her.

In the days that followed before the dinner, Marcia tried to dwell only on the agreeable aspects of the coming affair. So far she had not been to a real Japanese eating house and she would enjoy the novelty. It would be a pleasure to see Alan again and she was looking forward to meeting the gifted Madame Setsu. Of moody thoughts about Chiyo, she would, she told herself sternly, have no part. She would concentrate on playing the role of Jerome's wife in public for one last time as gracefully as she could. It was Chiyo, if anyone, who would be at a disadvantage.

On the afternoon of the dinner Jerome went to the

laboratory, leaving word that he would come directly from his work. So Marcia and Laurie went downtown with Nan. They took a cab because of the difficulty of parking in narrow, crowded streets.

The restaurant was one which did not cater to the general public and where no one spoke English. Guests came only by reservation and each meal was especially prepared and served in an individual room, so that only a few parties could be accommodated at any one time.

As they walked up a narrow side street toward the door, they passed three exquisitely gowned girls, elaborately painted, their hair combed in the stiff convolutions of an antique style.

"Are they geisha?" Marcia asked.

"Maiko," Nan said. "That's what apprentice geisha are called in Kyoto's Pontocho. That's the alley we just crossed which runs parallel to the Kamo River. It's a famous geisha quarter, but those little girls aren't the full fledged thing as yet. Here we are. And of course everyone, including the cook, is out to greet us."

There was the usual business of shoe-removing, to the accompaniment of much bowing and welcoming. Then a hostess in a dark kimono led them up a flight of narrow wooden stairs, with a special warning for Marcia to take care. The stairs were slippery and very steep, and there was no rail. The Japanese ran up and down agilely in their *tabi*, but Marcia found herself clinging to the edge of the steps as she climbed.

They were shown into an airy mat-covered room, with a low black lacquer table set in the middle of it and cushions all around. There was no other furniture and as usual no decoration except for the painting and flower arrangement in the *tokonoma*. More and more Marcia was coming to enjoy the uncluttered appearance of a Japanese room. When only one or two treasures were displayed at a time, and these were changed every few weeks, the beholder really saw and enjoyed them. In western houses, where everything was put on display, the owners quickly ceased to see what lay about them, and there could be little real savoring of beauty.

The other guests began to arrive at once. Chiyo looked like the proverbial Japanese butterfly in her flowered kimono with its graceful sleeves. Ichiro was sober for the moment and dressed to the teeth in a proper western business suit.

Marcia was grateful for Nan's presence and her readiness to make conversation. It was possible to greet the Minatos courteously and then move away from them, with as little to say to Chiyo as possible.

When Alan came in, Ichiro bowed to him so deeply and politely that Alan looked startled, though he shook hands with the former soldier in a friendly way. When they took their places on the silk cushions around the low table, Ichiro's interest in Alan did not seem to abate.

Yamada-san had discarded western dress for the occasion and wore a handsome kimono of dark gray, with his family crest in white on the sleeves and back. The kimono suited him and added to his essential dignity of manner. Mrs. Yamada, Nan explained, would not be with them. It was not the custom to take one's wife out to dinner. And in any event, Mrs. Yamada was in Kobe lecturing on birth control. Since Chiyo was

American born, her presence tonight was a different matter.

"Though I'm sure Minato-san wouldn't take her out to an affair of his own," Nan added in an aside to Marcia.

She placed Yamada-san on her right, and when Jerome arrived he sat on her left, with Chiyo next to him. In spite of her determination to carry the evening off with courage, Marcia could not help wincing at the elaborate consideration Jerome turned upon Chiyo. Once, across the table, he caught her look and Marcia saw how brilliant his eyes were with mockery. If he meant to bait her deliberately, then the evening might be worse than she anticipated.

The guest of honor was still absent and when Marcia asked Nan about Madame Setsu, Nan gave her a surprised look.

"Madame Setsu won't be here. She belongs to old-fashioned Japan and it wouldn't be considered proper for her to attend—even though we're celebrating publication of her book. What we foreign women do is, of course, another matter."

Ichiro Minato continued to grin and bow in Alan's direction, as if something had wound him up, and Nan, noting his efforts, spoke to him.

"You've read the book I loaned you, Minato-san?"

Minato drew in his breath with a hiss. "Hai—yess-ss," he said. "Is good book," and he beamed at Alan appreciatively.

"Marcia brought the Japanese edition of your book over to show me," Nan explained to Alan. "I thought she wouldn't mind if I let Minato-san read it. Apparently it has made quite a hit with him."

Alan looked puzzled. "But why should it? It's hardly a flattering picture of the Japanese—especially of the Japanese soldier."

Minato's grin grew a little wider and he reached cordially across the table for another western handshake. "Cobb-san, Minato-san, brothers," he said.

Chiyo came to her husband's aid. "Ichiro understands what you have written because he too was in a prison camp when he was captured in Malaya. That is how he got that scar on his forehead—when an Allied soldier struck him with the butt of a rifle."

Alan started to speak, but Chiyo, her delicate skin flushing, went on quickly.

"Those soldiers of the Allies were angry over what they found when they came into the country to free their own people. They had reason for anger. Since Ichiro was there, he took the punishment, though it was not his fault. He did not complain. But this is why he feels great sympathy for you, Mr. Cobb."

Alan returned Minato's smile. "The other side of the coin," he said. "I'm interested to know this, Minato-san."

One of the Japanese hostesses brought in a basket of white, flowerlike objects which Marcia couldn't identify for a moment. When the basket was offered her, she took one doubtfully and found that it was a warm, damp hand towel, which had been beautifully folded in the shape of a flower.

While the guests freshened themselves with the towels, Nan explained to Marcia and Alan that this was to be no *sukiyaki* dinner, such as Americans usually ordered. Tonight they were to be served a more formal type of Japanese meal. It began with tiny bowls of clear soup, in which bits of vegetable, fish and seaweed made undersea patterns. After that the succession of small covered dishes increased as course after course was set down around each place by the women who waited on them. Nothing appeared in quantity. The pattern of the dishes, the texture and color of the bits of fish, vegetables and meat were all part of an exquisite design. The Japanese must feed the eye first of all at a dinner.

Nan had placed Laurie next to Alan and after a few moments of odd restraint on Laurie's part, she had warmed to him as to an old friend, and was having a lovely time. Once or twice Marcia saw Jerome watching the two across the table and she did not find his expression reassuring. He looked as though he thoroughly disapproved of Laurie's friendship with Alan.

Everyone was being kind to Laurie, including Yamada-san, who went out of his way to suggest certain morsels as being especially worthy of her attention. A heady evening for a young lady of seven.

A heady evening for Ichiro Minato, too, as quickly became evident. A young woman sat at his elbow, pouring warm *saké* into his cup whenever he drained it, and before long he began to show indications of becoming the life of the party.

The Japanese, it appeared, did little drinking in their homes, and the men could become gay with considerable rapidity on a few cups of *saké*. Marcia could hear a boisterous group in another room of the eating house, where the men were already well into the spirit of the evening.

It was Chiyo, however, who brought about the most difficult moment as far as Marcia was concerned.

So far Chiyo had hardly glanced in her direction and had not spoken to her at all after the first greeting. But now, as if she wanted to distract the attention of the others from Ichiro, Chiyo addressed Marcia directly.

"I understand that you are going home to America very soon, Mrs. Talbot," she said.

There was a momentary silence, while everyone looked at Marcia, who had never felt more helpless in her life.

Laurie cried, "But you said we'd come here to stay! Why do we have to go home?"

Jerome ignored Laurie's outburst and added his own dry question. "Yes, my dear—you've kept us surprisingly ignorant of your plans. We'd all like to know exactly what they are."

Marcia said, "But I—" and fell unhappily silent. At that moment one of the Japanese serving women knelt beside Alan to fill his *saké* cup. Alan turned suddenly so that his elbow caught the little cup and knocked it out of her hands. There were a few seconds of confusion, just enough to give Marcia time to collect herself. Jerome waited for her answer and she gave it quietly.

"I haven't made my plans yet," she said, and met his eyes without wavering.

She knew suddenly that Alan had created the disturbance deliberately to save her humiliation, but she did not dare glance in his direction to thank him. All her will was concentrated on an outward poise that would get her through the evening without revealing her inward strain.

At the end of the dinner rice was served with a wooden paddle from a big lacquered box, and then fruit was set out on a large plate for the guests to help themselves. Of course green tea had been poured constantly all through the meal for those who were not drinking *saké*.

When they were through, Nan set the book of poetry called *The Moonflower* on the low table before her.

"I'm not going to make a speech," she said, "but a number of us have had a part in the publication of this book and I know we're all delighted with the result. It has been beautifully printed and bound, Yamada-san."

The publisher bowed his head in thanks for her words.

"Of course Jerry Talbot's role was pretty important too—since he took care of part of the cost of printing it," Nan went on. "So thanks for being a patron of the arts, Jerry. I'm glad I could find a publisher for it, and I'll send copies home to America with great pleasure when we get to the translation."

Marcia looked at Jerome in surprise. At no time had he hinted that he had taken any part in the publication of this book, though she remembered seeing it in his room and wondering about his interest in it.

"It would be nice, Jerry," Nan went on, "if you would read one or two of her poems. I've done a bit of free translation to help."

Jerome took the book and leafed through the pages. Then he read aloud the title poem about the moonflower, the "ghost white spirit flower" that met death at dawn. Marcia listened in surprise. She had never known that Jerome cared anything for poetry, or that he could read it so well. He chose another poem about the fall of the cherry blossom at its moment of glory, and then read several that must have grown out of the war. All carried the sadness and futility that seemed to be the keynote of so much Japanese literature.

"Nice job," Nan said shortly when he finished, and Marcia knew she was moved and trying to hide the fact.

Indeed, there was a note of emotion close to the surface and touching everyone except herself and Alan, who remained somehow on the outside.

"I will tell Madame Setsu about this," Chiyo said softly. "It will give her much happiness."

"Do you know Madame Setsu well?" Marcia asked, and was unprepared for the sudden silence that greeted her words. Jerome wore his usual sardonic expression, Chiyo stared at her hands in her lap, while Nan took the book back from Jerome and set it down on the table with a little slap, breaking the silence.

"Cat got everybody's tongue?" she asked. "Haruka Setsu is Chiyo's cousin. Didn't you know that, Marcia?"

Startled, Marcia shook her head. Chiyo's cousin? Then the woman in white who walked in the garden, the woman who had come so strangely in the night to stand beside her bed, the sick woman in the other part of the house, was the poet who had written these strange, sad lines. But there was an undercurrent of some meaning here that Marcia did not understand. And before she could seek the answer, Nan got up and stretched her cramped legs. The dinner was at an end.

As they were leaving the room and complimenting their hostesses, there was an incident near the stairway. By now Ichiro was not very sure on his feet and at the head of the stairs he lurched into Chiyo. Jerome, just behind him, pulled him back none too gently. Ichiro glowered at Jerome for an instant, and then seemed to sober abruptly and completely. But in that moment Marcia was aware of the sharp antagonism that existed just below the surface between the two men.

When they were downstairs and cabs had been summoned, Jerome asked Alan if they could give him a lift. He accepted and the Talbots, Nan and Alan got into one cab, while the others went their own way.

Jerome seemed in an affable mood as he sat beside the driver in the front seat, half turned so that he could talk to those in the rear. Marcia held a sleepy Laurie on her lap, the child's head against her shoulder.

"Sorry I haven't been able to set up a date with you sooner, Cobb," Jerome told Alan. "What about coming over to the house Sunday afternoon, if that suits you?"

"I'd like that," Alan said readily. "I'd like to have a talk with you."

They dropped him at his living quarters and went on.

"I like that young man," Nan said. "Though I had a look at his book, *The Tin Sword,* before I loaned it to Minato-san, and I must admit it's a pretty bitter outpouring."

Jerome raised dark eyebrows. "Bitter? From Cobb? I find that hard to believe."

"Don't underestimate him, Jerry," Nan said. "You're not always perceptive about people, you know."

Jerome seemed to take a rebuke from Nan when he would not from anyone else. He shrugged, dismissing Alan. But Marcia was interested in pursuing the subject of Alan's book further.

"What I don't understand is why the Japanese wanted to read his book," she said. "Why should it sell so widely here, considering what it's about? I should think they'd have hated it."

"I don't suppose they enjoyed it," Nan said. "But once the lid was off and they really found out what was going on, they had almost a compulsion to know the worst. Alan says every Japanese he has met who has read his book has been apologetic and eager to prove that Japan is no longer like that."

Laurie stirred against her mother's shoulder, not asleep after all. "Daddy," she asked, "why did you say Mr. Cobb was someone bad?"

Jerome laughed out loud, clearly amused. "That's a misquotation, I'm afraid. My point was slightly different. We'll talk about it sometime when you're awake. You're much too sleepy to make sense tonight."

Laurie let her head fall back on her mother's shoulder. Marcia held her close, but all her senses had been alerted. What had Jerome really told the child that Laurie should have such a notion? And why should Jerome try to undermine Laurie's friendship with Alan Cobb?

Nan's thoughts must have run along the same line, for when Jerome turned away to watch the road ahead of the cab, she leaned forward and tapped him on the shoulder.

"What are you up to, Jerry?" she asked pointedly.

But Jerome only laughed without mirth and gave her no answer.

FIFTEEN

BEFORE SUNDAY AND ALAN'S COMING, MARCIA TRIED to find out from Laurie just what it was that Jerome had said to her. But the little girl only repeated that Daddy said Alan was a bad person. Then she burst into tears and was so upset that Marcia did not question her further. Yet when she tried to reassure Laurie about Alan, she sensed a stiffening, a resisting, so that her words did not truly reach the child.

The long Japanese rainy season had set in and while it did not rain all the time, the skies were often gray and mists hung low over the mountains. The temperature rose and as it grew warmer, the humidity increased until there were days when one felt as if the air was wholly liquid and moving about was like swimming in a dim and murky aquarium. It was not an atmosphere conducive to optimism.

Yet in the rain Japan lost none of its beauty. Indeed,

it took on a new dimension, a new charm. In the garden a wet rock might have a satin gleam it lacked on a sunny day, and the sound of rain on tiled roofs made melancholy music. Pine trees shone brightly green when wet and in the bamboo grove beyond the fence the rain fell with a soft and murmurous rustling. Less romantic, perhaps, was the mud of unpaved streets, and the necessity for *geta*, which kept their wearers above the mud, became evident.

On Sunday it rained again; not hard, but steadily. Marcia lit every old-fashioned lamp in the drawing room and tried to brighten it with sprays of azalea and stalks of iris in vases.

Jerome looked in on her arrangements and cocked a quizzical eyebrow. "Why all the preparations? I thought this was business on Cobb's part?"

"Perhaps we can have tea when you're through," Marcia suggested mildly. "I'll stay away if you prefer, while you're talking about Alan's book."

"No need for that," he said. "In fact, I'd rather have you there. If it all gets too thick, I'll find an excuse and skip out. Then you can get rid of him."

Marcia turned away so he wouldn't see her distress. She had begun to count on this interview with Alan, hoping somehow that he would get through to Jerome. Alan, with his vigorous convictions, his concern for broader horizons than those of this house, might be able to reach him if anyone could. But Jerome's casual dismissal of Alan in advance did not bode well for her hope.

That afternoon Nan had dropped in to take Laurie away to tea at the Miyako Hotel. She was meeting some people from home, a couple who had a daughter about Laurie's age. Marcia was glad to have Laurie gone. She did not want Alan to glimpse the strange new distrust of him Jerome had planted in the child.

When the bell on the gate sounded, Sumie-san caught up the Japanese umbrella of oiled paper that stood handy near the front door and ran out to bring Alan dry through the garden. He carried a tall, paper-covered parcel and Sumie-san had to hop along beside him with the umbrella at full stretch to cover both Alan and the parcel.

"Brought you a *presento*," he told Marcia as she came to greet him, and set his burden down on the veranda edge. "I saw it in a flower shop and it reminded me of my boyhod in Manila. My mother had several of these and they always fascinated me. Besides, it's a flower arrangement you won't have to struggle with."

As Alan took off his shoes, she cut the string around the tower of paper and lifted off the covering to find a tall green plant in a handsome jar of Kyoto pottery. The dark green leaves were large and broad, and grew from tendrils that clung vinelike to a trellis of split bamboo sticks.

"There will be flowers later," Alan said, coming to stand beside her. "Do you know what it is?"

Marcia touched a green leaf with pleasure. "I don't, but I like it already."

" 'Ghost white spirit flower . . .' " Alan quoted, smiling. "It's a moonflower. I can remember watching the flowers on my mother's plants open at night. Though I'm afraid I was never around early enough in the morning to see them close. You'll like the perfume. It's quite haunting."

She wanted to thank him for more than the plant, but there was so little she could put into words. "It's a lovely gift," she told him. "I know how much I'll enjoy it." She gave the plant to Sumie-san to take into the house and led Alan into the drawing room.

As they came in together, Jerome rose to shake hands with his guest. He was taller than Alan, but not as broad, and his darkness of hair and complexion, his somberness of manner, contrasted with Alan's sandy head, fair skin, and air of easy cheerfulness.

Lucifer and the Archangel, Marcia thought and smiled at her own whimsy.

The two men took chairs near a window open upon the rainy garden, while Marcia drew a little apart and sat near the cold hearth where she might listen without intruding. Her thoughts were still busy with the contrast between Jerome and Alan and she did not pay much attention to their words.

There was, it seemed to her, a sureness about Alan that was lacking in Jerome. She had the feeling that a moment of danger would not easily defeat him. With Jerome it was never possible to tell what he might do in any critical circumstance. He might stay and laugh at danger. He might turn his back and walk out as though it didn't exist. Or he might battle with shadows and waste his energy on demons of his own imagination.

How strange to see Jerome so clearly, she thought, startled by her own musing.

Her husband's voice drew her back from her reverie.

"I can see the sort of thing you want for your Japanese chapter," he was saying. "There are of course hundreds of individuals in Japan who survived Hiroshima and Nagasaki. Even whole families. But the ashes have been combed fine since the war. Survivors are tired of telling their stories to the curious. There comes a day when a man shuts his door and says 'no more.' These people have their own lives to live."

"I understand that," Alan said. "And I don't want to force myself on anyone. But I've found that my purpose interests some of the people I've talked to. Interests them enough so that they want others to understand what they have been through, and how they've made new lives afterwards."

Jerome's laugh was dry. "Americans are great on self-help these days. How to face your dentist with equanimity. How to be married four times and find the courage to take on a fifth. How to meet disaster and come out a hero."

Alan did not ruffle easily. He ignored Jerome's tone and answered him quietly. "There's a lot in what you say. But understanding is very different from a superficial recipe for quick success. There's something to the phoenix out of the ashes business. I'm sure you've seen exactly what I'm talking about since you came to Japan after the war. Just as I saw it at Santo Tomas. What makes the phoenix struggle to rise when every count's against him? That's the thing that intrigues me."

Jerome sighed and began tamping tobacco into his pipe. "Yes, I know the cliché. The thing which distinguishes us from the animals. The magnificent, amazing, unquenchable human spirit. That's what you mean?"

"Why not? Maybe it's all we've got between us and the stars." Alan's smile was easy. "By the way, I ran into an old friend of yours the other day. A Japanese physicist named Ogawa, who worked with you on some experimental project when you first came to Kyoto. He sent you his regards."

Jerome said nothing at all. Casually Alan went on, though Marcia knew, as Jerome must know, that his words were far from casual.

"Ogawa sounded sincerely regretful because you'd turned to other lines of research. Lesser lines, he seemed to feel. Apparently he had a high regard for the work you were doing with isotopes. He said scientists have only begun to tap the peacetime possibilities."

Jerome made an angry sound of repudiation, but Alan continued as if he were musing aloud to himself.

"Ogawa put me to shame by quoting Eisenhower a lot better than I could on the Atoms for Peace project. Let's see—how do the words go? 'My country's purpose is to help us move out of the dark chamber of horrors into the light, to find a way by which the minds of men everywhere can move forward . . .' "

"The minds of men!" Jerome broke in harshly. "Spare me that at least." He turned to Marcia so suddenly that she was startled. "Will you fetch me something from my room? There's a carved mask on the wall above my bed. It will come off the hook easily. Please bring it here."

She went for the mask reluctantly. It was out of reach and she stepped out of her slippers and climbed upon the bed. At that level she came eye to eye with the fearful thing.

"I hate you," she said. "And I don't believe in you. You're nothing but a hobgoblin and you won't scare Alan Cobb." She tugged disrespectfully at the black chin whiskers and lifted the mask from the wall. But she turned it face down as she carried it back to Jerome. She did not like to look at the thing any more than she had to.

Jerome took it from her and held it up to the gray daylight of the window so that Alan could see the detail of the carving.

"It's a fine piece," Jerome said. "A copy of a famous original, but good in itself. What do you think?"

Alan took the mask from him and turned it about in his hands. "It's more than a carving. It's fairly alive. I don't think I'd care to meet the fellow who posed for this."

"You've met him," Jerome said. "You can see him wherever you look. The inner man. The fundamental core of all of us. The faces we show to each other are the true masks. I wouldn't give an old-fashioned Japanese sen for your magnificent human spirit. The mind of man! Test it in the clinches and this is what you find. I doubt that it's moving forward."

"That's not true!" Marcia cried, willing to listen no longer.

"Of course it's not true," Alan said calmly and smiled at her. He gave the mask back to Jerome. "I don't feel that I have to beat anyone else into agreeing with me. I gather that you prefer not to put me in touch with any of these people you might know?"

"I didn't say that." Jerome set the mask on a table beside him. "It's every man to his own poison. I'll fix you up with an interview with Chiyo Minato, if you like. Since she's a Nisei, she can talk to you without an interpreter. And she's been through plenty of horrors in the war."

"I'd thought of her," Alan said. "That would be fine."

Marcia was not sure that it would be fine. If Chiyo was so completely under Jerome's influence it was likely that she would give Alan only what Jerome chose to have her give. An interview with her was hardly likely to be spontaneous and from the heart. But there would be little use in saying this before Jerome.

She was about to ring a bell and ask for tea, when Sumie-san came hurriedly to the door, apologizing and bowing, and right on her heels came Chiyo herself.

"Please excuse me," Chiyo said formally to Marcia, and then spoke directly to Jerome.

"Ichiro will come here when he finds I'm gone. I had to speak to you first."

Marcia would have risen to leave them alone, but Jerome stopped her. "Don't go. This may be an example of the very thing I was talking about. The inner man as illustrated by our friend Minato-san. What's wrong, Chiyo?"

She went on breathlessly. "Ichiro is going to work for a shipbuilding company in Kobe. He wants to take me there to live!"

Jerome's face darkened. "There are many things against your going. Your children have a good home here. And what would your cousin do without you?"

"Ichiro says Haruka must come with us. He says he will be responsible for her."

"I can hardly see him being responsible for anyone," Jerome said.

Chiyo bowed her head and stared unhappily at the floor. Turning his back on her, Jerome walked to the window, where he stood looking into the wet garden.

"What do you mean to do?" he asked Chiyo over his shoulder.

"Haruka cannot be moved from her home," Chiyo said forlornly. "She is too easily upset. I must stay with her, of course. I have already told Ichiro that. He is angry and wishes to treat me like an old-fashioned Japanese wife."

With the stating of Chiyo's intent, a moment of crisis seemed to pass. Jerome turned, his eyes bright in his dark face. "Of course you must stay with Haruka. Don't worry about Ichiro. I'll handle him."

"Be careful . . ." Chiyo began and broke off because they could hear Minato's voice at the front of the house. He had not run through the side garden as Chiyo had done, but was making a proper entrance by way of the front door and in a moment Sumie-san brought him into the drawing room. Today he was informally dressed in a dark blue and white *yukata,* the cotton kimono everyone relaxed in during the summer.

He seemed sober enough and he was being stiffly polite in a somewhat military manner. His feet were bare, but he walked like a soldier and clicked his heels together, as if the very assumption of a familiar role might lend him the confidence to deal with his problem. He bowed stiffly to Marcia and to Alan and then addressed Jerome in Japanese. For his wife he had only a quick look of displeasure.

Jerome's Japanese was not as good as Nan's, but he seemed to understand the gist of Minato's remarks. "If you take this job in Kobe, you go alone," Jerome replied in English. "Your family must stay here. You could have work in Kyoto, if you wanted it."

Apparently Minato understood English better than he spoke it. He shook his head, his feet squarely planted on the floor, his air that of a man who did not mean to budge until he had what he wanted.

Jerome looked him over coldly, but Marcia knew that he restrained himself with difficulty. "Your wife doesn't wish to move to Kobe. If you bother her about this, or threaten her in any way, I'll turn you over to the police. That's all I have to say to you."

Minato's face had flushed a dark red, but he stood his ground, unmoved by Jerome's words.

"Soon I go Kobe," he repeated stubbornly. "Chiyo go Kobe."

Something seemed to snap into violence in Jerome. He jerked Minato to him by the front of his *yukata* and shook him like a spaniel. He was choking him when Alan thrust himself between the two. Under Alan's grip, Jerome's hands loosened and he let Minato go, turning his attention angrily to the American.

"This is no business of yours, Cobb. Get out of my way!"

Alan stepped aside, but Minato had taken the moment's respite to make his escape. Yet his exit was not so much a retreat as it was the dramatic departure of a samurai. He turned stiffly and marched out of the room with the exaggerated stride of a Kabuki actor.

Chiyo wept softly into her hands, but Alan paid no attention to her, or to the scowling Jerome. He turned directly to Marcia.

"I'm sorry," he told her. "I'll go along now."

She went with him to the door, shaken by what had happened.

"I didn't expect to find myself on Minato's side," he

said. "But that's where my sympathies seem to lie. I'm sorry I've been able to manage so little today. Perhaps I've made everything worse."

Marcia shook her head vehemently. "No! There must be something that will make Jerome face the future."

"He needs to face himself first," Alan said.

She looked at him anxiously. "What did this man Ogawa mean about Jerome giving his time to lesser research? I know he doesn't go regularly to the laboratory any more."

"I'm not sure and there's no use guessing about it now," Alan said.

"You'll tell me if you learn anything more?"

"I'll tell you," he promised. "In the meantime I don't like to see you living under this roof."

She tried to smile. "Don't worry, I'll be all right."

"Whistle if you need me." His voice was light, but his eyes remained grave.

She nodded, not trusting herself to speak.

"Take care," he said and turned away without touching her, though the very sound of his words was a light caress.

The rain had nearly stopped and she watched him following the stepping stones to the gate, a straight broad figure in his transparent slicker. Then she went back to the drawing room door.

Chiyo was weeping softly in Jerome's arms and he was comforting her. Marcia slipped away before they saw her.

She had come to the end of her endurance. It was time to face the fact that there was no longer any love in her for this man she had once cherished. There was nothing she could ever do for Jerome. There was no marriage left to save. Strangely, she could no longer feel jealousy of Chiyo, or resentment against Jerome. She was more concerned now for the loss to the world of the man Jerome had been than she was for his loss to herself.

Perhaps this was only a moment of vacuum, and pain would return later, but now she was moved only by a desire to get away from this house and from a Jerome who shocked and frightened her. Certainly he did not need her, and it was possible that she no longer needed him.

This was a thought too new to be accepted quickly in its full import. It left her drained and empty.

She stayed in her room until dinnertime, when Laurie came home from her visit with Nan. Then she faced the ordeal of sitting down at the table with her husband. Fortunately, it was Laurie who did most of the talking.

She was excited about the Miyako Hotel, with its many levels climbing up a steep hill, its gardens and grottoes and Japanese cottages. To say nothing of the pool, where Laurie and the visiting American girl had gone swimming.

"And what was this girl like?" Jerome asked, interested now, as he never used to be in Laurie's doings.

Laurie pursed her lips thoughtfully. "Well, she was sort of homely, with freckles and red hair. And she wasn't very smart. I could tell her anything and she'd believe it."

Marcia listened in silence, while Laurie, the loving and lovable, made unkind remarks about the people she had met that afternoon. Her father attended approvingly and added his own comments to encourage her.

Marcia waited until Laurie was in bed and then she went to Jerome's room and knocked on the door. When he called, "Come in," she stood quietly in the doorway and spoke to him, without entering.

"You've won," she said. "I'm going to take Laurie home as soon as it can be arranged."

Jerome sat at his desk across the room, and the bright intense look that had lately grown familiar mocked her words. "You mean, my dear, that your undying love for me has at length subsided."

She answered his mockery softly. "You told me the truth when I first came. The man I fell in love with disappeared a long time ago. You are someone I don't know."

He pushed aside the papers before him and came across the room.

"I'm glad you've come to your senses. It has been somewhat awkward having you here, I'll admit. But I couldn't very well put you out in the manner of a Victorian husband. However, your decision comes a breath too late on one score. You may go home, of course. I shan't stand in your way. But Laurie is my daughter and I'd like to bring her up myself. I want to see her educated realistically so she will be able to deal with life as it is. When you go, Laurie stays."

She heard him without believing. "But that's ridiculous! Of course Laurie will go home with me. How could you possibly hold her here?"

The dark brilliance glowed in his face. "She is already mine. More mine than yours. Ask her, if you don't believe me."

The expression on his face was frightening. It was difficult to speak quietly, but somehow she managed to keep her voice low and steady.

"You can't possibly hold her. Laurie will go with me."

He put his hands on her shoulders, and she would have drawn back from his touch, but his fingers tightened and held her cruelly in their grasp.

"Make no mistake about it. I'll keep her," he said. "And I'll smash anything that gets in my way. Try to take her away from this house, and I'll bring her back in a way you won't like."

He let her go and she turned and ran into the hall and back to her own room. She was more frightened than she had ever been in her life. Jerome lived in a world of his own where only his "truth" prevailed and the real truth had no meaning.

SIXTEEN

IT WAS NO LONGER RAINING, BUT MARCIA AWOKE TO A misty day. Gray light seeped into the room and she lay still, listening. Laurie breathed lightly in the next bed. From the rest of the house she could hear the sounds of Jerome's rising and breakfasting, and she lay tense and still through it all. She waited until he had left the house, then she got up and dressed quietly.

Sumie-san had placed Alan's moonflower plant in the dining room. Marcia saw it there and carried it upstairs to her favorite place on the upper veranda overlooking the garden. Since it had grown warm enough, she sat there often, where she could see garden and mountains, and the gray roofs of Kyoto.

She put the plant down near the rail where it could get whatever sun there was. How tall and green and strong it looked. When she searched among the leaves she could see the tiny nubs that would grow into the buds of moonflowers. The plant was tangible evidence of Alan's friendship. She wished she might talk to him.

Today she must talk to someone. Nan, perhaps? Nan had known Jerome for a long time. Nan might know how to deal with these dark aberrations as his wife did not. And Nan had seemed sympathetic lately. But first she must sound out Laurie.

When she returned to the bedroom, the little girl was up and dressing. Marcia brushed and combed her hair gently, braided the fine brown strands into long plaits.

"I think we will go home very soon now," she told her daughter. "As soon as we can get places on a plane. Will you be glad to see your friends again?"

Laurie swung about, jerking the braid from her hands. "Home? But home is here. Daddy says he needs me. He says I'm never, never to leave him again. In the fall he's going to start me to school here."

So he had gone as far as that with Laurie?

"I'm afraid that won't be possible," Marcia said. "Besides, you'll surely want to go back to your school in Berkeley where all your friends are."

"No!" Laurie's face had gone white in alarm. "I'm never going to leave my father again. If he wants me to, I'm going to stay in Japan with him always."

"But I am going home," Marcia said.

Laurie's face puckered and her lips trembled, but she held back from her mother. "I can't go home with you, Mommy. I have to stay here. I have to!"

Marcia kissed her cheek, and held the small, frightened face against her own for a moment, smoothing Laurie's hair back from a forehead suddenly damp with perspiration.

"Don't worry about it, darling. We'll work it out somehow. Let's have breakfast now."

But her casual words hid her inner fear. She could not forget the look in Jerome's eyes last night, or the sound of his voice raised in threatening abuse.

After breakfast Tomiko came to play and Marcia told Sumie-san to keep an eye on the children until she came home. Then she went up the hill to Nan's house.

Nan's small car was out in front and Marcia found her sitting on the entryway ledge putting on her shoes.

"Hi!" Nan called cheerfully as Marcia came through the gate. "You're abroad early. Anything I can do for you?"

Marcia hesitated. "I only wanted to talk to you. If you're going out, it can wait."

Nan tossed her shoe horn aside and stood up, looking vigorous and solid in her gray skirt and tailored pongee blouse. She studied Marcia's face for a moment and then picked up the handbag from the step beside her.

"Come along with me and we'll talk on the way. I'm going out to a miniature tree nursery to choose a tree for an American client. You may be interested and it will do you good to get away from that house. Where's Laurie? Want to bring her along?"

"No." Marcia shook her head. "I want to talk to you about Laurie."

"Trouble? Well, come on and we'll get started. Then you can tell me."

Nan could drive in Japanese traffic and listen at the same time, doing fair justice to both. As they followed narrow lanes toward a main road, Marcia related what had happened yesterday when Chiyo and Ichiro had come to the house. Their coming had been the prelude to Jerome's anger.

"I felt sorry for Minato-san," Marcia admitted. "I always thought the Japanese were an unemotional people. But there was plenty of feeling in Minato-san yesterday."

"We get that idea because of the training they have from childhood," Nan said. "There's not much suppression until they are five or six, and then the lid is clamped down. After that, it's bad manners to show emotion. If your mother is dying you smile. If you hate your mother-in-law you bow to her meekly and do her bidding. All this makes the Japanese seem a cheerful, happy people on the surface and it's certainly civilized to live with. No voices raised, no shouting in the streets. But watch them weep at a Kabuki play where they can let go a little. Watch them let down the bars on one cup of *saké*. And watch the emotions explode in unforeseen ways when steam builds up too long. I'd say Minato-san is a good example of emotions too long suppressed. He is thoroughly mixed up because of his indoctrination as a soldier in his youth, and then having the whole thing proved wrong from scratch. I hope he takes this job and goes to Kobe."

"Why doesn't Chiyo go to Kobe with her husband?" Marcia asked guardedly. "I should think she'd be delighted at the fact that he wants to sober up and get a job."

Nan drove for a block in silence. "It's not a simple matter. There's Madame Setsu, for one thing."

"We always come back to Madame Setsu. What *is* her illness? Why can't someone else care for her?"

Nan raised one hand from the wheel in a gesture of

impatience. "I'll confess that I'm getting tired of all this hush-hush to protect Haruka Setsu. Personally, I think you should have been told her story from the beginning. I've bowed to the wishes of others, but I've done that long enough."

"Then you'll tell me?"

"I'll tell you part of it, anyway," Nan agreed. "During the war she saved Chiyo's life. Chiyo feels her life belongs to this older cousin, for as long as she is needed. Haruka's sickness is a complete withdrawal from life. She goes nowhere, sees no one except those in her family. And at times I gather she has moments of being scarcely sane. Then she has to be watched."

They were passing a great red torii, the entrance to a shrine in the heart of Kyoto. Nan beeped her horn at a *tofu* vendor who chose that moment to step out in front of the car with his hand-drawn cart.

Marcia remembered the time when she had wakened to find Haruka standing beside her bed. She could no longer believe that had been a dream.

Nan turned out of the crowded street they were following and brought the car to a stop outside a bamboo gate. "Here we are. Can you hop out on your side? Cars aren't really a good idea in Japan because there's so little space for parking."

A bell tinkled as they opened the gate and walked into a spacious garden filled with row after row of long wooden tables on which miniature trees were growing in decorative pots.

"Here's where you learn about *bonsai*," Nan said. "That's what the Japanese call the art of raising miniature trees. Kato-san is a real artist, so be very respectful."

Kato-san was a miniature like his trees, small and wiry, with thin fingers strong enough to bend nature to his bidding. He bowed to them both and he and Nan exchanged courtesies in Japanese. Nan presented Marcia and he greeted her in English. Then he led them through the rows of trees to his house at the back, its entire side open to the garden. There they sat down for the inevitable cups of hot green tea, and Nan spoke about the tree she was searching for. Kato-san thought he had exactly the thing, but perhaps she would like to show her American friend the other trees first?

When they had finished their tea Nan and Marcia walked the aisles between the tables, admiring and commenting. There were trees and shrubs of every description—plum and willow and maple, azalea, wisteria. But the pine trees appealed to Marcia most. Such perfect replicas they were of their grownup counterparts, but with each branch wired when young to grow gracefully in the most delicate patterns. The slant of the trunk, the balance of the branches, the thickness of the foliage, all were controlled by a master hand. When the tree had been properly bent and trained in its youth, and the budding needles pinched back to proper thickness, the wires were removed and with care the tree would live to a great age in the small pot that contained it.

Kato-san left them to explore to their satisfaction and went to meet another visitor who had just come through the gate. As if there had been no interruption, Nan picked up the subject of Haruka Setsu where they had left it.

"The trouble is that she sometimes has the curious

notion that she is no longer part of the world of the living. She has the conviction that she belongs to the spirit world and she tries to run away in order to seek the place where her family's ashes rest. She has to be carefully watched, lest she come to real harm."

With a faint shiver Marcia remembered the curious fold of the white kimono—right side over left in the manner of death. And she recalled Nan's words the first time she had met her.

"This happens when the moon is full?" she asked.

"As a rule," Nan said. "Sometimes Chiyo isn't able to control her and Jerry has to go over and help. She will listen to him. Male authority, I suppose. But the rest of the time Chiyo is her main companion, her nurse, maid, everything. I suppose Ichiro would like to get his wife away from this if he could. But I think Chiyo will never leave her cousin as long as she is needed."

Nan reached out to touch the prickly needles of a small pine tree, her face sad and thoughtful. "It might be better for everyone if Haruka would die. Herself included. But I've hoped for that for too many years to have much confidence in its happening. She'll probably outlive us all. One of nature's little jokes, I suppose."

"Yet she writes those lovely poems," Marcia said, and remembered that Jerome had published a volume of them—for Chiyo's sake.

Nan shrugged. "Another withdrawal from life. Her writing is all melancholy, all beauty and death." She turned abruptly from the subject of Haruka. "You've talked to Chiyo, haven't you? Your children are friends. Why don't you urge her to go with Minato?

She could make her home in Kobe and leave this un-
natural life she has bound herself to."

Marcia stared at Nan, startled. "But then perhaps
Haruka would die, and Chiyo would blame herself—"

"Oh, let her die! Let her!" Nan cried with unexpected passion. "Wouldn't that be better for Chiyo in
the long run?"

She seemed bitter and angry in a way Marcia could
not understand. "But if . . ." it was hard to bring
herself to say it, but she must. "If Chiyo cares for Jerome . . ."

Nan's deep-set eyes turned their blaze upon her in
sudden impatience. "I only wish it were as simple as
that."

Kato-san's visitor had gone and he came toward
them again, bowing his apologies for leaving them.
Now he would show them the treasure they had come
to see. This way, please.

Marcia walked at Nan's side, but her mind was no
longer on miniature pines. No doubt the little tree
before which Kato-san paused in profound delight was
perfect in every sense with its tiny cones and five nee-
dled tufts. But she could not pay attention while Nan
discussed its virtues and possible faults and arranged
for its delivery.

What had Nan meant? That in some way Jerome's
hold on Chiyo was not through her love for him? That
Jerome loved her, but held her to him by other means?
Marcia was impatient now to return to the car where
she could push her questions farther. When Nan got
in behind the wheel, however, she would tell her nothing more.

"I've talked too much," she said a little crossly.

"Anyway, I don't think all this is why you came to me today. There's something else worrying you. Something newer than the set-up next door. Might as well get it out."

So on the way home Marcia told her of her decision to leave and of the way Jerome had met that decision—with a threat to hold Laurie. Nan, for once, was clearly angry with Jerome.

"In the beginning I thought you might help Jerry by staying, but I'm afraid I was wrong," she said. "When a person has been too long in the Orient, he finds it hard to go home. That's the way it is with Jerry. And with me too. But the time has certainly come for you to take Laurie and get away from Kyoto. She mustn't be submitted to his influence, nor you to his threats."

"What if Jerome tries to stop me? He sounded so wild and threatening that I was frightened."

"I know," Nan agreed soberly. "He can be dangerously determined when he's really stirred up. Don't do anything right away. For the moment you're safer right there in his house than you are anywhere else. Give me time to think of something. One trouble is that you're not very good at taking brutal action. And in the end brutal action may be exactly what's needed."

"I'll take it if I have to," Marcia said. "But he's changed so much that I hardly know him any more. You met him when he first came to Japan. What made him change?"

Nan answered indirectly. "You were a child when you fell in love with him. What did you know then about what he was like?"

"I married him," Marcia said.

"Sure, sure. And I didn't. Though goodness knows I tried hard enough before I realized it was no use."

Marcia looked at her in dismay. Somehow she had not imagined this. Not since her first doubtful meeting with Nan. Nan as a loyal friend to Jerome, yes. Nan as someone to lean on, or to seek out for advice, or—

Nan broke in on her thoughts with a dry laugh. "Go ahead and say it. You didn't take me for the romantic type that goes in for unrequited love? Is that it? Well, relax. I'm not. All that's over long ago. But tell me what you think Jerry was like before he came out to Japan."

"He was a dedicated sort of person," she recalled. "Wrapped up in his work and devoted to my father. He couldn't see anything outside of his work."

"To what purpose? I mean where was his work going?"

"I don't know exactly. Of course he was working on various secret projects for the government, but I don't think that was the purpose that held him. I think he always looked beyond the nearest test tube for the effects of what he was doing. I mean the use of his work for long-range purposes."

Nan said, "Look, here's a stretch of park. Let's get out and sit on a bench and talk this through. I'm tired of splitting my attention."

Marcia was willing. Nan parked the car nearby and they found an empty wooden bench near a pond where lily pads floated languidly. They could turn their back upon the gray city and look up at the green Kyoto hillside.

"I met him in Hiroshima, as you know," Nan said.

"He'd had his first look at the results of the bomb by that time. It hit him pretty hard."

Marcia nodded. "I knew he had changed when he came home from Japan that first time, but I didn't dream how much."

"During the first years I knew him, he began to lose touch with everything good in the human race," Nan said. "When the news came of your father's death, I was afraid of what might happen."

"What do you mean?" Marcia asked.

"That's another story. It doesn't matter now. The immediate problem before us is what to do about you and Laurie."

"I suppose we could go to Tokyo," Marcia said, "and get aboard the first plane we could take for the States."

Nan shook her head. "Too obvious. That's exactly what he'd expect."

"Could he really stop me?"

"He could follow you if he chose and I wouldn't want to face him when he gets into one of his wild moods. The consequences don't matter to him then. You can't apply ordinary rules of reasoning to a man who is using another set of rules."

Marcia thought of the moment when Jerome had tried to choke Ichiro and could only agree.

On a street nearby a school had let out for the day and children began to pour through the park past them; a flood of boys and girls in the summer uniform, white blouse and dark skirt, white shirt and dark trousers. They moved downhill decorously, gay enough, but with none of the racing and screaming which American children indulged in when they got out of school. Some wore shoes and socks, but many of them clapped along on *geta*.

Several small ones paused in front of the bench where Nan and Marcia sat, and stared with wide, shoe-button eyes, their mouths slightly open. Nan spoke to them in Japanese and they smiled and came a few steps closer, more curious than shy.

"We'd better go back to the car," Nan said. "In no time we'll have fifty kids standing around gaping at us. Makes a fellow self-conscious. They're fascinated by our queer round eyes and big noses. Kyoto doesn't get as many foreigners as Tokyo does."

The children followed them to the car and watched with continued interest as they got in. Marcia waved as they drove away and several of the children waved back before scattering happily about their business.

"This humidity must be getting me down," Nan said. "I don't usually lose my patience like that. I'll be glad to get off to Miyajima."

"You're going away?" Marcia asked.

"For a short vacation. Early in July I'll go down to the island of Miyajima and loaf and feed my soul."

If she were still here, she would miss Nan, Marcia thought. The older woman's presence in the house up the hill had been something to count on.

"Well, here we are," Nan said. "I'm afraid I haven't helped you much today. But give me a little time to figure something out. And don't do anything too suddenly, will you? We'll get you away before it's too late."

As she went into the house, Marcia thought over Nan's somewhat ominous words. Was it too late already? Was she to be trapped here by a reign of terror on the part of a man who was beyond reason?

Laurie was still playing in the garden with Tomiko, and Marcia went upstairs to the low comfortable chair she had placed on the veranda, the spot she found the most peaceful and pleasant in the house, now that the weather was warm. There she sat looking out over the garden and the rooftops of Kyoto. How strange to think of Nan's being in love with Jerome long ago. Strange and sad. Had he known? she wondered. Certainly he seemed to count on Nan and take her friendship for granted, as he well might if he were aware of her old feeling for him.

At what opposite poles were Jerome and Alan Cobb. She recalled the sight of the two of them together yesterday—that glimpse of light and dark. Thinking of Alan, she turned in her chair to admire the plant he had brought her, and saw that it was no longer on the veranda where she had left it. That was strange. Perhaps Sumie-san had seen it there, decided that it belonged elsewhere and carried it away.

Marcia stepped to the rail and called to the children, playing by the fishpond. "Laurie, is Sumie-san in sight? I'd like to speak to her for a moment."

Before Laurie could answer, Sumie-san herself came out of the house and looked up at Marcia inquiringly.

"Before I went out," Marcia told her, "I brought the new plant upstairs. Have you seen it?"

"*Yu gao* plant?" Sumie-san said and shook her head.

"You didn't move it from upstairs then?" Marcia asked.

"No see, no take," Sumie-san said, disclaiming all knowledge.

Marcia let her go. There was no use asking Yasuko-san. The cook never came upstairs. And if Laurie had moved the plant, she would have admitted it by now. She was staring up at her mother with a bright, interested look.

"Maybe the plant is what the lady from next door wanted when she came over," Laurie said.

"Lady from next door?"

Laurie got up from her knees and came closer to the house. "Yes. The beautiful lady in the white kimono. A little while ago I looked up and she was standing right where you are now bending over the plant." Laurie lowered her tone to a whisper. "She's sort of spooky, isn't she? I never really saw her good before. She's so beautiful—like a lady out of a dream. Or like that lady in white in the picture in Daddy's room."

Marcia listened, startled and chilled. "Then what happened?"

"I don't know. Tomiko wanted something and I went to help her. And when I looked back at the veranda the lady was gone. Like a ghost. I never heard a sound. She was just there, and then she was gone."

"And the plant?" Marcia asked.

"I don't know. I guess I didn't notice the plant after that."

"All right, dear. Thank you," Marcia said.

Laurie went back to her play and Marcia studied the veranda for a moment. The narrow gallery on this side led straight to the partition door to the other side of the house. Thoughtfully Marcia went over to it and grasped the knob. It turned quite easily in her hand and the door gave a crack as she pushed it.

Someone had left the door between the two households unlocked.

SEVENTEEN

FOR JUST A MOMENT THE URGE TO FLING THE DOOR open and look into the other half of the house was strong in Marcia. But she felt a little frightened as well. Nan had said gently that Madame Setsu was not quite sane. And Marcia had no desire to open a door into the presence of a madwoman. Certainly this door should not be left unlocked. Tonight she would have to ask Jerome about it and tell him what had happened.

She said nothing at the dinner table before Laurie. Jerome ignored his wife, addressing himself only to Laurie, and as usual the child responded with the excitability her father all too easily aroused in her. When the meal was over and Laurie had gone outside to play in the soft dusk of the garden, Marcia stopped Jerome in the hallway to speak to him.

"Something odd has happened," she said. "Alan

Cobb brought me a moonflower plant yesterday and this morning I put it on the veranda upstairs. Laurie says the Japanese woman from next door—Chiyo's cousin—came through into our part of the house and was looking at it. When I went upstairs later this morning the door was unlocked and the plant gone."

Jerome reached into his pocket to take out a key chain with several keys on it and studied them. "I'll look into the matter," he said curtly.

The next day when she went upstairs to sit on the veranda she found the door locked and all as it had been before, except for the missing plant. Even as she noted its absence she hoped the moonflower would give poor Madame Setsu pleasure.

These were days of inner turmoil for Marcia. Before she fell asleep at night she tried to steel herself to take action the next day. In spite of Nan's warning, she must make an effort of her own. She could at least get her plane tickets for the States, even if she set the date a little ahead. Then she would have time to convince Laurie that she had no choice but to go home with her mother. Yet every morning she awakened fearful of forcing the issue with Jerome and taking the actual step.

So the days slipped one into another and the moment for action was pushed ahead. She had the feeling of being caught helplessly in a trap from which there was no escape.

Then Alan phoned her one night when Jerome had gone out again—gone next door, in all probability.

"Tomorrow's Sunday and it promises to be a fine day," he said. "Would you and Laurie like to come on a picnic?"

She accepted the invitation eagerly. Anything to get out of this house and away from her own treadmill of futility. Perhaps an afternoon in Alan's company would clarify her thinking, strengthen her will to act.

Laurie was getting ready for bed when Marcia returned to their room with news about the planned picnic.

"I'll ask Yasuko-san to fix us a nice lunch," she told Laurie. "Mr. Cobb is coming for us around eleven. He says there are some wonderful temple grounds within walking distance of this house that he'd like to show us. Something different from Kiyomizu."

Laurie brightened at the word "picnic," but when Marcia mentioned Alan's name, the light went out of her face and she turned her back and went to stand before the empty fireplace. Marcia watched her uneasily.

"Don't you feel well?" she asked.

"I feel all right," Laurie said. Her eyes were upon the Japanese doll Alan had given her; the doll which still wore the demon mask Laurie had placed over its face.

"You've always loved picnics," Marcia said. "So what's the matter?"

"It's not the picnic." Laurie would not look at her mother. "It's that Mr. Cobb. Daddy doesn't like him. He thinks that little mask is—" She broke off unhappily. "Oh, never mind. It doesn't matter."

So that was why Laurie had been crying over the mask that time, and had flung it away into the garden. Jerome had connected it in some sneering manner with Alan.

Gently Marcia picked up the doll and removed the

mask from its face. "There," she said. "That's better, isn't it?"

Laurie took the doll from her mother's hands, studying its plump cheeks and slanted dark eyes, the lovable innocence of the round face that mirrored other young faces they had seen in Japan.

"Why did you want it to wear the mask?" Marcia asked. "I think it's much nicer without. Now it can be itself. Just the way Mr. Cobb can be himself, if you don't go thinking up queer notions about masks."

Laurie didn't answer. But she took the doll with her as she crawled into bed and set it against her pillow. Her expression was one of puzzlement and uncertainty.

Marcia sat down on the bed and took Laurie's hands into hers. "What is it that's worrying you, darling? Won't you tell me?"

"Daddy doesn't like Mr. Cobb," Laurie repeated, studying the face of the little doll.

"Your father hardly knows him," Marcia said. "On the plane you liked Mr. Cobb a lot."

"I know." Laurie's brows drew down as she struggled with some inner problem. Then, as if, within herself, she took a step in a positive direction, the strain lifted from her face and she smiled at her mother. "I think the picnic will be fun," she said.

When Laurie was asleep, Marcia took the little mask and hid it beneath the handkerchiefs in her dresser drawer. She did not know the details of what had happened concerning that mask, or what poison Jerome had tried to plant in the child's mind, but her instinct was to hide the mask and give Laurie time to forget it.

On Sunday Jerome worked in his room and did not

come out to greet Alan when he arrived. Marcia and Laurie were ready and they left quickly, with Yasuko-san's generous lunch in a wicker basket that Alan and Laurie swung between them.

Alan took them across a main highway and through a tunneled gateway in the hillside. Beyond the tunnel was another world of small houses, gardens, bamboo fences. The day was sunny and clear and the sweltering humidity had lifted.

The temple buildings occupied a low stretch of ground in a pocket formed by two arms of the hills. At the main entrance a vendor sold refreshments and Alan bought a green cellophane bag of Japanese *sembi*, the tiny, salty crackers browned in soy sauce. Laurie had already become addicted to *sembi* and nibbled content-edly as they walked along. Marcia was relieved to find that her manner toward Alan seemed normal and friendly, as if the inner cloud had lifted completely.

As always before, Marcia experienced a sense of re-laxation in Alan's company. His cheerful calm seemed to banish the miasma of fear and doubt that haunted her and befogged her path so that she could choose no road with confidence.

Marcia looked about in delight as they entered the grounds. Tall cryptomerias with smooth, reddish bark lifted their great heads high in the air. These giant Japanese cedars were a match for the great buildings gathered toward the rear of the widespread area. They were simple, rather austere buildings, with sloping tiled roofs and carved eaves. Gray tile shone like silver amid green foliage and everywhere was the rustle of wind high in the trees, and the rushing sound of a stream nearby. Distant white walls marked the limits of the enclosure.

"These buildings always seem to me more strongly masculine than Kiyomizu," Alan said. "Kiyomizu is prettier, more delicate and feminine. But I like this best."

She felt the difference too. Beyond the first entrance rose a second gateway—massive and wide, with a dozen or more weathered brown columns of wood set in concrete. The great doors, with enormous bolts and hinges, stood open. It was a gate for a giant, towering several stories high, with two tiers of roofs and an upper gallery. Beyond the gate they could see a venerable Buddhist priest in a brown robe, leaning on a peeled staff as he tossed scraps of food to several little brown dogs. He paid no attention as Laurie ran ahead into the shadow of the great gate and jumped onto a doorsill that was at least two feet high.

Alan and Marcia followed her more slowly.

"I like this place because it's always so peaceful," Alan said. "The crowds don't seem to throng here as they do to some of the temples. I come here whenever I want to be quiet and think."

To be quiet and think. Marcia breathed the pine-scented air deeply and let the tenseness flow out of her nerves and muscles.

"This is a perfect place for a picnic right here in the gateway," she said. "Do you suppose anyone will mind?"

"They never seem to," Alan said. "This isn't the temple proper and the Japanese always use the grounds of a temple as if it were a public park."

They sat down on the high doorsill at the base of a

tree-like column, enjoying the breeze that blew through the gateway. Azaleas were at their last flowering and the low bushes were all about, flaming with bright color.

In many ways she would miss Japan, Marcia thought. It had given her so much of loveliness and new experience. If only she could have seen it at a happier time.

When they unpacked the lunch, Laurie ate her sandwiches with a greater relish than she had shown for a long while. Once the upheaval, the wrench of taking her away from her father had been made, perhaps she would become her normal happy self again. There was a risk involved of course, but it was a risk Marcia felt she must take.

Laurie finished her lunch and was at once eager to explore. When she wandered off through the cryptomerias, Alan turned to Marcia.

"I've discovered where your husband goes when he's not at the laboratory," he said.

"Yes?" Marcia was suddenly tense.

"He's doing something completely out of his own line—research in a Japanese medical center. Some sort of work in medical chemistry." Alan's voice hardened. "The sort of work a thousand other men are better fitted to do."

"But—but why?" Marcia whispered. "Why, with all his background and experience in—"

"I don't know," Alan said. "My purpose wasn't to spy on him, and I hadn't the knowledge of Japanese to get the full answer. Ogawa speaks English. If I see him again, I'll ask for details." He was silent for a moment, lost in his own thoughts. Then he said, "Nan has told me about the problem that's facing you."

She felt only relief. "I'm glad you know."

"Nan says she's afraid of what Talbot might do if he's pushed too far, but you can't stay on in that house and let things grow gradually worse. I worry about you. I think about you quite a lot."

She thought of him too, she realized. He stood for someone to be counted on in her troubled world, but more than that, someone increasingly dear. It was good to be here with him now in this ancient temple gateway, removed for a little while from the fear that haunted her days.

For a moment she did not want to hurry ahead toward something new, but only to hold to this quiet contentment of being with Alan, of not asking anything more. But nothing ever stood still and the moment was fragile. A word, a touch of his hand would shatter it. She was like a woman wakening in a strange country, not yet sure of herself, or of what the new land would bring into her life. She must be quiet for a little while so that she could become accustomed to change and be able to face it with purpose and courage. There was portent here, but the grip of the past was too fiercely upon her and she dared not look toward the future.

She leaned her head back against a wooden pillar and closed her eyes. "Talk to me, please. Don't let me think about myself. Then perhaps when I go back everything will seem clearer and I can do what must be done."

"What shall I talk about?" Alan asked.

She kept her eyes closed. "Tell me about you. Tell me about Santo Tomas."

For a little while he was silent. She lifted her face to the breeze and listened to the peaceful sound of rushing water and of the wind in the great cryptomerias. If he chose to tell her, he would. If he did not, it wouldn't matter.

"Santo Tomas?" Alan said at last. "It was a university, you know. And is again. But it was only meant for a day university, so there were no dormitories. We were jammed into a forty acre area that was never meant to house four thousand internees."

"What did you hate most about being there?" Marcia asked, her eyes still closed. "Aside from having your liberty taken away, of course."

He thought about that for a moment. "I think I missed privacy more than anything else. We were so crowded in upon one another. Of course we thought about food all the time as our supplies went down. Everyone was hungry. A good part of the time we lived on smuggling from friendly Filipinos outside who helped us at the risk of their lives."

"Did you know what was going on in the world outside?"

Now she watched his face as he spoke of those years from which he must have thought he might never emerge.

"The garbage truck was our source of information." He smiled faintly. "It smuggled in our news reports every day. And there was a fellow who'd been a radio commentator in Manila who kept us posted by the records he played over the public address system in the prison. The Japs had a system for speaking to us whenever they wished and he operated it for them. The day of the Luzon landing he played 'Hail, Hail, the Gang's All Here!' and the Japs never understood how we knew."

Marcia could feel the tightening in her throat, but she said nothing, waiting for him to go on.

"It wasn't all bad. Nothing ever is. We could watch the sunsets over Manila Bay. And some of the internees used to hold gospel meetings in a patio. There was a serenity about those that helped us. We made a few good friends, of course."

"Have you kept in touch with any of them?" Marcia asked.

"Not many. I stopped off in Honolulu on the way out here to see one friend from that time. Of course some never left Santo Tomas. I remember one girl, a nurse. There was supposed to be no communication between men and women in the prison, but we managed to get around that. And of course the nurses were allowed to attend us."

His face had softened as his thoughts turned back. "Her name was Susan. Everybody loved her. She didn't just nurse our bodies with the few medicines she was able to get hold of. She cared about what went on inside us too. She helped keep our spirits up. I was lucky because she cared about me especially. And I about her. We'd have married, I think, if we had come out of Santo Tomas together. On the last Christmas Eve we thought we'd make it. Army Liberators flew overhead and dropped Christmas card greetings from the President and the Armed Forces. We knew it would be over soon, if we could just hold on. But Susan gave too much of herself. She was always sharing her rations with the sick, or giving them away altogether. She ran on spunk and courage almost up to the end. I blamed the Japs for her death and hated them pretty fiercely for a while. I suppose that's why I could hardly wait to write *The Tin Sword* when I got home. I had a lot of spite to get out of my system in those days."

There were tears in Marcia's eyes. He lifted her hand and put it to his cheek for a moment.

"Sometimes you remind me of her. Not in appearance—she was very different—blond and rather small. But you have something of the same spark. Something that won't be quenched."

Her throat tightened at the touch of his cheek against her hand—a light, quick gesture that released her at once.

"I had a bad time when I was freed," he said. "They flew my mother home, but I came back the slow way on a transport ship. I suppose I was in pretty bad shape from malnutrition and I'd lost my grip on life besides. Maybe I didn't even want to live at first."

She stayed very still, waiting for him to continue. He got up from the sill and his movement broke the thread of emotion that had drawn too taut. He stretched widely and smiled down at her.

"Anyway, here I am! And I'll confess my taste for life has never been stronger."

"When we first met you," Marcia said, "you told Laurie you were coming to Japan to find out something about yourself. What did you mean?"

He rested a foot upon the step beside her and leaned on his knee. "After I got that book off my chest and spilled out all my hatred of the Japs on a pretty personal basis, I quieted down and began to get my bearings. I realized that I'd been writing about an inhuman species called 'Japs.' But I didn't really know anything about the Japanese. I kept wondering what made them tick and what I'd think of them at firsthand after what I'd experienced."

"And now that you've had a firsthand chance?"

"I've learned a lot," he said. "For one thing I can better understand how the Japanese soldier was stamped into a mold when the tin sword was put into his hands so early."

"What do you mean?"

"The modern Japanese soldier had no use for a sword. But the physical sword they gave him was a psychological sword as well—the samurai sword of his fathers. Devotion, sacrifice, all the stuff of honored history. And the blade was kept sharp, to assure death rather than dishonor and surrender. But even with all the early, harsh training they were given, not all of them were brutal. War gives the brute a better opportunity to show himself, whatever his race."

"And how do you feel about the Japanese now?"

He answered without hesitation. "I like them personally. And I admire them tremendously. They've taken complete defeat and the devastation of a good deal of their country and they've built upon it through hard, courageous work. They haven't whined and they haven't sulked. Japan is beginning to hold her head up among nations again, not because of a war machine and superior power, but because she can be respected for what she is doing. The country's gaining a new self-respect that the people have needed for a long time."

Marcia nodded. "I've felt that too in the little I've

seen." She looked up at him and saw the softening in his eyes as he watched her.

The past seemed to fall away, and the dark present. It was as though she had only to reach up to him and he would lead her out of all trouble, away from her fear of Jerome and her concern about Laurie. Yet even as a comforting warmth engulfed her, she knew it was illusion. She could not reach out to him until she had loosened the bonds that held her in fear to Jerome.

Laurie came running back, out of breath. "Oh, do come and look!" she cried. "I've got something to show you. Please come and see."

Alan held out his hand and pulled Marcia up. Afterwards he did not let her go, but held her fingers lightly in his as they followed Laurie beneath the great crypto-merias.

Ahead Laurie skipped along toward the place where an arched brick viaduct, almost Roman in design, carried the rushing stream they had heard. Beneath the main arch stone steps climbed the hillside to a level where more temple buildings were ranged and priests moved serenely in the sun.

Marcia watched as Laurie darted under the arch, and ran up the steps to a point where she could look down on the flowing water, charmed by every new discovery. It was good to see her once more vitally alive without the nervousness that beset her when she was with her father.

When they had explored the hillside for a distance, they started home, walking slowly, holding to this new, unspoken companionship between them for as long as possible. Alan went with them to their gate, and Marcia held out her hand in wordless thanks.

His eyes were grave. "Don't let yourself be panicked," he said. "But get away from this house soon."

She nodded mutely and followed Laurie through the gate. But before she and Laurie had reached the house she stopped her daughter and rested her hands lightly upon her shoulders, looked into her wide brown eyes.

"Never forget how kind Mr. Cobb is," she said. "Don't let anyone talk you out of believing in him."

A cloud went over Laurie's face, but she agreed dutifully. "Yes, Mommy. He is nice."

That evening before she went to bed, Laurie played again with the Japanese doll. And she did not think of the demon mask, or inquire what had happened to it.

EIGHTEEN

THE NEXT DAY JEROME WENT OUT EARLY AND WHEN HE had left the house Marcia hurried downtown and booked passages home by plane. She set the date for three weeks ahead, not daring to force the issue at once, even if she could get space during the busy tourist season.

On the way home from her errand a plan came to her which might aid in solving the problem of getting Laurie away without too much of a disturbing upheaval. It had occurred to her that she might find an ally in Chiyo.

When she came home from getting her tickets, she went to the Minatos' gate and rang the bell. When the maid answered, she asked for Mrs. Minato and was shown in. Before she saw Chiyo, she heard the soft, plaintive singing she had so often heard before. Upstairs someone picked at the strings of a samisen.

On the evening when Minato-san had brought her here, the wooden shutters had been placed around the lower floor, closing it in for the night, so she had seen little of the house. On this warm, drizzly July day the paper *shoji* had been slid back, and even one or two of the inner *fusuma,* which served as walls between the rooms, had been removed. Thus most of the downstairs was open to the garden and any possible stirring of air. There could be no concealment in such a house. Chiyo sat on the *tatami* polishing something slender and shining, singing as she worked. As she turned the object in her hands, Marcia saw that it was a long, slightly curved sword.

Chiyo stopped singing at the sight of her guest and bowed to Marcia. While her emotions were well-schooled and she revealed no surprise, it seemed to Marcia that there was an uneasiness in her, a concealed tension. Once she glanced upward as if the samisen music disturbed her.

Marcia stepped out of her shoes and sat down on the cushion Chiyo offered. "So it's you I've heard singing," she said.

Chiyo smiled. "It is an accomplishment I learned after I came to Japan. Madame Setsu likes to hear me —she finds it soothing. But sometimes I sing only for myself."

"But always such sad songs," Marcia said.

"When the heart is sad, so must the singing be," Chiyo agreed. She motioned to the long weapon she held and to another shorter sword which lay beside her in its scabbard. "My husband's swords."

"You mean he carried these as a soldier?" Marcia asked.

Chiyo looked shocked. "Oh, no! These are the swords of his family. They belonged to his great-grandfather, who was a samurai, and to several ancestors before that. Perhaps you have never seen a samurai sword before? This one is a work of art." Chiyo picked up the shining blade by shielding it in a silk cloth and held the hilt toward Marcia.

The hilt had been bound in strands of silk and leather, with diamond-shaped openings in which ornaments had been set. Marcia bent to examine them, without touching the sword.

"These are the *menuki*," Chiyo said. "That means the 'fist place.' The great metal workers of Japan created beautiful sword ornaments. These are copper and gold—a design of heron flying. Of course this is a ceremonial sword, worn only for dress occasions. In the old days a warrior had three swords. One for ceremony, one for fighting—and then a short sword, like this one here."

Chiyo gestured toward the straight, stocky sword which also had an ornamental hilt and carved guard.

"What was the short sword for?" Marcia asked.

"This one was the samurai's constant companion. His fighting sword had to be left at the door when he went visiting, but this one he never took off except when he slept. And then it was probably ready to his hand. The samurai's rank and his honor were vested in this sword. And if his honor was destroyed he committed *seppuku* with it and died. What you call *hara-kiri*."

Chiyo gave the long blade a last brisk polishing and slipped it carefully into a scabbard which had a great bow of silk tied around it. Then she rose and made a little bow to Marcia.

"Excuse me, please. I have something which must be returned to you."

Quickly she crossed the *tatami* to the steep Japanese staircase and went up it to the floor above. Marcia, waiting, looked about the spacious airy rooms, unmarred by the westernization of the other half of the house. Outside in the garden she could hear the children playing. The samisen music had ceased and there was a soft murmur of voices upstairs. In a moment Chiyo came down again, carrying the moonflower plant.

"This should have been returned to you," she said. "Madame Setsu finds it hard to understand that others live in this house. I don't know how she got the key, but she must have gone into your part of the house and when she saw the plant standing there, she believed it to be hers. I have explained to her and we are both very sorry."

"I understand," Marcia said gently. "Tell her I wish her to keep the plant if it gives her pleasure. I know she must like moonflowers. That poem—"

"The *yu gao* is her favorite flower," Chiyo said. "But I will get her another. She must not take yours." She set the plant down and knelt again on the cushion beside Marcia. "There is something you wish to tell me?"

"Today I booked my flight home to the States," Marcia said. "Laurie and I will leave in three weeks' time."

Chiyo said nothing. Her eyes were downcast and she waited in silence.

"When I came here," Marcia went on quietly, "I didn't know what it was that kept Jerome in Japan.

Now I understand and I do not hold it against you. I've changed, as Jerome has changed, and now it no longer matters. But when I go home I mean to take Laurie with me. You, as a mother, can understand that?"

Chiyo bowed her head in agreement.

"Then will you help me?" Marcia asked. "My husband opposes my taking Laurie away. He has threatened to stop me if I try. But if you wish you can surely persuade him to let her go. He will listen to you as he will not to me."

Now Chiyo looked frankly puzzled. "Why should he listen to me?"

"Because—" Marcia made a small, helpless gesture with her hands, "because he loves you and you can influence him. I am giving him up to you, Chiyo. When I leave Japan I will never come back. Surely you can do this much for me."

"Ma-ah!" Chiyo made the Japanese exclamation of dismay and shook her head, as if she repudiated Marcia and refused any promise of help. Then, surprisingly, she bent her head and covered her face with her hands.

"What is it?" Marcia cried. "What's the matter?"

For a long moment Chiyo remained as she was, rocked forward. Then slowly she straightened and faced Marcia again and now shocked dismay was written openly on her face. As she rose from her knees she seemed uncertain and concerned. Softly she went to the foot of the stairs and looked up before beckoning to Marcia.

Bewildered, Marcia went to stand beside her and Chiyo gestured upward.

"Go upstairs," she whispered. "Go up quietly. Make no sound."

"But—why?" Marcia asked, having no desire to encounter Haruka Setsu.

In her gentle way Chiyo was imperious. "Go!" she said. "It is better if you see for yourself."

Hesitantly Marcia climbed the stairs. The murmur of voices was audible again, and she paused at the top step, looking about. Opposite her, across a small hallway was a closed paper *shoji,* its white panes glowing from lamplight beyond. A shadow lay across the paper panes—the shadow of a woman in Japanese dress, and beside it, even as she was about to turn away, a second shadow stirred. For just an instant the profile of a man showed in silhouette against the light, then he turned his head and the shadow was blurred.

But that single clear instant was enough. The man in the room beyond was Jerome Talbot.

Quickly Marcia crept down the stairs, her feet sliding on the slippery wood in her haste. In the room below Chiyo waited for her pityingly.

"One time Ichiro brought you here so you would know," she said. "But you did not understand."

"No," Marcia said, "I didn't understand. I've been wrong from the beginning."

"You must not remain here now." Chiyo spoke in a whisper. "I am going out. Will you come with me? I wish to speak to you away from the house."

Shock possessed Marcia. She knew that horror lurked in this discovery and that sooner or later she must face it. Now there was urgency in Chiyo's request and she gave in to it.

"I'll come with you," she said.

Chiyo carried the moonflower and they left it inside Marcia's gate. Then they went down the lane toward a cross street where the tram cars ran. Both women were silent on the trip downtown. At Sanjo Bridge they left the car and Chiyo led the way down an embankment along the river, where a group of school children sat on the stones, busily painting pictures of the scene. Chiyo paid no attention to the familiar sight, but led Marcia farther along the bank away from the young artists.

"Here it is quiet," she said. "Soon I must go to my drum lesson nearby, but first we can talk." She reached into her kimono sleeve for a piece of tissue and dabbed at her nose, clearly close to tears.

Marcia waited, feeling drained of all emotion.

"It is my husband, Ichiro," Chiyo began. "He wants very much to go to Kobe to work and he still insists that I go with him. Because of my cousin Haruka I cannot go. It is impossible to leave her. Also your husband wishes me to stay to care for her. Yet it is best for Ichiro to take this work in Kobe. He has been too long what the Japanese call a 'useless person.' He says now that he will leave me if I do not go with him. I don't know what to do."

"Perhaps it would be better for you if he went away?" Marcia asked.

Chiyo looked shocked. "He is my husband. There is no other man for me."

And all this while, Marcia thought, she had not seen what was there before her eyes. She had always used the wrong key. Jerome's kindness toward Chiyo, his consideration for her, all stemmed from the fact that she was indispensable to him in caring for Haruka.

"When I first met him," Chiyo went on, "Ichiro had just returned from Malaya. He was very sick. Not in his body, but in his spirit. His family had died in Tokyo during the war, as mine had also. Many turned away from him, as happened to returning soldiers who came home in disgrace. He needed me very much, though I was so young—only sixteen. I had no one but Haruka, and he accepted her too, and the—the circumstances under which we had to live if I was to care for her. Even now he has great kindness for Haruka and he would take care of her, if I could take her away from here."

"Then why don't you?" Marcia asked. "Perhaps it would be better for everyone."

"She is so good, so brave," Chiyo went on, as though Marcia had not spoken. "And she is so very—beautiful. And pitiful. I disliked you at first for coming here because I thought you might hurt Haruka. Now I believe it would be better for her to be hurt and stop this thing."

"Jerome is in love with a woman who is—" Marcia faltered and paused.

Though she did not speak the word, Chiyo understood. "What is madness? Which one of us is not mad in some way? Your husband perhaps too! Even you for coming all this way to get him back. How foolish I thought you when I first saw you here. Yet I do not think you foolish now. Or mad. Perhaps Haruka is the wisest of us all, because she is so very close to the other life. It is necessary to watch her always, lest she step across."

She turned back toward the street and Marcia went with her.

"It is unfortunate that you cannot take your husband home with you," Chiyo said. "That would be the best thing. Haruka would be sad, but she would come with Ichiro and me and perhaps she would recover from the sorrow of his going. But if your husband stays, there is no way out for any of us."

"He will never go home with me," Marcia said, and did not add that she no longer wanted him to.

"I will tell Ichiro that I must stay here," Chiyo said sadly. "There is no other way. Now it is time for my lesson. Would you like to come and watch?"

There was something so gentle and apologetic in Chiyo's tone that Marcia could not refuse. They followed the narrow alley that ran parallel with the river and was called the Pontocho section of Kyoto—one of its principal geisha quarters. Cutting into this alley was a still narrower street, hardly more than a slit of walk between the close-set little houses. Chiyo turned up this slit just as it began to rain again, and stepped into the entrance of a two-story house. From above Marcia could hear the beat and chant of the drum music.

They left their shoes at the entrance and went up the narrow stairs. The large main room upstairs was for the teacher and her pupils, with a smaller room of mats adjoining for visitors or those who waited for their lessons.

Chiyo went in quietly and bowed low to the woman teacher, while Marcia sat down on cushions in the visitors' room to watch. She had the strange sensation of moving in a dream. Sooner or later appalling reality would sweep back upon her, but for the moment she welcomed distraction.

The teacher wore a dark gray kimono and sober-hued obi. Her black hair was pulled straight back into a knot behind. She sat on her feet before a large polished block of wood and in each hand she held a stick of white leather, rounded at the handle, but flattened at one end like an elongated spatula. With these she sounded the beat, whacking the sticks vigorously against the wooden block.

Each of the four girls held a hand drum, shaped rather like an hour glass, with a diaphragm at each end. One hand held the drum near shoulder height by its silken cords, while the other hand patted it.

The teacher not only sounded the beat with her leather sticks, but also accompanied it with a vocal chant, and the drum players echoed the chant at certain places in the music.

The far side of the room was completely open and overlooked a veranda of the next house, across a narrow roof. Marcia watched the rain spattering on wet tile. A pair of white *tabi* had been pinned to a wire over the gallery and flapped back and forth gently in the breeze as the drums began.

The lesson was advancing serenely, when a man's voice sounded suddenly downstairs. At once Chiyo set her drum down, murmured apologies and rose from her knees. Ichiro had come for her unexpectedly, but only the swiftness of her movement betrayed her alarm.

Marcia went downstairs with her, to find Ichiro waiting. He bowed somewhat absently to Marcia and began to speak to Chiyo in Japanese. Earnestness and entreaty sounded in his voice and Marcia heard him repeat the word "Kobe" several times.

Chiyo attempted to hush him until they were away

from the house, but he had been drinking again and *saké* seemed to release his natural restraint. Not wanting to be part of this domestic crisis, Marcia tried to make an excuse and get away, but Chiyo pleaded with her to stay.

"Please—perhaps you can make Ichiro understand that what he asks is impossible."

Her escape barred, Marcia found herself walking through the drizzle toward home, while Minato-san beseeched his wife.

Once Chiyo turned to Marcia in explanation. "He finds it hard to talk to me at home because of Madame Setsu. He does not wish to hurt her feelings, but thinks his own family comes first."

"Perhaps he's right," Marcia said.

"No, no!" Chiyo cried. "You do not understand. But one thing is clear—Ichiro must go to Kobe. This I am sure of now. He must go soon. If he stays here something terrible will happen."

She spoke gently to her husband in Japanese and, while his expression did not change, Marcia saw despair in the bending of his head. An increasing sympathy for Minato-san was growing in her, but no effort at persuasion seemed to have any effect on Chiyo and by the time they had walked home, Marcia was convinced that Ichiro was wasting his time in an effort to change his wife's mind. Something held her adamant.

When Marcia reached home, Sumie-san came to meet her.

"Where is Laurie?" Marcia asked.

"Have come inside," Sumie-san said cheerfully, but it developed that she did not know where the child was at the moment.

Laurie did not answer her mother's call and Marcia began to look for her, suddenly uneasy. She was not in the bedroom, or drawing room, or dining room. Nor was she upstairs. There was only one place left to look.

Marcia opened the door of Jerome's room and saw her daughter at once. Laurie sat on the floor before the empty fireplace and for a moment Marcia did not realize what she was doing. Then she stepped closer and saw in horror that Laurie, with a concentration that shut out everything else, was systematically crushing in the head of the Japanese doll. Her weapon was a brass paper weight from her father's desk and she raised and lowered it fiercely, smashing in the fragile plaster until her mother caught her hand and held it.

Laurie looked up at her stonily for a moment and then burst into wild sobs. Marcia went down on her knees and held the child close, rocking her gently back and forth, whispering to her softly, trying to keep her own trembling from showing itself to her daughter.

"We're going home soon, darling," Marcia crooned. "Soon we'll be on the plane for home and then everything will be all right again. Hush, darling, hush."

But Laurie sobbed on in abandonment and would not be comforted.

NINETEEN

THE EPISODE OF THE DOLL WAS MORE FRIGHTENING TO
Marcia than anything else that had happened. Laurie
ended by being violently sick to her stomach and Marcia put her to bed, sat beside her, soothing her, reading to her when she felt a little better.

The broken doll she hid away in a drawer, sick at the
sight of the mutilated head. Yet she did not want to
throw it away. Laurie had some sort of confusion
about the doll and it would be necessary to get to the
bottom of it. Whatever it was, she was sure the cause
led back to Jerome and his sway over his daughter. Any
reproach she might make to him on this score would
be useless, but she wanted him to know what had happened, to see this clear evidence of his unhappy influence.

At dinner that night, with Laurie absent from the
table, Marcia told him what the child had done, and

how ill she had become as a result. To her surprise Jerome did not laugh the matter off. He shoved his chair back from the table as if he did not want any more dinner.

"Bring me the doll," he said curtly.

When she returned to the bedroom, Marcia found Laurie asleep. She was able to open the bureau drawer without waking her, and take out poor little Tomi, her broken head wrapped in a handkerchief. She carried the doll to Jerome at the table in the big dark dining room, and laid it before him.

He picked it up, almost as if in dread and turned it about, examining the broken head. Laurie had not completed her destruction, for only one side was crushed in. One plump cheek remained, and part of a merry smile, while one black, slanted eye regarded them innocently.

Jerome pushed the broken toy away from him on the table and covered his face with his hands.

"What is it?" Marcia cried, more disturbed by his show of despair than she would have been by anger.

"Never mind," he said. "Don't bother me now. But you can do something for me. I had agreed to take Cobb to see Mrs. Minato tonight and I don't feel up to it. When he comes, tell him I can't see him. Make any excuse you like, so long as you get me off."

Sumie-san tiptoed in, frightened, to clear the table, but Jerome sat on, unheeding, his face in his hands. When she began to load dishes on a tray, he rose and went past Marcia to his room, looking white and strained. Marcia returned to Laurie, hiding the doll in the drawer again. She stood beside the child's bed for a little while, listening to her regular breathing. Then she went to the window and stood looking out into the garden.

O Tsuki-sama ruled the world again tonight. All traces of rain had been swept away by rising wind and the moon rode the cloudy sky, full and clear. The small pine trees made a black pattern against the silver light, but the garden lay peaceful and still.

Yet there was no peace in the scene for Marcia. She remembered Chiyo's words. How fine was the boundary line between sanity and madness? At what point did one step across? And where did the area of danger begin?

Alan was coming here tonight. That was the one consoling thought she could cling to.

When the bell at the gate jangled, she did not wait for Sumie-san, but ran hastily to answer it. It was not Alan at the gate, however, but Chiyo, all the Japanese restraint gone from her.

"Ichiro is in trouble!" she cried. "He went out after we came home today, and now the police have called and they are holding him at the station downtown. Oh, please, please—Talbot-san must do something."

Marcia led her into the hallway and rapped on Jerome's door. He heard Chiyo's voice and he came to see what the matter was. Marcia half expected him to shrug Ichiro's troubles aside, but he did not. He was always kind to Chiyo.

"I'll go down to the station at once," he told her.

"I will come with you," Chiyo said. "If he is in trouble he will need me."

They went out together, Chiyo bowing apologetically to Marcia. When Marcia returned to her room,

Laurie had turned over on her stomach, but she still slept, exhausted from her emotional bout.

Half an hour later Alan arrived. Jerome and Chiyo had still not returned.

"I'm glad you've come," she told him. "Jerome had to go out unexpectedly, and Chiyo went with him. Something has happened to Minato-san. He's been drinking again and the police phoned his wife. I'm afraid he's in trouble."

"I see. And what about you? There's been trouble for you, too?"

In the drawing room she sat in a stiff Victorian chair and told him about the doll and about Laurie's subsequent emotional upheaval. He heard her through.

"It's you I'm worried about," he said when she finished. "Laurie will grow up and for her all this will fade. But what's happening to you, Marcia?"

She kept her voice steady by an effort. "I got our plane tickets for home today. In a little while I can take Laurie away. If we can just get through the next three weeks."

"Not here," he said. "You need to leave this house. You need to get away from Kyoto."

She knew this was so, but she could see no practical move that would get Laurie safely away from Jerome.

"Nan said to be careful," she began.

"Listen!" Alan said and moved suddenly to a window. "There's something going on next door."

Marcia went to stand beside him. She could not see into the next garden, but she heard a voice calling anxiously in Japanese, then the sound of someone running.

Sumie-san came into the room a little out of breath.

She explained in a rush that the maid from next door had just come to tell her that Haruka-san had run away and she had been unable to stop her. The fox had taken possession of her again and she might come to harm.

Marcia didn't hesitate. There seemed only one thing to do. "We'll have to go after her. Sumie-san, stay with Laurie. Don't leave her for a moment. We'll be back soon."

She did not ask if Alan would go with her. He came at once. As they hurried out to the front lane she explained.

"It's full moon again tonight. Nan says when the moon is full Madame Setsu becomes melancholy. She has a strange idea that she belongs to the spirit world, and she goes seeking the spirits of those she loved, so she can rejoin them."

In the lane they saw no one and turned downhill to the first cross street. Alan held out his hand so they could run together as they caught sight of a slight figure in a white kimono disappearing around the corner at the end of the street.

"She's heading toward traffic!" Marcia cried. "We've got to stop her."

But Haruka Setsu, for all that she wore a costume that was scarcely made for running, glided ahead of them as smoothly and swiftly as the spirit she felt herself to be. The ends of the flowing silk scarf over her head floated behind her, shimmering in the soft moonlight.

In view of the highway they could see her clearly, but they were not in time to stop her as she ran directly into the evening traffic. Miraculously, nothing struck her, but Alan and Marcia were held up for a moment or two before they could get across. By that time Haruka had darted into a path up the hillside.

"That's the way we took for the temple the other day," Marcia said, as they ducked hand-in-hand under the nose of a *bata-bata*.

"Perhaps that's where she's going," Alan said.

It was like following a will-o'-the-wisp. When clouds darkened the moon, only the luminous flicker of a white kimono guided their direction. She was far ahead now, and any turn of the crooked lane might lose her for good. But she moved always in the direction of the temple and they were in time to see her flee through the gate where Alan and Laurie and Marcia had entered the Sunday of the picnic.

Now they lost her completely and the moon was dark, the temple grounds haunted and shadowy. There were a hundred places where she might hide in this vast place, if she suspected that anyone pursued her.

"Wait," Alan said, and his voice was hushed as the stillness about him, hushed as the rushing whisper of water and the sighing of wind in the cryptomerias high overhead. The grove of great trees rose black and tall on their right, and the scent of cedar was all about them. Directly ahead the tremendous inner gate with its huge columns and high doorsill made a block of massive shadow. Beyond, near the temple buildings on the hillside, were a few scattered lights.

Marcia and Alan stood close together and she felt his fingers strong about her own. They waited, breathing quickly, striving to pierce the soft darkness, to catch some gleam of white that would give them direction.

"Perhaps if we call to her?" Marcia whispered.

"No," Alan said. "We might only frighten her into hiding."

The scene about them lightened a little, then grew increasingly bright as the great opal moon came out from behind streamers of clouds. The earth seemed awash with silver now, and Marcia could almost feel the moon intoxication touch her, as it must have touched Haruka. The gate loomed darkly sinister and black with shadows, only its tiled roofs gleaming in the moonlight. Then came the glimmer of white for which their eyes searched and Marcia's clasp tightened on Alan's fingers.

Haruka Setsu was no longer fleeing. Nor, apparently, did she know she was pursued. Slowly she moved out of the deep shadow of the gateway, out from between tall columns, until she stood on the edge of the raised platform that made the floor of the gateway. The great roofs and columns dwarfed the slight figure in white, yet they made the woman a focus of all interest, as a figure spotlighted on a stage.

She was half turned toward them now, as she faced the moon. The white scarf fell back from her head and face. She raised her arms as if in supplication to O Tsuki-sama, and the long flowing kimono sleeves hung from her arms in a line of classic beauty.

Alan made no sound, but his hand drew Marcia with him. It was as if they sought to capture a wild heron which raised white wings for flight there in the lambent moonlight.

Now they were close, close enough for Marcia to see the woman's profile clearly for the first time. In the clear pure light her face was lifted in all its terrible beauty. A strange frozen beauty, like that of a young girl whom the years could not touch. As they watched, caught in a spell which held them quiet, Haruka let one arm fall to her side out of sight. The other slender hand remained outstretched, suppliant, pleading. It was as if she beseeched the moon goddess to let her follow the moon path away from earthly suffering.

Alan stirred. This was their chance. They were so close to her now. But a loosely graveled walk circled the gateway and when Alan's foot struck the fine pebbles they made a tiny clatter. At once the woman on the platform shrank back and flung the scarf over her head to hide her strange, terrible beauty. As a spirit of the dead, she must be faceless, in true Japanese tradition.

Alan spoke to her gently. "Madame Setsu? Don't be afraid. We've come to take you home."

The woman moved, but this time Marcia moved more quickly. She ran up the stone steps of the gateway and approached her, speaking softly.

"I am Chiyo's friend. Do you understand English? We have come to take you home. Please—*dozo,*" and she gestured in the direction from which they had come.

The woman turned and came to her, moving lightly on her elegant *zori* sandals. She seemed to peer at Marcia through the thin scarf. She murmured words in Japanese, but Marcia was helpless to understand. At least Haruka did not seem to be afraid of them. Her attitude was more one of sorrow, of hopelessness, perhaps. As though her quest for those she would rejoin had been defeated once more, and she could do nothing but give in with good grace.

She slipped past them and went down the steps, but when they moved quickly after, one on each side of her, she did not seek to escape, but walked proudly between them in the direction of home. Marcia did not touch her, knowing that the Japanese were not given to laying hands upon the person of a stranger, but she was aware once more of the illusive perfume the woman wore. Haruka moved more moderately now, and when they reached the highway she waited between them until it was safe to cross.

Little was said on the way home, though she seemed to understand something of their English when they addressed her. She did not come with them in the manner of a captive being retaken into custody, but as a distinguished lady who does honor to her companions by accompanying them.

When they reached the Minato gate, she bowed very low to each of them in turn.

"Arigato gozaimasu," she murmured her thanks in a low sweet voice. And with the veil still hiding her young face, too youthful for her years, she went through the gate and into her own part of the house.

They heard the maid come to greet her, and then Chiyo's voice, raised anxiously. A moment later Chiyo came hurrying after them as they turned away from her gate.

"Thank you for bringing her back!" she cried. "I was thinking of Ichiro and I forgot."

"Was it serious about your husband?" Marcia asked.

Chiyo nodded. "Yes, serious. Talbot-san got them to let him off. For this one time. But nothing like this must happen again. Good night. I must go to my cousin now. Thank you again so very much."

Alan walked with Marcia around the corner to the Talbot gate. "Shall I come in with you?"

She shook her head. "No. He won't see you tonight. It's better if you don't."

"All right. But I'll see you soon. We'll work this out somehow."

"Thank you." She gave him her hand, longing to say more, but this was not the time and she turned away, her eyes bright with tears, and hurried into the house.

Jerome was in his own room and he did not come out. Apparently he had not yet been told that Haruka was missing. Marcia went into the bedroom she shared with Laurie and found the child awake. She was sitting up in bed, with Sumie-san beside her and they were playing *jan-ken-po*, the scissors-paper-stone game that Japanese children loved.

When she saw her mother, Laurie got up in bed and flung her arms about her neck. "Why did you go out and leave me? What happened, Mommy?"

Marcia held her tight and soothed her, while Sumie-san slipped away.

"It was only for a few moments, darling. The lady next door, Madame Setsu, went out and Alan and I were afraid she might get hurt. So we brought her back. She isn't very well, you know."

"The lady in white?" Laurie asked. "The dead lady?"

"Honey, she isn't dead," Marcia protested, coaxing Laurie down into the bed with gentle hands. "She's only ill."

Laurie's slender arms twined about her neck again, holding her in a frantic clasp. "No, she's dead! That's why she always wears white like the Buddhists do for a funeral. She's dead like my doll Tomi is dead. Mommy, what did you do with the doll?"

"I have it," Marcia said gently. "Snuggle under the sheet now, and I'll sit here beside you. Would you like to hear how we found her in the temple grounds and brought her home?"

Laurie always loved a story and Marcia turned this one into a romantic tale of a Japanese princess bewitched by a moon spell. Laurie listened and at length grew sleepy. But before she slept, there was a moment in which her eyes opened wide and she looked up into her mother's face.

"Does Mr. Cobb really wear a mask to hide what he is like? A nice mask that hides something cruel and ugly?"

Marcia put her cheek against her daughter's soft, warm one. "Whatever makes you think such a terrible thing? Of course there's no mask. Mr. Cobb is very good and kind and . . ."

"But Daddy says everyone wears a mask. You too, Mommy. Because everyone is wicked inside. Inside we're all like that horrid face on the wall in Daddy's room. If we didn't try to hide our wickedness from one another we—we'd all go crazy and die. Like Madame Setsu."

The sickness of horror rose in Marcia's throat. She could only hold Laurie close, denying her words fiercely, striving to reassure her. But how could she find words to undo such evil? At least Laurie seemed to take comfort in her closeness, her murmured reassurances and she slept at last in Marcia's arms.

Marcia tucked the sheet about her and turned off the lights in the room until only one was left burning.

Then she pulled the window draperies against the eerie moonlight. She had no intention of undressing tonight. Someone must keep vigilance in this house, hold away the dark power that could emanate from the mind of one man.

When she grew weary, she lay down fully clothed on the other bed, but her mind remained endlessly alert and it was as if every nerve in her body listened and waited.

Once she got up and went softly to open the door into the dark hallway. The old house sighed and creaked, and she listened tensely for the sound of a door opening upstairs, for the sound of *tabi* on the wooden treads.

But no door opened and she closed her own as soundlessly as she could. A half hour later she heard the quiet opening of Jerome's door, and his step in the hallway. Her heart beat suffocatingly in her throat when his footsteps hesitated outside her door. But they went by and she heard him go up the stairs.

Once more she opened her door and stood in listening stillness in the dark. Above, the "nightingale floor" of the gallery creaked, she heard a key turn in a lock and another door opened. It closed again quietly and everything was still.

So Jerome had gone to Haruka again. But now she felt only a pitying sadness for the tragedies in Haruka's life that had left her with a man so embittered and isolated. Yet perhaps he showed Haruka the tenderness she herself had once known from him, and perhaps Haruka brought him a certain peace he could not otherwise find.

Nevertheless, long after, as Marcia lay awake beside Laurie, she heard another sound far away in the stillness of the night. It was the soft, heartbreaking sound of a woman weeping.

TWENTY

IN THE MORNING MINATO WAS GONE.

Chiyo came running over shortly after breakfast to tell Jerome before he left the house. Marcia went to the door to let her in and as they stood in the entryway Chiyo blurted out the news.

"He went away in the night," she said. "Or before dawn this morning. He left a note for me on his bed and I found it when I woke up."

Jerome came into the hall and she turned toward him anxiously.

"Ichiro has gone to Kobe. I wanted him to go, but now he has gone without telling me, without saying good-by."

Jerome's face looked worn this morning and a little gray, but the burning in his eyes was bright as ever.

"A good thing," he told her. "For a long time I've

275

said you ought to be rid of him. Now he'll be off your hands."

"But I love him," Chiyo said helplessly. "This is what you do not understand. He needs me. He cannot manage without me."

"A common notion with women," Jerome said and threw Marcia a sardonic glance. "He'll manage without you."

"Do you know the name of this place where he hopes to find work?" Chiyo asked.

"Yes, I know. And if you insist, I can probably get him discharged and sent home. A few words about his reputation here, about . . ."

"No, no!" Chiyo cried. "That is not what I wish."

Jerome shrugged. "If you're wise you'll get over him. He's certainly not worth your attention. Let him go and forget him."

He went past them out of the house, and Chiyo sighed unhappily.

"He doesn't understand," Marcia assured her. "You'll surely hear from your husband. How is Madame Setsu this morning?"

"Well enough," Chiyo said sadly. "She always weeps after she has run away. But she will be quiet now. All the will to act has gone out of her. She will cry when she is alone, and read sad poetry. After a time she will write a new poem of her own and then she will feel better. This is the pattern. She never runs away twice in the same moon. But what am I to do about Ichiro?"

The bell at the gate jangled as they stood there talking and Marcia looked up to see Alan crossing the stepping stones. Her quick surge of happiness told her that she had been longing for him to come.

He greeted them cheerfully, but wasted no time in coming to the point of his visit. "Can you get over to Nan's right away?" he asked Marcia. "She has a plan in mind for you."

"Of course," Marcia said, and then glanced at Chiyo. "Come with me. Perhaps we can talk about your trouble too."

Chiyo agreed and Marcia called Laurie. They went over to Nan's with Alan, but he did not come in with them.

"I think you'd better do what Nan suggests," he said. "Marcia, this is good-by for a little while."

"Good-by?" she repeated, startled.

"You'll be hearing from me," he said. "And don't worry—you're in good hands."

She wanted to keep him there, but he was already on his way, and there was nothing to do but go inside to see Nan.

Isa-san took Laurie into the kitchen to play with a new kitten and Nan shut the study door so they could talk without interruption.

Through Alan, Nan already knew what had happened the night before, but she had not heard about Ichiro and she listened in silence while Chiyo told her. Then she smoked soberly for a few minutes, lost in her own thoughts.

"Until now," she said at last, "I've always stood by Jerry Talbot. I've kept my own council and I've never sided against him. I've tried not to get involved." She looked directly at Marcia. "But I am involved now. And I can't believe that what he's trying to do is right for anyone, including himself. Not in the long run."

She opened a drawer and drew out a strip of paper which seemed to be a ticket and held it out to Marcia.

"I was leaving for my vacation tomorrow. You'll go in my place. We'll get another train ticket and Chiyo can go with you."

Both women stared at her and Chiyo began to shake her head. Nan stopped her at once.

"Wait. Don't tell me it isn't possible because of Haruka Setsu or your children. Eventually you'll have to leave her and go to your husband. Let Jerome deal with the problem himself. He has made it his problem and he has no business saddling you with it for life. And your children will be fine with the maids. You know they'll be given good care."

"You don't understand," Chiyo began unhappily. "It is not for Mr. Talbot I wish to stay. I owe my cousin . . ."

"Yes, I know," Nan broke in a little impatiently. "You owe your cousin your life, and you have paid for it many times over since the war. Since that time she has come to owe you hers. Besides, she belongs to the past and you belong to the present, to the future. Your children and your husband are more important. I don't see how Ichiro has stuck the situation for as long as he has. You should be proud that he got up the nerve to go away."

Plainly Nan's firm manner abashed Chiyo, who said a little timidly, "But still, I don't see."

"Go to Miyajima with Marcia," Nan said. "It would be awkward for her to go alone when she speaks no Japanese. I was to stay at a Japanese inn there and the reservation is already made. They will take Marcia in my place, and you also, Chiyo. I've already phoned. It will not be expensive, and this will be a practice trip for you. You'll be away only a short time and then you can see how your cousin manages in other hands. I know a friend of Yamada-san's—a woman who was a nurse in wartime. I think she'll come and stay with Madame Setsu. Let Jerry pay her. If it works out, you'll have more confidence when Minato-san writes that he wants you in Kobe."

"But if he wants me while I am away?" Chiyo asked.

Nan grinned at her. "Let him stew for a while. It won't hurt him."

This time Chiyo managed a smile. "Thank you," she said softly. "Thank you with all my heart. Now I will go home. There are many things to be done."

She bowed herself out and when she had gone Marcia said, "But your holiday, Nan? What a shame for you to give up your own plans."

"I'm only postponing them," Nan said. "Somebody's got to stay here to keep an eye on Jerry. Maybe that's my job. Alan's right that you ought to leave Kyoto, get away to a quiet place where you can find your bearings and be out of Jerry's reach."

Marcia smiled her gratitude. "Of course I'll do what you say."

"Good!" said Nan matter-of-factly. "Suppose you go home now and get packed. You can bring any extra stuff you want to leave over here. Then you won't have to return to the house at all before you catch your plane. Or even return to Kyoto. I can send your things along to Tokyo for you. Stay one more night in Jerry's house so he won't guess what you're up to."

Marcia was glad to accept Nan's suggestions, and that night she slept more peacefully than she had for a long time. Once, after midnight, Laurie wakened from a disturbing dream, crying aloud, and Marcia took the child into her own bed. One more night in this house, she thought, only one more. Then they would be free of it.

Never again need she fear the brooding evil that centered in that mask in Jerome's room. Never again would she step into the crowded Victorian drawing room that seemed so out of place in this age and this country. She would never need to listen again for creaking floors in the night, or for the melancholy sound of a samisen. She would be free of all this for good, once they were away.

But even as she told herself these things, she could not quite believe them. It was as if the house held her in a closed fist and would not let her go. These were the gloom-ridden thoughts of the night, however. By morning she was able to throw them off and dismiss them as foolish.

She did not get up until Jerome had left the house, and then she told Laurie casually of their plans. It sounded like an adventure to Laurie, a vacation visit, and she did not argue with the fact that they weren't telling her father good-by. Marcia explained that he was working very hard and wouldn't have time to see them off, hoping that her story would serve its purpose.

Chiyo came over with a small straw suitcase and a few things for the trip tied up in a *furoshiki,* the cloth square which still served the Japanese as a carryall, even in this modern world.

Nan drove them to the train and until the last moment Marcia hoped that Alan might find time to come to the station and wave them off. But Nan did not mention him and Marcia could not bring herself to ask if he knew when she was leaving.

Chiyo seemed nervous and uneasy. Nan assured her that all arrangements had been made, and that she would hardly be out of the house before the nurse would come. She could count on the woman's tact and sympathy, since Yamada-san vouched for her. Living in her own dream world, Madame Setsu might not miss her cousin as much as Chiyo expected.

Japanese trains were remarkable for their efficiency and this one left Kyoto at the exact moment the schedule called for. Once the station platform had been left behind, Marcia drew a deep breath and began to feel the strain go out of her. For a little while she and Laurie were safe. This breathing space would serve to renew and strengthen them for whatever lay ahead.

Throughout the car passengers were making themselves comfortable for the trip. All the electric fans had been promptly turned off and several windows opened. This seemed to make everything hotter and dirtier, but no one seemed to mind. The passengers were good-natured and as informal as the Japanese ever became in public. There were no first class cars these days, only second and third. First class had been discontinued as undemocratic after the war, and with its abolishment had gone certain refinements of travel.

As the train left Kyoto's environs it turned toward the seacoast, the great industrial city of Osaka, and the seaport of Kobe. Chiyo leaned against the window, studying the landscape with interest. The last time she had seen these cities the bombing had left everything devastated. But now look at them, she cried—completely built up and thriving. Ma-ah! it was amazing.

After Kobe the towns were small and the sea curled inland, dotted now with the tiny improbable islands of a Japanese print. The neat small hills rolled along on the land side, with mountains beyond, and occasional volcanic cones rising abruptly in solitary independence. How green Japan was, how brightly green, with the ever-present paddy field, and the darker green of pine-forested hills.

Now and then the train stewardess, neat in her blue-gray uniform, her cap set jauntily on one side of her bobbed and permanented hair, would come through to see that all was well.

At lunchtime two girls rolled a cart of refreshments back and forth throughout the train. But though there was a dining car as well, Chiyo suggested that they get a Japanese *bento* at the next station. When the train pulled to a stop she leaned out the window and waved her hand to a woman with a tray slung about her neck and piled high with flat wooden boxes. For a few yen —the equivalent of cents in America—Chiyo purchased three boxes and three small earthenware pots of tea.

Laurie loved the fun of such an unusual picnic and Marcia was grateful for the distraction which kept the little girl occupied and happy. For her own taste the *bento* was prettier to look at than to eat. It was made up mostly of neat rolls of cold rice, wrapped in thin black sheets of seaweed and decorated with bits of fish, vegetables and briny pickle. Wooden chopsticks were provided and the covers of the little teapots made tiny cups. When lunch was finished, one simply disposed of the remains by dumping them somewhat casually into the aisles, through which a porter came along eventually and swept everything up.

In the afternoon as the train sped along the beautiful Inland Sea, Marcia saw that Chiyo was, for some reason, becoming nervous again. She watched the flying countryside intently, her hands clasped tightly in her lap, her mouth pinched as if she suppressed some inward emotion. When Laurie tried to attract her attention to some sight out the window, Chiyo seemed hardly to hear her.

At length Marcia leaned toward her in the seat opposite. "Are you feeling all right, Chiyo? Is anything wrong?"

Chiyo moistened her lips with her tongue and her eyes looked a little strange, as if they saw past Marcia to something only she could glimpse.

"It is the place we are coming to. I lived here after our home was destroyed in Tokyo."

They were running through city environs now—a city that sprawled over a wide level plain, with hills partly rimming it.

"It is like six islands," Chiyo said, "built on the arms of a river delta."

In the distance Marcia could see what had once been a domed building. Now the dome was only naked girders, the concrete walls broken, windows standing empty to the sky. The glimpse vanished as newer buildings cut in, but somehow that dome had a familiar look to Marcia. Quite suddenly she knew where they were. She had seen that building before in a picture.

"Ground zero," she said softly.

Chiyo threw her a quick, half-frightened look, and

when she spoke her voice was hushed. "This is Hiro-shima."

She ceased to look at the buildings they were passing —new and well built, with no signs of ruin. Instead she was staring up at the sky. When she spoke Marcia felt a prickling up her spine.

"I will never forget the light," Chiyo whispered. "So golden-white and terrible, flashing everywhere all at once. Haruka was with me in the street and she clutched me to her, shielded me with her body before the concussion came and leveled buildings all around us. The roar stunned our ears and we were pelted with a dreadful rain of molten glass, and hot tar from a nearby road-repairing job. Being a small person, I might have been killed if Haruka had not shielded me against her side. I was fortunate to be wearing a light-colored kimono which reflected the rays. Haruka wore the dark-colored *mompé*—the baggy overalls women wore during the war—so she was not so well off."

The train had pulled into the station, but Chiyo paid no attention to the passengers getting off. Laurie had drawn close to her mother and Marcia put an arm about her as Chiyo went on.

"We were stunned for a few minutes. But we were alive, though others lay dead in the street near us. A dreadful brown cloud was rising over the city. I re-member the flashes of bright color on the underside, and a redness like blood. A muddy rain began to fall as the windstorm moved in after the blast. A storm of flame and wind and debris. We must have been only a few blocks from the edge of total destruction. Yet we were alive."

"I didn't know," Marcia murmured. "I thought you were in Tokyo during the war."

"That was in the beginning. My family in Tokyo were killed in the bombing there. So I had come to live with my cousin and her children in Hiroshima. Haruka's husband died in the fighting in the Pacific islands. Her old mother and three children died here. I was in the street with her on the way to market, or we would have died too, in the ruins of her house. As it was, she saved my life."

Chiyo's face twisted in sudden pain.

"You see how it is with my cousin? This is how she has suffered."

"Yes," Marcia said softly. "I see."

"I must never forget. I must pay my debt. Soon, I think, I will return to Kyoto."

The train took on a few new passengers and pulled out of the station. Chiyo seemed to rouse herself and return to the present.

"The next stop is Miyajima-Guchi," she said, "where we take a ferry for the island."

TWENTY-ONE

THE WATERS OF HIROSHIMA BAY REFLECTED BLUE OF SKY and green of mountains as the little ferryboat approached the island of Miyajima. Somewhere on shore the strains of "Auld Lang Syne" were drifting from a loudspeaker, a little startling to hear in these Japanese surroundings.

High, wooded peaks rose in a central ridge ahead. In the shallow water near the shore stood the great red torii sacred to the island, forming a gateway to the heart of the famous waterfront Shinto shrine. Far above, a many-tiered red pagoda lifted its pinnacle against the green hills. Nearby were temple roofs and small teahouses clinging to wooded cliffs.

"So beautiful," Chiyo said wistfully. "Never have I seen this island before. It is good to come here."

On shore a porter from their inn awaited them and led the way to a jeep which served as the hotel car.

287

Away they bounced over rutted roads, through narrow twisting streets with open shops on every side. The little town was gray—like every Japanese town. When they were first built, the unpainted wooden houses glowed beautifully golden for a time, but they weathered at length to shades of gray and dusty brown. When gray tile roofs were added, the overall picture was a dull monotone. No wonder exclamation points of vivid color were needed in torii and shrine.

At the gate of the *ryokan,* the Japanese-style inn, they left the jeep and followed stepping stones through the garden to the entrance. An entourage of the inn help came gaily to greet them and carry in their pieces of baggage from the car. On the veranda several women in kimonos knelt in low bows, greeting them with the usual welcome of *"Irasshai!"* Eager hands helped with shoes and the smiles were interested and genuine. The woman who led them upstairs made much of Laurie and she was able to air a little of the Japanese she had learned in Kyoto from Sumie-san and Tomiko.

Down narrow hallways with polished wooden floors, up flights of steps and down another maze of corridors they went until their hostess opened the *shoji* to the room Marcia and Laurie were to share. Chiyo was given a room adjoining.

Marcia's first impression was one of sheer beauty. Not because the room with its honey-colored mats, its *tokonoma* alcove and painting, was any different from other Japanese rooms, but because the art of the Japanese house was more clearly illustrated here than Marcia had ever seen it before.

The simplicity, the lack of decoration made the view

it framed on its open side all the more perfect. The outdoors became a part of the room's decoration. Beyond the *tatami* was a narrow strip of veranda, with low modern chairs of beige wood, and a small table set between them beside the rail. Beyond and a story below lay a miniature mountain gorge, with a waterfall tumbling over wet rocks and gushing into a flowing stream that dipped toward the sea. On the far side of the stream a hill rose, steep and green, and at a place where the stream deepened and quieted, a curved wooden bridge spanned its width. Through the open wall the sounds of waterfall and stream came in and were a part of the room.

The smiling maid brought freshly starched and clean-smelling blue-and-white *yukata* for them to put on. It was pleasant to slip into the cool cotton kimono and sit on the floor unhampered by tight western clothes. Tea was served at once, and small pink and green cakes with a thick soy bean jam between crisp layers.

A back rest was produced for Marcia, so that sitting on the floor would be comfortable. The guests were assured that the bath was ready for them whenever they wished—the hot bath of a natural spring.

"Oh, let's not take baths now!" Laurie objected. "Let's go explore, before it gets dark."

But Marcia was all for the bath and she gathered up towel and soap and followed the maid outdoors. The bath house was at a distance from the inn, which might make it awkward when it rained. Marcia had slipped into *geta* and was discovering that it took a little practice to learn the proper tipped-forward walk that enabled one to keep the clogs on the feet.

She was relieved to find that the bath had been reserved for her alone and would not be a communal Japanese affair. The maid let her in and left her at the door. Marcia stepped into a huge-steamy room with a tiled floor and a sunken pool, large enough and deep enough to swim across, filled to the brim with piping-hot water.

By now she was accustomed to the luxury of the Japanese bath, and when she had washed with soap and rinsed away grime and suds, she lowered herself slowly into the pool and sat on a ledge, with the water to her neck, soaking away all physical and mental strains.

In this warm, cavernous room, with the water laving her body, it was possible to think quietly as she had not been able to do in Kyoto. Now she could face clearly and without confusion that moment of discovery when she had known that it was not Chiyo to whom Jerome was tied, but Haruka Setsu. What pain and dark unhappiness there must have been for him in that relationship. She knew now that there had been times when he had longed to break away to a more reasonable life. His marriage must have been a deliberate step in that direction. Yet always Haruka had drawn him back to her through his unhappy obsession. Here in Miyajima, where she was safe, Marcia could think of Jerome with pity.

She thought of Alan too, and wondered when she would see him, before she left Japan. Wondered without anxiety because the question was only one of "when." Somewhere he would come to her, and she would be ready for the next step, whatever it might be.

She climbed dripping out of the pool and stood on

the tiled floor, while she toweled herself dry. Then she stretched, arms high above her head, her slim body warm and languorous as a cat's. She slipped into the *yukata,* careful to fold the left side properly over the right, and tied the narrow green sash about her waist. When she returned to her room she felt rested and calmer than she had been in weeks.

A Japanese dinner was brought to their room, where Chiyo ate with them. Again there were the small bowls, the tasty dabs and bits, the fluffy, steaming rice. The meal seemed especially appetizing served by two smiling, kimono-clad maids, while the odor of pine, the murmurous sound of the stream, filled the room, and the hillside opposite grew dark in the fading light.

After the meal they went for a brief walk along narrow, busy streets, looking into the shops. When they returned to the inn, the maids had taken the bedding from the cupboards in their rooms and set out their beds for the night.

The *tatami* itself, being a stuffed matting, was not hard, but springy, and upon this had been laid piles of three purple and brown *futon*—the thick padded quilts which served as mattresses. Chiyo said that three were a concession to the pampered western body. In the other room she herself would sleep on only one. White coverings sewed to the quilts served as sheets, while the pillows were small and came in a hard variety that felt like a sandbag, as well as a slightly softer version. At least the old wooden pillows upon which the Japanese had once slept were no longer popular. They belonged to the day of elaborate head-dresses, when a lady combed her hair for the week and wanted nothing to disturb it.

Sliding wooden shutters gave them privacy, and a low cylindrical parchment lamp had been set on the floor near the heap of bedding to serve as a night light.

Laurie, already in pajamas, bounced about on top of the beds, sampling them for softness, delighting in everything that was different. Yet she seemed too keyed up in her enthusiasm and Marcia tried to quiet her.

"Tomorrow's another day and there will be lots to do. So do pop into bed, honey, and go to sleep." Laurie, however, had found that a *tatami* was wonderful to turn somersaults on, and would not be quieted.

Marcia, kneeling on a cushion before the tiny Japanese dressing table that was like a doll's dresser, brushed her hair and braided it. Then she crossed the hall to the wash-room—a bare room with a wooden floor and a sink along one side. There were two taps, both running cold water. Adjoining was the room known to all tourists as the *benjo*. No Japanese lady would think of using the word—there was a more elegant term which meant "wash-hands." But the simple name had stuck as far as foreigners were concerned. The little wooden door had a latch, which could also be opened from the outside. There were special slippers which one wore in the *benjo,* though the polished floor was scrupulously clean. A long porcelain basin was set into the floor, and near it had been placed a blue vase containing a single lily. The combination made a surprising still life.

When Marcia returned to her room she found that Laurie had slid open one of the wooden shutters on the little veranda so that cool night air blew in from outdoors. Marcia stood beside her, looking out at the dark, pine-scented night. They could see white froth where the little waterfall spilled over rocks and up the stream a little way were a few scattered lights. The rushing sound of the water mingled with the sighing of wind in the Japanese pines.

"It's so beautiful," Laurie said in a hushed voice. "Our house in Kyoto isn't like this."

"Try to forget Kyoto for now, dear," Marcia said. But she did not add that they would not be returning there. Laurie had not yet come far enough from her father.

They left the sliding door open and snuggled down in their wonderfully comfortable Japanese beds. Nothing could have been warmer or more cozy. The little night light shed a faint golden glow in its immediate vicinity, but it did not brighten the room too much. In her keyed-up state Laurie did not fall quickly asleep and Marcia heard her moving and turning for a long while before her breathing became even.

Marcia lay awake, thinking over the long day, remembering Hiroshima and all the things Chiyo had said, pitying poor Haruka Setsu, who had lost everything in the blast.

The next few days in Miyajima were tranquil and lovely. The weather held clear and they climbed the hills, roamed the shore, and visited the beautiful shrine on the water. Marcia began to have the feeling that the island was cut off from the rest of the world, out of reach, out of touch. There was no word from Jerome, as she had half feared there might be. Nan did not write, nor did Alan, but Marcia was content to mark time and dream a little. It was enough to watch Laurie relax and grow less nervous.

Only Chiyo seemed restive and troubled. Marcia

knew she was concerned about Haruka, that she missed her children and worried about Ichiro. But so far she had made no attempt to leave for home. Surely everything was all right in Kyoto, Marcia assured her, or Nan would let her know.

Late one afternoon, when Marcia had gone for a walk alone, she came back to the inn to find Laurie in a state of eager anticipation.

"Something wonderful is going to happen tonight!" she announced. "One of the maids just came up to let us know. Tell her about it, Chiyo!"

"We are very fortunate," Chiyo said respectfully. "You have seen the stone lanterns on the shore of the island? There are more than a hundred of them, as well as many bronze lanterns in the shrine. When someone gives a handsome sum to the shrine, the priests light all the lanterns. A wealthy Japanese has asked that this be done tonight. It is a good night because there are clouds. The moon will be hidden, and the tide will be high. On a dark night when the tide is full this is a very famous sight. We must go down after dinner to see it."

One treated all "famous" sights in Japan with reverence, as Marcia was beginning to learn.

After dinner, when it was fully dark, they walked down the winding little street to the waterfront where a glowing new world had come to life.

Lighted stone lanterns made a bright passageway of the road along the shore. The several low red buildings of the shrine were connected by broad galleries built out over the sea. Now, at high tide, the shrine seemed to float upon the water, glowing with light, a curved red-lacquer bridge spanning a stream at one point to reach it. Reflected lights shimmered in the water and in the distance lights shone along the shore of the mainland.

Laurie could not be restrained. She would dart away to see something the grownups were too slow about reaching, then come dancing happily back. Her eager smile made quick friends for her among the Japanese and she found a little girl her own age to talk to, with a few words and a good deal of sign language. This was Laurie as she used to be, and Marcia hoped that nothing would obstruct the healing.

Chiyo found a place where they could stand near the water and look back along the magically lighted shore. Tonight there was a wistfulness about her, as if present beauty made memory all the more poignant. When Laurie danced off with her new friend, Chiyo began to speak in her low, musical voice, and her words were of the terrible time after the bombing.

Listening, Marcia forgot the enchanted world of Japanese lanterns, the gay holiday crowds.

"We lived like animals in the ruins," Chiyo said. "Haruka had been hurt by the glass and hot tar and she had developed radiation sickness. Her body had been between me and the flash, so I was not so badly injured, only a little cut on one hand. But ill as she was, Haruka would not leave the place where her home had been. She believed that if we waited there her children and her mother would come back to find us. She would not believe them dead, though I knew there was no hope. Some stranger gave us food on the second day. We ate nothing on the third. Then I learned about a place where the injured were being cared for, and I made Haruka come with me because I knew she would die if she was not tended. But there were so many, so many, and so few to help. And this was a new sickness which doctors did not know enough about. We had no family left in all Japan and Haruka's husband was long dead in the Pacific. So we lived in a shack of wood and tin that I built with my own hands —a child's hands, really. And I became like a wild thing, fighting for my life and for Haruka's."

There was a starkness in Chiyo's face as she remembered.

"Talbot-san found us there. He saw how ill Haruka was and he took her into his care. At first I was bitterly angry with the Americans for what they had done, but they were my people too, and I could not continue to hate them. I want now to be Japanese because this is my husband's home. But I hate only war."

"I can see now," Marcia said softly. "I can understand a little better."

Chiyo did not look at her. "Talbot-san was not there when the bomb fell on Hiroshima, but he too was burned by the blast."

"Yes," Marcia said, "I know."

In the light of many lanterns there was a shine of tears in Chiyo's eyes.

"I wanted to hate you when you came," she said. "Because of Haruka. But hating hurts only the one who hates. That house has been bad for us all. I am glad Ichiro has gone out of it. Soon I must take my children and leave it too. That is the only way. But there is always Haruka. How am I to save her?"

Marcia had no answer for her question.

Laurie, who had been in sight a moment before, had disappeared through a group of approaching Japanese, and Marcia moved to follow her. She had a feeling of deepening affection for Chiyo as they walked together between the rows of glowing lanterns.

On ahead Laurie had managed to find an American in the crowd and had gone up to him unhesitatingly. As she turned and the man came with her, Marcia's heart thudded unexpectedly, for the American was Alan Cobb.

As he approached the gleam of lanterns fell across his face, highlighting its firm, strong lines. Laurie danced along at his side in delight. With her father's shadow lifted, there was no mistaking her affection for Alan.

"Komban wa," he said. "Good evening."

She had known he would find a way, Marcia thought. She had known he would come and she made no effort to hide her joy in seeing him. His eyes studied her for a moment, as if he reassured himself that all was well.

"My classes are out for vacation, so I came here as soon as I could get away," he said.

Chiyo bowed politely, but she did not seem overjoyed at the sight of him.

The four walked along the shore together. Marcia felt no need for speech. There was promise and hope in Alan's presence and for the moment she need only take joy in his being here.

When they had seen enough of the festive night they walked back toward the inn. Alan was staying at a western-style hotel near the ferry, but he came up the hill with them. When they reached the inn, Chiyo and Laurie went on ahead, while Alan held Marcia at the gate for a moment.

"I'll only be here for a day or two," he said. "I want

to see you. Will you come for a walk with me tomorrow morning? Just you alone?"

"Of course," she said, and put her hand into his.

He said good night gravely and turned away. Laurie had taken off her shoes and gone inside, but Chiyo waited for Marcia.

"I must stay with you now," she said. "If this man is here, then it is better if I stay."

"What do you mean?" Marcia asked.

But Chiyo only looked at her without expression and went into the inn.

During the night it began to rain and the tumbling sound of the stream past their window increased to a roar. But it was a lullaby sound that did not disturb the sleep of guests in the inn.

TWENTY-TWO

IN THE MORNING THE DOWNPOUR WAS STEADY AND drenching and Marcia woke to see the little stream turned into a torrent, its tributary swollen, the waterfall leaping its rocks in a fury of foam. In disappointment she remembered her promised walk with Alan.

The maid came in to open the shutters and clear away the bedding, shaking her head over the rain. When Chiyo looked in on them, the girl explained that there was a typhoon off Kyushu and they were getting the edge of it. The rain was likely to continue all day, according to the radio.

Chiyo ordered the reasonably western facsimile of breakfast, though somehow a bowl of soup arrived after the *hamu-ando-egu* and there was an apple for dessert.

Paying no attention to the weather, Alan turned up by nine o'clock and waited in the shelter of the entrance veranda, sending word up to Marcia. When she came downstairs she found him wearing rubber boots and a long slicker.

"If you've got rain togs, fix yourself up," he said. "We're going for that walk. I've borrowed a Japanese umbrella from my hotel."

Marcia ran upstairs and put on her rain things. There was a moment's difficulty with Laurie, who wanted to come along, but Chiyo managed to interest her in the prospect of learning some Japanese games. So Marcia went back to Alan ready for a walk in the rain.

Her galoshes fitted snugly about the ankles and her raincoat had a high collar. She tied a bright silk scarf about her head and clung to Alan's arm as they stepped into a roaring world. The oiled paper of the big umbrella, pulled tautly over ribs of bamboo, was like a drum beneath the rain and they had to raise their voices to speak above the uproar.

When they left the crooked streets of the little village behind, they set off along a winding road that led upward on a hillside of maple and pine and bamboo. The green look of the hills seemed intensified in the rain, and even the wet tile of roofs and brown rocks by the road took on a satiny sheen. A stone lantern wore a cap of wet green moss, and a torii gleamed bright vermilion, as if it had just been painted. The fragrance of wet pine was everywhere in the clean, spiced air.

With her arm through Alan's, Marcia could feel the strong sure movement of his body beside her own as they climbed the hill. A long flight of steps turned upward toward a temple far above, and they climbed toward it slowly, pausing at times to look down upon the mist-hidden sea and the great red torii rising near the shore. Halfway up they came to a small pavilion where a roof and platform had been built to house a big bronze bell.

"Let's stop a moment," Alan said.

The drumming roar quieted as he lowered the umbrella and set it streaming against a post of the open pavilion. Here they were out of the downpour, but the very air was liquid with mist and Marcia could feel the drops gather upon her face.

The platform was on a level with the tops of tall cryptomerias which grew in a ravine cutting steeply down below the bell pavilion. Yet there was still more hillside above and they could glimpse the gate guardians of the temple farther up—two fierce statues of pinkish-red stone, gigantic in proportion, scowling at any insignificant human who paused before them.

They could talk, now that the drumming had quieted.

"You saw Nan before you left?" Marcia asked.

"I saw her a few days ago, briefly. But she'd had no word then from Talbot, if that's what you're wondering."

Marcia sighed. "I don't know what he may do, what he may be planning."

"You have only to keep out of his way until you're aboard your plane," Alan said.

It seemed simple enough as he put it and she wished she could make herself believe in his words. But she could almost feel the strange pull of that house in Kyoto, as if it drew her back to some inevitable reckoning.

She moved farther into the pavilion where she could

look up at the great bronze bell overhead. The underside of the roof above it was hung with hundreds of white prayer papers, fluttering when the wind touched them. An entire tree trunk had been peeled of its bark and suspended so that it could be freely swung by anyone who wanted to strike the bell.

"Do you suppose we might ring the bell?" Marcia asked. "I'm sure there must be luck in ringing a temple bell."

"That sign probably invites us to," Alan said. "But only one boom at a time. I understand these bells are used as fire alarms when they're rung steadily."

She reached for the braided red and white cord that swung the log back as far it would go, then released it to strike the side of the bell. The sound was a musical whisper through the woods and Alan laughed out loud.

"We can do better than that!" He caught at the cord and set the log to swinging rhythmically back and forth before he released it and the deep-toned voice of the bell trembled on the air and mingled with the sound of rain and tumbling stream. Then he held the log until it hung quiet again, so that it would not strike the bell a second time.

Marcia moved to the wet railing and looked down upon the rolling green of the treetops. Alan was close beside her and the moment was suddenly alive with promise. The wet mist against her face, the smooth dripping rail under her hands, the freshly washed colors, even the taste of rain upon her lips—all added to the acuteness of her senses.

She turned to him, knowing that this was the moment she had been moving toward ever since the night on the plane when he had lowered himself into the seat beside her.

He saw the turning of her head, the way her chin lifted, and he bent to kiss her mist-wet mouth. Strangely his touch was not altogether gentle. There was a demand in him now, even something of impatience that brought a swift response surging through her. Then he released her almost angrily.

"Let's find a place where we can be dry," he said. "There are words we need to get out of the way between us."

She gave herself up to his lead, pulling her raincoat about her throat, slipping her hand through his arm as he raised the umbrella. Once more they stepped into the rain, retracing their steps to a lane that curled along the hillside. They followed this until village roofs were visible once more, clustered below, and here in this high place they found a teahouse.

The single-story building was built at the cliff's edge, with a stone supporting wall slanting beneath. There were stepping stones leading to the door and lilies growing in the garden. At the entryway a woman came to help them out of their wet things. They went through the clean, open rooms to a place where they could sit on cushions before a low black lacquer table. Here they could look out through the open side of the room at the view below, while the wide overhang of the roof shielded them from the rain.

No one spoke English here, but Alan knew the word for tea—*ocha,* and the woman smiled and bowed.

While they waited, Alan said little and she saw a sternness in his face that disturbed her. He stared out at the red and black pines on the hillside, lost in thoughts she could not share. But when he sensed her anxiety and looked at her, his eyes softened and she knew, whatever the anger that stirred him, it was not for her.

The tea came quickly and the small flowerlike cakes with sweet bean jam between layers. The pungent green liquid warmed after the chill of the rain as Marcia drank it, holding the hot cup gratefully in cold fingers.

"You've made your decision?" Alan asked her suddenly. "You're going to break away from this marriage to Jerome Talbot?"

"My marriage with Jerome was over long ago," she said. "I came out here to save something that was already gone."

"Nevertheless, you came to Japan. You came absorbed by one man. You came out here in love with him."

"That's true," she said sadly. "I'd been running blindly for a long time after something that wasn't really there. Sooner or later I had to stop. I couldn't go on loving him when I found out how he had changed, what he was really like."

He said nothing and she sensed a waiting in him. Somehow she must make him understand. She must be as honest about herself as it was possible to be.

"When you run for a long time and then find that you no longer have a goal, there's only one thing to do," she said. "You have to stand still for a while. Completely still, as if you were in a vacuum. Maybe for a time you're afraid of any movement at all, because movement means pain, and you've had enough of pain. You don't really want anything new to run after."

He reached across the table and covered her hand with his. Quietly she went on, her look unwavering as she met his gaze.

"That day when we picnicked at the temple I was standing still. I was afraid to move in any direction, and yet there was a sort of peace for me that day because I was with you."

"I knew you weren't ready," he said. "But I couldn't be sure you ever would be. I came here to find out."

She turned her hand palm up beneath his. "Emptiness isn't what I want. I want to move again, to feel again. But not with my eyes closed. I don't want to move blindly toward something that's only part of my own imagination."

"You'll be safe this time," he said gently. "I'm waiting for you, Marcia."

"It's not only safety I want," she told him.

He leaned across the little table to cup her face in his hands, and this time there was no anger or impatience in his kiss.

It was still raining when they put on their things and started back toward the inn. They walked close together in the dry little world beneath the Japanese umbrella and Marcia knew that she would remember these as moments of intense happiness, no matter what the future held.

Once, as they rounded a turn, a farmer in a straw rain cape and shaggy straw hat went past them, looking somewhat askance. Marcia laughed softly, remembering the symbolism of the umbrella in Japanese prints.

They found their way downhill to the inn more quickly than they had come up. Alan went with her to the veranda, where maids came running out to be of service. They exclaimed over Marcia's wet stockings and damp clothing, and took away her raincoat, murmuring solicitously. But at the same time they seemed to be trying to tell her something as well. Something that had them plainly excited.

"Will you wait while I run upstairs?" Marcia asked Alan. "Perhaps Chiyo can translate."

He sat down on the ledge and she hurried upstairs past her own empty room and into Chiyo's. Neither Chiyo nor Laurie were in sight. One of the maids had followed and now she began to make gestures, as if to indicate that Chiyo and Laurie had gone out.

Puzzled, Marcia went into her own room and looked around to see if Chiyo had left any sort of message. Laurie's things had been picked up and her suitcase was missing. As she stood there, suddenly frightened, groping for some reassuring explanation, she heard Alan's voice calling to her from downstairs.

"Marcia! There's a telephone call for you. Can you come down here and get it?"

She was breathless by the time she reached the telephone and heard Chiyo's voice at the other end.

"We're in Miyajima-guchi." Chiyo's words came in a rush. "We're taking a train in a few minutes. Ichiro is here. He came to Kyoto to see me and found me gone to Miyajima. Your husband sent him after Laurie because he could not leave Madame Setsu and come for himself. Talbot-san has threatened to cost Ichiro his job in Kobe if he does not do this. I could not stop Ichiro, so it is better if I go with them."

"But, Chiyo—" Marcia began desperately.

Chiyo's voice was suddenly faint. "I must go now.

Ichiro is calling me. Don't worry—I will look after Laurie. But come soon to Kyoto."

The receiver went dead. Marcia hung it up limply and returned to Alan.

"I'll have to go back," she told him. "I knew we would never get away as easily as this."

"I'll go with you," Alan said. "Hurry and pack. We'll get the next train we can catch for Kyoto."

TWENTY-THREE

JAPANESE VACATIONERS WERE LEAVING THE ISLAND THAT day and there was a crowd on the dock to see friends off on the boat. Several gay young men stood in the bow and tossed serpentine streamers to pretty girls in kimonos on the dock. The loudspeaker wailed the music of "Auld Lang Syne" and everyone was properly sentimental. For such an occasion the emotional lid was off.

Marcia stood beside Alan at the rail and watched Miyajima slip away as if her heart went with it. Among the trees she could see the roofs of the temple above the bell pavilion, and the teahouse with its sturdy supporting wall, where she and Alan had sat talking as if the problems that faced them could be easily solved. There was the shore with its hundred stone lanterns, the lovely shrine and the famous red torii in the water. No tears came into her eyes, for this was no time for weeping. Now she needed to pour all her strength into the meeting of forces that lay ahead.

As she had known it must do, the house had pulled her back to its secret life, so strangely twisted and hidden from the world. Now she must face it again and find the way to resolve the hold it had upon her, once and for all.

The colored serpentine streamers broke and fell into the water, trailing limp and wet behind the ferry. Alan drew her away from the rail and they found seats in the cabin until the ferry docked at the mainland.

There was little talk between them. Alan was grave and thoughtful and he understood without question that she must go back to the house, that she must be with Laurie.

Once he said, "Don't give up. There's a way out of this. We'll find it."

She did not answer. There seemed to be no means by which she could take hold of her problems. By the time the law moved its slow, ponderous machinery, Laurie might be lost to her for good, and, more important, lost to herself. For the moment Marcia knew only that she must return to the house in Kyoto and take up her life from that point on. She dared not think of Alan. She dared not take comfort in the touch of his hand, or the affection in his eyes.

They caught a local to Hiroshima and took a Kyoto train from there. It seemed to Marcia that she had always traveled on Japanese trains. As the mountains slipped by on one side, the island-dotted sea on the other, she felt that all this was as familiar as the coast of California.

The train was a slow one and they reached Kyoto in the evening.

Alan took her as far as her gate. "You can reach me through Nan, if you need me," he said. "I'll keep in touch with her."

His hand rested lightly on Marcia's arm. She nodded and turned quickly away because her throat was tight with aching and she could not speak.

As she walked through the garden she could see the lights burning in her own room, though Jerome's was dark. Sumie-san came joyfully to welcome her and said that *danna-san*—the master—was out. But *Raurie-san* was sad and cried much.

Marcia hurried into the bedroom and found Laurie in bed, her eyes puffy from weeping. She flung herself into her mother's arms and clung to her fiercely.

"Minato-san made me come!" she cried. "When I didn't want to leave you, he said Daddy was very sick and wanted me right away. But it wasn't true—it wasn't true at all! Mommy, I don't want to stay here any more. I'm afraid of Daddy the way he is now. We were happy on Miyajima—please let's go away again."

"We'll go away soon, darling," Marcia said. "But now I'm here, so you can sleep and not worry. No one is going to take you away from me."

She sat beside Laurie's bed and pretended to read until the child fell asleep. Then she went into the wide, dim hallway she had hoped never to see again.

Up the dark stairs she went, to the upper floor. Here in this quiet place on the veranda perhaps she could think, plan. As she must plan somehow. The moon-flower was there where she had left it, and now she saw that it had been transformed. There among the large green leaves were three enormous ghostly blooms, scenting the night with their sweet, spicy odor. Marcia bent over it, breathing the heady scent. What was it the odor reminded her of?

She was still there when she heard the key turn in the lock of the partition door. Moving swiftly in her stockinged feet, she stepped onto the *tatami* of the room behind and drew herself back in a shadowy corner.

Once more she saw the woman in white. Madame Setsu came smoothly along the gallery, her silk kimono sleeves rippling with her movement. For once she wore no scarf about her head and her long black hair hung down her back, caught loosely with a tortoise-shell clasp. In the dim light the scarlet of her obi looked almost black. Her perfume blended with that of the moonflower and the similarity was evident.

Marcia leaned against the wall, holding her breath, and felt beneath her fingers an electric switch. She could light the veranda if she wished, but she held her hand still, watching.

Madame Setsu went straight to the plant and bent lovingly above the white flowers. One graceful hand reached out to touch them lightly. Then, before Marcia could move, Haruka plucked the three blooms from the vine and held them up in her hand.

Marcia cried out faintly in dismay and the woman turned, startled. The switch was there beneath Marcia's fingers and as she pressed it the veranda sprang into light, its full radiance falling upon the face of the woman who stood there.

Always afterwards Marcia was grateful for the way she managed to stand absolutely still. She did not cry

out in horror, or shrink away as she might so easily
have done. For in that moment of looking full in
Haruka's face, she knew horror as she had never known
it before in her life. One profile was frozen in beauty,
as it had been more than ten years ago; the other was a
mask of pure horror—the empty eye socket, the twisting scars of terrible burns, keloid welts pulling and dis-
torting. Even as she stared into the light, momentarily
stunned, the woman raised the hand which did not
hold the blossoms and put the contracted claw of it up
to hide her scarred face.

Marcia spoke as gently as she could. "I'm sorry I
startled you, Madame Setsu. *Gomen nasai*—forgive me,
please."

Haruka's sigh was like a soft moan. She glided
swiftly to the open door and through it to the other
side. Sick with shock, Marcia turned off the light and
stood trembling in the dark. Haruka had dropped the
moonflowers in her flight and they lay white and luminous upon the dark floor. Still shaken, Marcia bent to
pick them up and then went downstairs to her room.

Laurie lay sleeping quietly, but Marcia could not un-
dress at once and go to bed. Now she could understand Chiyo's love and loyalty for this recluse who had
withdrawn to hide the dreadful thing she had become
from the world. It was to this that Jerome had bound
himself, keeping alive what he had felt over Hiroshima, tying himself to a love that was forever self-
punishing, that fed always on horror and renewed itself
incessantly at a fount of despair.

Marcia sat stiffly in her chair, the white blossoms
clasped in one hand. She opened her fingers slowly and
stared at the fragile blooms, bruised now and begin-

ning to wilt. Had Haruka wished to strip the plant of its beauty, just as her beauty had been stripped from her?

How lovingly all those about her had kept her sad secret. Not even Nan, who must have seen Haruka in those early days in Hiroshima, had betrayed her by so much as a word. There was another of the poems in *The Moonflower* that Jerome had read aloud the night of the dinner that returned to Marcia's mind.

> Monstrous flowers of cloud
> Blooms above the city;
> Flower of death."

It was possible now to understand Haruka's obsession with death, her wish to be one with the dead.

Laurie tossed suddenly in her bed, muttering beneath her breath and Marcia dropped the blossoms and went to her quickly.

"Wake up, darling. It's only a dream. Everything's all right. I'm here and you're in your own bed."

Laurie opened her eyes and stared at her mother in terror. "It was the lady in white. The lady with only part of a face. She took the scarf away and she was coming closer and closer—"

"Hush, darling. It was only a bad dream." Marcia rocked her daughter gently back and forth in her arms.

That time when Laurie had looked up to see Haruka on the gallery above the garden, she must have seen her only in profile, just as Alan and Marcia had beheld her that night in the temple grounds. But now it was clear that Laurie had seen her again. When? How?

"The lady in white is a very sad, unfortunate person,

honey," she whispered. "But she is gentle and she would never try to hurt you. How did you know about her face?"

"Daddy took me to see her," Laurie said. "He told me I was never to tell you. He said this was the wicked thing human beings did to one another. He said this was why I must never trust anyone."

Abhorrence for the thing Jerome had done left Marcia sick and shaken. Her last vestige of pity for him shriveled at the realization that he would inflict such horror on a child. Then she remembered something— the doll!

It must have been after Laurie had seen Haruka that she had smashed in one side of the doll's face. All the miasma of sickness in this house seemed to center about the smashing of the doll. Yet until Laurie could be withdrawn completely from her father's reach, she would be under the spell of all these things—a hostage to evil.

Tomorrow, Marcia knew, she must face Jerome and win Laurie back to all that was balanced and sane. Now at least she held a weapon in her hands. Nan had said there was a time when one must take brutal action. Jerome had left her no other choice.

TWENTY-FOUR

WHEN JEROME CAME HOME DURING THE NIGHT SHE DID not know, for once she fell asleep, Marcia slept heavily until morning touched the windows. Then she came sharply awake. As she sat up in bed she saw the reminder of withered blossoms on the floor by her chair where they had fallen, and knew that today she must cut the last strands that held Laurie—and herself—to this house.

Laurie heard her stir. "Is my father home?" she asked, and there was the new note of dread in her voice.

"I don't know," Marcia said.

"If he is, do I have to see him?" Laurie asked. "Will he take me away from you the way he said?"

"Not ever again," Marcia told her gently. "Stay in bed for now, darling. I'll see him first."

Jerome was at breakfast when she went into the dining room and he greeted her sardonically.

"Good morning. So you decided to return to Kyoto after all?"

There was a trembling in her, but she answered him evenly. "I came after Laurie, of course." There was no point in reproaching him for his actions. Her words would fall on deaf ears.

He shrugged and pushed back his chair. "As you please, my dear."

"I'm going to take her home to the States," Marcia said. "I want to talk to you about that."

He paused beside her on his way to the door. "You never know when you've gone far enough, do you? You never know when to give up?"

"I'm not giving up," she said. "I must talk to you."

"Sorry, not this morning," he said and brushed indifferently past her out the door.

A few moments later he was gone from the house and Marcia called Laurie to get up for breakfast.

During the morning a sad and subdued Chiyo came in to see her and Marcia told her how Haruka had come through into this part of the house last night and stripped the moonflowers from the plant.

Chiyo bowed her head in distress. "At some time she has taken the key from Talbot-san and she will not give it back. I do not know where she hides it."

"I saw her face," Marcia said quietly.

"Ah—*so desu, ne,*" said Chiyo, lapsing into the familiar Japanese phrase that meant "it is so." "I am sorry —it is better not to see. She has been ill while I was away. I know now how much she needs me. I am very sorry about what happened in Miyajima. There was nothing I could do."

"I understand," Marcia said. "What about Ichiro?"

"This is what I have come to tell you. This morning he has gone back to Kobe. There is no other way. In a week or two I will follow him there."

"That's the best solution," Marcia agreed. "But what of Madame Setsu?"

"She will come with me," Chiyo said. "I have already talked to her and she has agreed."

"She is willing to leave this house, to leave Jerome?" Marcia asked in surprise.

"She understands more than I realized." Chiyo bowed her head. "She says she cannot let me sacrifice my life and my happiness for her. If trouble came between me and Ichiro because of her, she would never forgive herself. And she feels that she has turned Talbot-san away from the great work he should do."

"What did she mean by that?"

"She spoke with deep understanding," Chiyo said, "and I was ashamed because I did not know her thoughts or feelings. She remembers that when Talbot-san first came to Japan he was wrapped up in plans which excited him. He wanted to pay something of the debt he felt he owed because of the bombs on Hiroshima and Nagasaki. So he meant to give himself to peacetime work with nuclear energy. He meant to work here in Japan at the side of Japanese scientists for whom he had great respect."

"Yes, this is all true," Marcia said. "But why did he give it up? What changed him?"

"Haruka changed him." Chiyo's tone was sorrowful. "She did not wish to, but he looked at her and suffered. And as time passed he saw about him in the course of his work the great suffering of many others. Human beings so maimed and disfigured that surgery and skin grafting could do nothing for them. More and more he began to search in the laboratory for some means of bone and tissue regeneration. He wanted to believe that this could be found. He did not see that this was work for others, and that he was turning back, instead of moving ahead. He looked at Haruka and his mind grew obsessed, until only this one desire ruled him. His true work was forgotten. The men who believed it an honor to work at his side, left him for their own projects. For a long time he stayed in the laboratory alone, struggling in a field which was not his own, trying to learn a new science."

"Without success?" Marcia said.

"That is true. He became angry and bitter and went more and more along a road he walked alone. At last he gave up and went to work with doctors who knew more than he did—but always in frustration and futility, for this was not where his true genius and knowledge lay."

"Haruka knew all this?"

"She knew and suffered because she knew. But there was no way in which she could turn him back toward the old way. Now she feels that I have given her the answer. If she goes out of his life, perhaps—"

"I wonder," Marcia said. The solution seemed too easy somehow, and Jerome's reaction to it might be violent.

"The only way is to try," said Chiyo. "As soon as we can make ourselves ready we will go to Kobe. The thing I fear now is to tell Talbot-san. Always in the past he has been kind to me. But I think he will not be kind when I tell him this."

Marcia made her decision quickly. "Let me tell him," she said. "There are other matters I must speak to him about also. Don't worry, Chiyo. I have a plan. Go back to Haruka now and tell her everything will be all right."

There were tears in Chiyo's eyes. "Thank you. You are a good friend."

Marcia went with her to the gate and then turned back to the lonely house. There was nothing more she could do, no step she could take until Jerome came home. She could only hope that her promise to Chiyo would then be turned to fact.

All day long Jerome did not come. At dusk, when Laurie was playing with Tomiko in the garden, Marcia went upstairs to look at the moonflower plant and saw that two more buds were slowly opening. She watched in wonder as the creamy white petals unfolded slowly, almost imperceptibly, before her very eyes. The closed buds seemed to swell to fullness and then, with a tiny pop, the petals were released and the flowers opened to the twilight.

When she heard the bell at the gate, she went down the stairs to face Jerome. He saw her there in the dim hall, waiting for him.

"I suppose you still want to talk to me?" he asked. "All right, let's get through all this unpleasantness," and he led the way into the drawing room.

She followed him and turned on the cold light of the chandelier. She did not sit down, but remained standing near the door, while her husband crossed to the far side of the room. The moment was upon her and she dared not flinch.

"Ichiro has gone back to Kobe," she told him.

"Good riddance." Jerome took out his pipe and began to fill it. "How did you enjoy your little idyll in Miyajima with Alan Cobb?"

She let the sudden attack go and continued, her voice steady. "In a week or two Chiyo will follow her husband to Kobe and she will take her children there with her."

Jerome did not look up from lighting his pipe. "We've been over this ground before. I'll have to deal with Chiyo. She can't go, of course. She has just seen how much Haruka needs her."

"Haruka is going with her," Marcia said.

He flicked out the match in his fingers and stared at her.

"Haruka is going to Kobe with Chiyo," she repeated. "She understands the circumstances and she wants to go." Marcia's breathing quickened. "Jerome, you must let her go."

This time she knew she had confounded him. Anger came alive in his eyes. "If you've meddled in this affair, I promise you—"

Her heart beat heavily, thickly, but she went on. "You must let her go. And you must let me take Laurie home to the States."

"You're out of your mind," he said. "As you very well know, I'll do none of those things."

She touched her dry lips with the tip of her tongue. "I've seen Haruka," she said. "I've seen her face."

He balanced his pipe on his palm, studying it. "Yes?" he said.

"All these years you've protected her. You've given her a separate world to live in where she could be loved and honored and hidden from anyone who might look at her with horror. You've given your life to this. Surely you won't want it all wasted, thrown away?"

There was a moment of tight silence between them.

"Exactly what do you mean?" he said.

She took a deep breath to strengthen her resolve. "I'll make a bargain with you. Let Haruka go with Chiyo to Kobe. Let me take Laurie home to the States without opposition from you."

He seemed frighteningly still. "And if I refuse?" he said.

"Then I will go to the press with Haruka's story. The foreign press and the Japanese press. It's a romantic story and a sensational one. You still have a name in the world. Reporters will interview her. This house isn't a fortress, you know. They'll manage. You're newsworthy anywhere. Haruka's peace will be gone for good."

He took a step toward her and she saw his eyes. The dark brilliance was in them again and suddenly she was afraid of him in a new way. Her palms were damp with physical fear as he came slowly toward her. She dared not cry out, or move so much as a muscle. She had the instinct of the hunted thing to remain quiet when flight was impossible.

Before he reached her, he seemed to recover himself to some degree, but his sudden smile was more disturbing than a sober visage.

"So?" he said. "You'd expose Haruka to the reporters? You'd throw her to the sensational presses of the world cold-bloodedly, without a qualm?"

The trembling in her would not let her speak. She could only nod wordlessly.

He laughed at her then, softly, though there was little amusement in the sound. "For a moment you almost fooled me. For a moment I forgot how well I know you. Because of course you will never go through with it. If you've seen Haruka's face, then it isn't in you to injure her so cruelly. Your bargain's lost its potency, my dear."

Because all he said was true, she could not speak at all. This was the thing she had meant to hide. The weapon she had picked up was useful only if he did not guess that the point was blunted by her own compassion.

The anger seemed to go out of him and leave a strange emptiness behind. He went past her out the door as if he had forgotten she was there, and she heard his own door close after him.

Marcia fled into the garden, where Laurie still played and caught the child by the hand.

"Come quickly, darling," she said. "I'm taking you over to Nan's."

The child looked into her face and came with her at once. They hurried around the house to the gate, without going inside at all.

Alan was there when they reached Nan's and Laurie turned to him in happy greeting. She too was finding in Alan a haven of reassurance.

"May Laurie stay here tonight?" Marcia asked Nan a little breathlessly.

"Both of you can stay, of course," Nan said.

But Marcia shook her head. "I must go back. Nothing is settled yet. I must go back and wait for an answer."

Nan would have grumbled a little, but Alan understood. He came with her part way along the lane. The dusk was deepening now and in the shadow of a bamboo grove he drew her into his arms. She clung to him for a moment as if she would draw strength from the very feeling of his arms about her.

"I'll go in with you, if you like," he said.

"No," she told him quickly. "I must go alone. I don't know yet whether I've won or lost. He behaved so strangely . . ."

He tilted her chin and kissed her mouth warmly before he let her go. She ran back to the house with the feeling of his kiss upon her lips and the assurance of his love fortifying her.

The light was on in Jerome's room and she hesitated for a moment outside his door. But instinct told her this was not the time to face him. She must wait until he was ready to come to her.

Softly she stole upstairs to the gallery overlooking the two gardens. How peaceful it seemed here in the Japanese twilight. The moon was rising in a darkening sky and the noises of the city seemed far away from this hillside. Yet how little peace there was within the Japanese house. Beneath this roof there was separate torment for each one, with little promise of relief anywhere.

She moved to where the tall plant stood beside the rail, remembering how she had watched its great blossoms open only a little while ago—so very long ago. But now there were no white blooms there amid the green. She stared at the plant for a moment and then moved quickly to the door of the partition. The knob turned beneath her hand and she pushed it open.

A Japanese bed had been spread upon the *tatami*, but the covers had been flung back and there was no one in it. From the gallery that edged the room, she could look down into the Minatos' garden. On the far side something white fluttered in the dim light. White and scarlet. The white of a kimono, the scarlet of a long obi, untied.

"Chiyo!" Marcia called down the stairs. "Chiyo, go quickly into the garden!"

She heard Chiyo answer, heard her hush the children. A moment later Chiyo ran into the garden and Marcia heard her sharp cry of anguish.

By the time Marcia reached the head of her own stairs, Chiyo had come through the gate between the gardens and was running through the hall, calling for Jerome. He came out of his room at once and Chiyo said, "It is Haruka—in the garden."

He strode past her out of the house and Marcia came down the stairs to Chiyo.

"Tell me," she said softly.

"This time she has found her spirit world," Chiyo murmured, her head bowed in sad acceptance.

Haruka had chosen a bough of the old camphor tree, she said, and her own red silk obi, knotted.

"Red is the color of passion," Chiyo murmured. "A great lady of the old court died for love in this way also. Haruka admired her greatly. She did not mean to go to Kobe. She chose another way."

They followed Jerome into the garden and Chiyo hurried back to her house to quiet the frightened children. Marcia waited in the gateway. Reflections from the lighted house and pale illumination from the rising moon lay upon the garden. She could see Jerome clearly now.

Walking carefully, steadily, he came toward the house, bearing Haruka in his outstretched arms. Her face was turned gently toward his shoulder and one long white kimono sleeve trailed toward the earth. The scarlet band of the obi was lost in the folds of her kimono.

But it was Jerome's face of which Marcia was most aware. It was a face of stone from which all emotion had been swept away. She did not move from the gate, or speak to him, but when he saw her there, he paused and looked at her.

"Go home to America," he said. "Go with Alan. And take Laurie with you."

"But what of you?" she asked softly.

Before her eyes the stone mask seemed to dissolve and beneath it was the face of a man who sorrowed deeply.

"My work has been waiting for a long while," he said. "Haruka has sent me back to it. I want to do something for her people as well as for my own."

He went into the house then, carrying Haruka Setsu to the place Chiyo had prepared for her.

With tears wet upon her cheeks, Marcia moved toward the ancient camphor tree. White petals on the ground caught her eye and she bent to pick up the withered blossoms of the moonflower.

The words of the poem Haruka had written out of her melancholy whispered through Marcia's mind.

>   "Ghost white spirit flower
>   Open to the moon;
>   Death comes at dawn."

Moonlight lacquered the garden and dawn was far away. Marcia lifted her face to the light touch of a breeze from the mountains.

Born in Japan of American parents, Phyllis A. Whitney is the bestselling author of over 35 books. She is recognized as one of America's most successful writers of romance and suspense. Her most recent novel, RAINBOW IN THE MIST, was a *New York Times* hardcover bestseller. Ms. Whitney lives in Virginia.

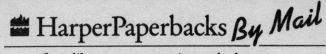

♦ HarperPaperbacks *By Mail*

If you like romance, passion and adventure, you're sure to like these...

4 *Unforgettable Romantic* Love Stories

These four novels are filled with intrigue and suspense and overflow with love, passion and romance.

PRIDE OF PLACE by Nicola Thorne. Judith Prynne sees the opportunity of a lifetime. Follow her from London to all of Europe, in a passionate quest for money, power and the love of a man who could take it all away.

THE HOUSE OF VANDEKAR by Evelyn Anthony. A family dynasty struggles for five decades against its two obsessions: love and betrayal. They weave an intricate web of love and lies that trapped them all.

A TIME TO SING by Sally Mandel. Fate brought them together and bonded their

hearts in a dreamed-of perfect life. Then fate returns and tries to take it all away. This is a story of star crossed love that you will never forget.

SPRING MOON by Bette Bao Lord. Spring Moon was born into luxury and privilege. Through a tumultuous lifetime, Spring Moon must cling to her honor, to the memory of a time gone by and to a destiny, foretold at her birth, that has yet to be fulfilled.

Buy All 4 and $ave. When you buy all four the postage and handling is *FREE*. You'll get these novels delivered right to door with absolutely no charge for postage, shipping and handling.

Visa and MasterCard holders—call 1-800-562-6182 for fastest service!

- -

MAIL TO: **HarperPaperbacks, 10 E. 53rd St., NY, NY 10022 Attn: Mail Order Division**

YES, send me the love stories I have checked:

☐ **Pride Of Place**
0-06-100106-6. . . .$4.95

☐ **The House Of Vandekar**
0-06-100050-7 . . .$4.95

☐ **A Time To Sing**
0-06-100066-3 . . .$4.95

☐ **Spring Moon**
0-06-100105-8. . . .$4.95

SUBTOTAL . . . . $_____

POSTAGE AND HANDLING* . . . . $_____

SALES TAX (NJ, NY, PA residents) . . . . $_____

Remit in US funds, do not send cash   **TOTAL: $**_____

Name_____

Address_____

City_____

State_____Zip_____

Allow up to 6 weeks delivery. Prices subject to change.

*Add $1 postage/handling for up to 3 books...FREE postage/handling if you buy all 4.

HP-12 -12 11 10 9 8 7 6